EVERYMAN, I will go with thee,

and be thy guide,

In thy most need to go by thy side

Æsop's and other Fables

AN ANTHOLOGY

INTRODUCTION BY
ERNEST RHYS

POSTSCRIPT BY
ROGER LANCELYN GREEN

Dent London Melbourne Toronto
EVERYMAN'S LIBRARY
Dutton New York

© Postscript, J. M. Dent & Sons Ltd, 1971
All rights reserved
Printed in Great Britain by
Biddles Ltd, Guildford, Surrey for
J. M. DENT & SONS LTD
Aldine House, 33 Welbeck Street, London
This edition was first published in
Everyman's Library in 1913
Last reprinted 1980

Published in the USA by arrangement
with J. M. Dent & Sons Ltd

No 657 Hardback ISBN 0 460 00657 6
No 1657 Paperback ISBN 0 460 01657 1

INTRODUCTION

THE fame of Æsop, however we look at it, has this advantage, that it is thoroughly in keeping with his book. There are all the elements of fable in the old story of his life, and the man himself has been made into a folk-tale creature, as if to suit the atmosphere that surrounds "The Lion and the Fox" and "The Frog and the Mouse" in his pages. Sir Roger L'Estrange in the "Life" which opens his fine seventeenth century folio of the Fables, has described the fabulist with lineaments that have become distinct as the crookback of Richard III.

Æsop was a slave, says Sir Roger (following Camerarius), already twice bought and sold when the record opens, and we see him first on the road to Ephesus to be sold a third time. In his person he was "deformed to the highest degree: flat-nosed, hunch-backed, bladder-lipped, baker-legged," with a long, misshapen head, and "his complexion so swarthy that he took his very name from it, for Æsop is the same with Ethiop." In fact the "most scandalous figure of a man that ever was heard of," and so tongue-tied that people could hardly understand what he said. This we feel is just as it should be, for it at once brings Æsop into range with the beast-fable and the wonderful array of folk-tale animals that start up in his world. In the frontis-piece to L'Estrange's book, he appears surrounded by these creatures. An ape and a fox are at either foot; a lion is behind him; a hare is being devoured by an eagle before him. On the tree over his head are grouped a peacock, an owl, and what looks like a mythological jackdaw. Then, to aggravate his own deformity, his hunched shoulders and his protuberant front are encased in steel armour. Final touch of all, he holds in one hand a scroll inscribed "Utile Dulci" and in the other a style.

In the following account of his going to Ephesus with

other slaves to be sold, his wit at once appears. When the burdens they had to carry were allotted, Æsop chose a pannier of bread twice as heavy as the bales the rest lifted, which made the other slaves call him a fool for his pains. But as the bread was to feed the slaves on the road, by the afternoon his burden was reduced by half, and before evening he had nothing to carry but an empty basket. Fables to the fabulist: we see how finely this episode falls into place in the Æsop legend. When we turn from the proverbial Æsop and try to get at his actual or his literary beginnings, we have to go back to the father of history, who again tells us that Æsop was a slave. Herodotus has the pull over the later biographers in that he is able to get into the page an allusion to the pyramids. The pyramids bring him to Rhodopis, a Thracian by birth and the slave of Iadmon, and one of her fellow-slaves was Æsop. And as the death of Marlowe is able to add a deeper tinge to his poetry, so the murder of Æsop is made by Herodotus to add a touch of reality to his fables. "The Delphians," he says, "proclaimed that if any one asked compensation for Æsop's death, it should duly be given to him. But the only man to come forward was a grandson of Iadmon, bearing the same name."

This serves to bear out the fact that he was the older Iadmon's slave, and it lies very near the base of his history. It confirms the popular idea of him as a slave, and it leaves us with the belief that he really was murdered, or as we should say executed, in accordance with the sentence of the Delphic oracle, and in all likelihood because some of the fables had been held to convey a seditious meaning that may or may not have been intended by himself. Ergo, if this be true, Æsop, like Socrates, suffered for his wisdom. As Crainquebille went to prison for saying "Mort aux vaches,"[1] so we may conjecture Æsop went to his death because he told too feelingly the fable of "The Ox and the Frog" or "The Oak and the Reed."

[1] Can M. Anatole France have recollected, one wonders, how in the Indian fable the tiger confessed to the unpardonable sin— the killing of cows?

The earliest fable of Æsop of which there is any record is found in Aristotle's *Rhetoric*: "The Fable of the Fox and the Hedgehog," and it is worth notice that in this there is a reference to embezzling the revenues of the State. In other early references Æsop appears to take on some of the features of a court-jester. We see him as one who had freed himself from slavery and had come to the Court of Crœsus, and, while Solon edified that monarch, Æsop taught him by inuendo, drollery, riddle and fable. We see him afterwards moving in a kind of fabulous progress from city to city. At Corinth he warned his hearers against mob-law in a fable which Socrates used afterwards. At Athens he taught prince and people by the fable of "The Frogs and Jupiter." Finally, he was sent by Crœsus—so the tradition goes—with a sum of money due to the Delphians, and they repaid him, being afraid, no doubt, of his wit, by a cry of sacrilege. It is said that he tried to save himself by appealing to their known reverence for the laws of hospitality, and his appeal was of course a fable, that of "The Eagle and the Beetle." But it was in vain, and the story goes that he was taken to one of the Phædrian precipices and hurled headlong from its summit.

Even this was not all: his very death attained an immortality; and the proverb of "Æsop's Blood" lived to remind the Delphians and his own countrymen that the blood of a slain man cries to Heaven. As some sort of reparation, a statue to him was put up two hundred years after his death in front of the statues of the Seven Sages. However we read these memoirs of "the Real Æsop," we are driven at length to see him in the light they throw over him, and to take him once and for all as the type of his kind. But having decided that, we have to admit that the beast-fable did not begin with him, or in Greece at all. We have, in fact, to go East and to look to India and burrow in the "tales within tales" of the *Hitopadesa* to get an idea of how old the antiquity of the fable actually is.

"The Father of all Fables," Sir Edwin Arnold suggested the *Hitopadesa* should be called, as from its various adaptations and translations have come Æsop and Bidpai or

Pilpay, to say nothing of Reinecke Fuchs in later time. So deep is the Indian impress it lays on all its later migrants, that one cannot read of a mouse in a fable without remembering that the little beast, as Gunesh's emissary, was of great account in Hindoo legend; or of a crow without thinking of the Indian bird of that name with its grey hood; or of a serpent without recalling Vasuki or Ananta, chief of the snakes that have human heads and live in the subterranean land, Pátála.

Max Müller even prepared a kind of family tree to show the descent of the modern fables that sprang from this antique stock. He traced one in particular, the fable of Perrette as we know it in La Fontaine's "Milkmaid and her Milkpail"; and showed how it went back to the Indian story of "The Brahman and the Pot of Rice." In this, Perrette's Indian ancestor has a jar into which he puts one day some butter and honey, left over after his repast, and hangs the jar on a nail. Then, leaning back on his couch, a stick in his hand, he falls to musing on the high price of butter and honey, and thinks that when the jar is full he will sell what it holds, and buy ten goats with the money. In two years, he calculates, the ten goats will be four hundred; and these can be sold and turned into cattle. So he goes on; adds flock to flock, field to field; and builds a great house, and sets up a great family, with a son and heir. If this son is good, all will be well; if not?—at this point the Brahman raises his stick—"I shall beat him over his head with my stick!" So saying, he strikes the honey-jar and breaks it, and the honey and butter pour down over his head.

Some centuries later and the story has reached the milkmaid version in the "Dialogue of Creatures Moralised" (1517).

"It is tolde in fablys that a lady uppon a tyme delyvered to her mayden a galon of mylke to sell at a cite, and by the way, as she sate and restid her by a dyche side, she began to thinke that with the money of the mylke she wold bye an henne, the which shulde bringe forth chekyns, and when they were growyn to hennys she wolde sell them and

by piggis, and exchaunge them in to shepe, and the shepe
in to oxen, and so whan she was come to richesse she
sholde be maried right worshipfully unto some worthy man,
and thus she reioycid. And whan she was thus mervel-
ously comfortid and ravisshed inwardly in her secrete solace,
thinkynge with howe greate joye she shuld be ledde towarde
the chirche with her husbond on horsebacke, she sayde to
her self : ' Goo we, goo we.' Sodaynlye she smote the
ground with her fote, myndynge to spurre the horse, but
her fote slypped, and she fell in the dyche, and there lay
all her mylke, and so she was farre from her purpose, and
never had that she hopid to have."

This is, however, from a Latin original, "Dialogus Crea-
turarum Optime Moralizatus."

As we turn on from Indian to Persian fables, and then
from Greek to Latin, or Latin to English, we do not find
much which we can set apart as due to classic sources in
the most typical and proverbial of the beast-tales. But,
indeed, it is one of the tests of a good fable that it has an
air of innocence in all its sleight or subtlety, and belongs to
the childhood of the world. It does not seem to depend
on any one language or race for its character. It turns
upon the relation of man to the beasts, in whose doings he
can trace the droll pattern of his own human nature. As
men went on, and grew literary, it was still possible for a
writer of wit like La Fontaine, or a philosophical artist like
Lessing, to adapt the old mode. But we are conscious, in
all the new play of their wit and fable fantasy, of something
less than the real Simon Pure ; something which is not
Æsop, but his shadow.

The puzzling thing is that, when we set about tracing
some of the fables to their origins, often at the further
Oriental remove, we are carried beyond the pitch of sim-
plicity and come to a much earlier literary incarnation.
Mr. Joseph Jacob in his interesting account of the Oriental
Æsop points out, for instance, a Jataka variant of the
fable of "The Wolf and the Lamb." It occurs in the
"Dipi," translated by Dr. Morris in the *Folk-lore Journal.*
In this story the Panther meets a Kid, and complains

that the Kid has trodden on his tail. The Kid says that as the Panther's face was towards it, how could it have trodden on the end of his tail? But the Panther replies that his tail is so long and reaches so far that it covers the earth in its four quarters, therefore the Kid must have stepped on his tail. The Kid thereupon explains that it came through the air and did not touch the ground. The fatal end may be foreseen. The Panther insists that the Kid, by coming through the air, startled the beasts and spoilt his food and his chances of a dinner. So saying, he falls upon the Kid, tears its throat, and greedily devours it. The same writer suggests that the Greek fable of "The Wolf and the Lamb" is merely a simpler version of this story, arrived at by omitting the Indian exaggeration of the world-wide tail and the flying Kid. As it appears, there is also a Thibetan version in which the two actors have already become the Wolf and the Sheep, and of course the next metamorphosis to the familiar form we know is easy.

What we learn from this instance is that a fable, which on the face of it looks like the natural beast-fancy of a childish mind, may be a bit of an older myth; just as a ballad, which looks like the pure outcome of the border life, some-times turns out to be nothing more or less than a piece of stolen romance. This may help to account for that lurking air of hidden meanings and immemorial mythical signs which we find in some fables, recalling a people, wise and childish at once, who had built up a theory of the world ages before Æsop was born. However, when we have decided that any fable may have this enormous pedigree, we can save ourselves the trouble of trying to carry it back and simply read it for entertainment, like any listener who sits by the winter's hearth.

Not much need be said about the make-up of this enlarged "Book of Æsop" and his fellow-fabulists. It begins with some of the very earliest versions that found their way into English through the printing-office of old Caxton. The bulk of those that follow are, for the convenience of the modern reader, borrowed from the translation of Thomas James, made some four hundred years later. Sir Roger

L'Estrange's folio supplies some of the later classical fables by Æsop's imitators, and Phædrus, and Æsop's far ancestor in the *Hitopadesa*, are not forgotten. One or two English and Welsh tales, and La Fontaine, Lessing and Gay carry on the tradition; and at the end Tolstoi brings it within reach of our own day This does not by any means exhaust the vast store. But the book, it must be remembered, is intended, first of all, to give pleasure to those eternal tale-lovers, who are the only true Æsopians and still belong to the childhood of a new time; and it only gives what they are likely to care for. A word of thanks is due finally to those revisers, including Mr. Vaughan Lloyd, Mr. W. Hughes-Jones and B. R., who have helped to prepare new versions of certain Indian, Russian and other fables.

ERNEST RHYS.

FABLES—BY WAY OF POSTSCRIPT

THE splendid collection of Fables made by Ernest Rhys sixty years ago needs no excuse in its latest reprint. The Fable is as much a part of our mental heritage as the proverb or the literary allusion—indeed it has an even wider grip on us, for it embraces both the literate and the illiterate with equal kindliness and often comes more readily to mind than either when we seek "to point the moral or adorn the tale".

In his Introduction Ernest Rhys dealt with Fables with becoming seriousness: perhaps a postscript may be allowed what Stevenson described so delightfully in *The Wrong Box* as "a little judicious levity".

For Fables *do* need some apology—an apology to the animals who figure so largely in them and are made to exhibit so many human frailties and follies of which they could never have been guilty!

In his poem to Æsop preluding an edition of the *Fables* in 1889, Andrew Lang allowed the animals to answer back for the first time:

> He sat among the woods, he heard
>   The sylvan merriment; he saw
> The pranks of butterfly and bird,
>   The humours of the ape, the daw.
>
> And in the lion or the frog—
>   In all the life of moor and fen

Postscript

In ass and peacock, stork and dog,
　　He read similitudes of men.

"Of these, from these," he cried, "we come,
　　Our hearts, our brains descend from these."
And lo! the Beasts no more were dumb,
　　But answered out of brakes and trees:

"Not ours," they cried: "Degenerate,
　　If ours at all," they cried again,
"Ye fools, who war with God and Fate,
　　Who strive and toil: strange race of men,

"For *we* are neither bond nor free,
　　For *we* have neither slaves nor kings,
But near to Nature's heart are we,
　　And conscious of her secret things.

"Content are we to fall asleep,
　　And well content to wake no more,
We do not laugh, we do not weep,
　　Nor look behind us and before;

"But were there cause for moan or mirth,
　　'Tis *we*, not you, should sigh or scorn,
Oh, latest children of the Earth
　　Most childish children Earth has borne."

They spoke, but that misshapen Slave
　　Told never of the thing he heard,
And unto men their portraits gave,
　　In likenesses of beast and bird!

Ten years later the cause of the Beasts was taken up even more force-fully by Kenneth Grahame, who pointed out that Æsop (and all proper fabulists after him) dared not accuse his fellow men to their faces, and had to find some way of disguising the reproof he was intending to level at them in his tales—and so saddled the poor, uncomplaining Beasts with all our human faults and foibles.

Whether the Beasts had been maligned by the Fabulists before the Philologists joined in the hunt seems uncertain. But philological aspersion is rife to this day in our general conversation. Do not some of us lead a dog's life, wolf their dinners, bully their inferiors, cow the weaklings, take the lion's share, behave sheepishly or cattily or cockily, and fox or badger their friends? Is it natural or fabulous to be as proud as a peacock, as brave as a lion or as busy as a bee—when we know that it is more fabulous than natural to be a dog in the manger, or a country mouse, or to count one's chickens before they are hatched?

Of course, as Kenneth Grahame pointed out, it was obvious that Beasts would have their own views of human characteristics, and themselves make up Fables that would surprise us. And, as one would expect of the man who understood so clearly what the wind in the willows was saying, he was able to overhear several of them, including one made apparently by a monkey:

> A frolicsome ape, who in much careless ease inhabited a lordly mansion in Regent's Park, lounged up one afternoon to certain bars, on the other side of which selected specimens of humanity were compelled to promenade each day for the instruction and diversion of philosophic apes. A little maid in a Leghorn hat having timidly approached the bars, her large fat mother, shaking her imperiously by the shoulder, ordered her to observe the pitty ickle monkey, so mild and so gentle, and give it a piece of her bun at once, like a good, kind, charitable ickle girl. The small maiden, though herself extremely loth, proffered her bun to the ape, who possessed himself of it with a squeal of delight, and bit her finger to the bone as well: for he had bitten nothing more juicy and succulent than a neighbour's tail for a whole week past; and tails are but gristly things at the best. But the large, fat mother, falling upon the already shrieking little girl, shook and cuffed her unmercifully, protesting that of all the naughty, tiresome, self-willed little trollops, and that never, never, never would she take her a-pleasuring again.

Like all good art forms, Fable lends itself well to parody. Kenneth Grahame's examples of the Beasts' version of Æsop go at least half way in this direction, and nearly twenty years earlier when "Stalky & Co." were at school at Westward Ho!, their school magazine, *The United Services College Chronicle*, had produced a series of "Fables for the Young" specially suited to hungry schoolboys who were inclined to help themselves to the natural produce on the local farms. It was perhaps Beetle who wrote the Fable of "The Caitiff and the Canine" in the number for 20th March 1882.

> A person having occasion to visit a henhouse secretly, was attacked by a large and tenacious mastiff. Stripping off his outer garment, he permitted the ferocious canine to attach himself firmly thereto. Then carefully conveying the animal for the distance of some hundred yards down the lane, he re-donned his habiliment and presented himself in tears before the pitying farmer, who gave him food and severely chastised the faithful hound.
>
> Thus it is plain that deception is the better part of valour.

But parody is as sincere a form of flattery as imitation, and Kipling like many other writers turned later in his life to the more subtle use of Fable: and such stories as his "Children of the Zodiac" and "The Mother Hive" show how Fable may be used to the best possible advantage and become the background of really great literature:

> When all the world would keep a matter hid,
>   Since Truth is seldom friend to any crowd,
> Men write in fable, as old Æsop did,
>   Jesting at that which none will name aloud.
> And this they needs must do, or it will fall
> Unless they please they are not heard at all.

ROGER LANCELYN GREEN.

SELECT BIBLIOGRAPHY

William Caxton, *Æsop*, 1485; Sir Robert L'Estrange, *Fables of Æsop, Barlandus, Avianus and Abstemius*, 1694; John Gay, *Fifty-one Fables*, first vol., 1727, second vol., 1738; Gotthold Lessing, *Fables*, translated by J. Richardson, 1773, and anonymously 1860; *English Fables from old chap-books*, 1801–3; Jean de La Fontaine, *Fables*, Bohn's Library, translated by E. Wright, 1842; *Iolo Manuscripts* (Welsh Fables), by Edward Williams, 1848; Thomas James, 'Æsop', 1848; *Phaedrus*, Bohn's Library, 1848; Pilpay, *Fables*, translated 1852; *Hitopadesa*, translated by Sir William Jones, 1851; Krilof, *Fables*, translated 1869; Lokman, *Fables*, 1869; Leo Tolstoi, *Fables, Tales and Stories*, 1872; *The Fables of Bidpai*, 1888, and *The Fables of Æsop*, edited by Joseph Jacobs, 1889; G. M. Bussey, *Book of Fables* (for Florian and others), 1890; *A Hundred Fables of Æsop*, edited by Kenneth Grahame, 1899; *Babrii Fabulae Æsopeae*, edited by J. P. Postgate, Oxford 1919; *Babrius and Phaedrus*, newly edited and translated into English, together with an historical Introduction and Comprehensive Survey of Greek and Latin Fables in the Æsopic Tradition, by Ben Edward Perry (Loeb Classical Library), 1965.

CONTENTS

Contents

Contents

xviii   Contents

Contents

IV. ÆSOPIAN FABLES

(ATTRIBUTED TO PHÆDRUS)

V. ENGLISH FOLK TALES

VI. WELSH FOLK TALES

VII. FABLES FROM HITOPADESA

Contents xxi

Contents

XII. FABLES FROM LOKMAN

XIII. FABLES FROM FLORIAN

XIV. FABLES FROM LA FONTAINE

Contents

xxiii

xxiv　　　Contents

XVII. FABLES FROM KRILOF

XVIII. FABLES FROM TOLSTOI

A VISION OF ÆSOP

By Robert Henryson

I

In middis of June, that jolly sweet season,
  When that fair Phœbus, with his beamis bright,
Had dried up the dew frae dale and down,
  And all the land made with his lemys [1] light;
  In a morning, between mid-day and night,
I rose and put all sloth and sleep on side,
And to a wood I went alone, but [2] guide.

II

Sweet was the smell of flowris white and red,
  The noyis of birdis right delicious;
The bewis [3] broad bloomèd above my head,
  The ground growand with grasses gracious;
  Of all pleasance that was plenteous
With sweet odours and birdis harmony,
The morning mild, my mirth was more forthy.

III

The roses red arrayed on rone and ryse, [4]
  The primrose and the purple viola;
To hear it was a point of paradise
  Sic mirth the mavis and the merle couth ma. [5]
  The blossoms blithe brake upon bank and brae,
The smell of herbis, and of fowls the cry,
Contending who should have the victory.

---

[1] Rays.   [2] Without.   [3] Branches.   [4] Bushes and twigs.
         [5] Blackbird could make.

IV

Me to conserve then frae the sunis heat,
    Under the shadow of an hawthorn green,
I leanèd down among the flowris sweet,
    Syne [1] made a cross and closèd both mine een :
    On sleep I fell among the bewis been,
And, in my dream, me thought come through the shaw [2]
The fairest man that ere before I saw.

V

His gown was of a claith as white as milk,
    His chymers [3] were of chamelot purpure brown ;
His hood of scarlet, borderèd with silk
    In heckle wise, [4] untill his girdle down ;
    His bonnet round was of the old fashion ;
His beard was white, his eine were green and gray,
With lokar [5] hair, whilk o'er his shoulders lay.

VI

A roll of paper in his hand he bare ;
    A swanis pen stickand under his ear ;
An inkhorn, with pretty gilt pennair, [6]
    A bag of silk all at his belt he wear.
    Thus was he goodly graithèd in his gear.
Of stature large, and with a feirful [7] face ;
Even where I lay he come a sturdy pace ;

VII

And said, "God speed, my son ; " and I was fain
    Of that couth [8] word, and of his company.
With reverence I salust [9] him again,
    "Welcome, father ; " and he sat down me by.
    "Displease you not, my good master, though I
Demand your birth, your faculty and name ;
Why ye come here, or where ye dwell at hame ? "

---

[1] Then.   [2] Wood.   [3] Cymar.   [4] Meaning obscure.   [5] Curled.
[6] Pen case.   [7] Grave, austere (?).   [8] Kindly, known.   [9] Saluted.

VIII

"My son," said he, "I am of gentle blood;
  My native land is Rome, withouten nay;
And in that town first to the schools I yude,[1]
  And civil law studied full many a day.
  And now my winning is in heaven for aye;
Æsop I hecht;[2] my writing and my work
Is couth and kend to many cunnand clerk."[3]

IX

"O master Æsop, poet laureate,
  God wot ye are full dear welcome to me;
Are ye not he that all thir fables wrate,
  Whilk in effect, suppose they feignèd be,
  Are full of prudence and morality?"
"Fair son," said he, "I am that samen man,"
  God wait gif that my heart was merry than.

X

I said, "Æsop, my master venerable,
  I you beseik,[4] heartly for charity,
Ye would dedane[5] to tell a pretty fable
  Concludand with a good morality."
  Shakand his head, he said, "My son, let be;
For what is worth to tell a feignèd tale,
When haily preaching may nothing now avail.

XI

Now in this world methinks that few or none
  Till Goddis word that has devotion;
The ear is deaf, the heart is hard as stone;
  Now open sin, without correction
  The ee inclinand to the eird[6] aye down;
Sae rusted is the world with canker black,
That my talis may little succour mak."

[1] Went.   [2] Am named.   [3] Skilful scholar.
[4] Beseech.   [5] Deign.   [6] Faith.

XII

"Yet, gentle sir," said I, "for my request
Not to displease your father-head, I pray,
Under the figure of some brutal beast
A moral fable ye would dedane to say.
Wha wate nor I may lear [1] and bare away
Something thereby hereafter may avail."
"I grant," quoth he, and thus begouth ane tale.

[1] Who knows but that I may learn?

I. FABLES FROM CAXTON'S ÆSOP
(1484)

THE FOX AND THE GRAPES

A hungry Fox stole one day into a vineyard where many bunches of Grapes hung ripe and ready for eating. But as luck would have it, they were fastened upon a tall trellis, just too high for Reynard to reach. He jumped, and paused, and jumped again, in the attempt to get at them. But it was all in vain. At last he was fairly tired out, and thereupon, "Take them who will," he cried, THE GRAPES ARE SOUR!"

THE RAT AND THE FROG

The Rat went on a pilgrimage, and he came by a River, and demanded of a Frog that she should be his ferryman, and ferry him over the water. And thereupon the Frog bound the Rat's foot to her foot, and in that wise she swam with him to the middle of the River. But when they were come thither, the Frog ceased to paddle, and came to a halt; to the end that the Rat should be drowned. Meanwhile a hungry Kite, seeing them there in mid-water, swooped down upon them, and bore them both off. This fable made Æsop for a similitude profitable to many folks. For he that thinketh evil may chance to find that evil fall on himself.

THE WOLF AND THE SKULL

A Wolf found a dead man's head, which he turned upside down with his foot. And he said, "Ah ha! how fair hast thou been, and pleasant. And now thou hast in thee neither wit nor beauty; and thou art without voice and without any thought." Therefore men ought not only to behold the beauty and fairness of the body, but also the goodness and the courage.

5

THE LION AND THE COW, THE GOAT AND THE SHEEP

Men say that it is not good for a servant to eat plums with his lord; and to the poor, it is not good to have partage and division with him which is rich and mighty; whereof Æsop rehearseth such a fable.

The Cow, the Goat and the Sheep went once a-hunting in the chase with a Lion, and they took a Hart. And when they came to have their part and share in it, the Lion said to them—

"My lords, I let you wit that the first part is mine, because I am your lord; the second because I am stronger than ye be; the third because I ran more swift than ye did; and whosoever toucheth the fourth part, he shall be my mortal enemy!"

And thus the Lion took for himself alone the Hart. And therefore this fable teacheth to all folk that the poor ought not to hold fellowship with the mighty. For the mighty man is never faithful to the poor.

THE PILGRIM AND THE SWORD

An evil man may be cause of the perdition or loss of many folk. As rehearseth unto us this present fable of a Pilgrim which found in his way a Sword, and asked of the Sword, "What is he that hath lost thee?" And the Sword answered to the Pilgrim, "A man alone hath lost me, but many a one have I lost."

And therefore an evil man may be lost, but ere he be lost he may well harm many a one. For by cause of an evil man may come in a country many evils.

THE OAK AND THE REED

A great Oak would never bow him for no wind, and a Reed which was at his foot bowed himself as much as the wind would. And the Oak said to him, "Why dost thou not abide still as I do?" And the Reed answered, "I have not the might which thou hast." And the Tree said to the Reed proudly, "Then have I more strength than thou."

And anon after came a great wind which threw down to the ground the said great Tree, and the Reed abode in his own being. For the proud shall be always humbled, and the meek and humble shall be enhanced, for the root of all virtue is obedience and humility.

THE FOX AND THE COCK

A Fox came toward a Cock and said to him, "I would fain know if thou canst as well sing as thy father did." And then the Cock shut his eyes and began to cry and sing. And the Fox took and bare him away. And the people of the town cried, "The Fox beareth away the Cock!" And then the Cock said thus to the Fox, "My lord, understandest thou not what the people saith, that thou bearest away their cock? Tell to them that it is thine and not theirs." And as the Fox said, "It is not yours, but it is mine," the Cock escaped from the Fox's mouth and flew upon a tree. And then the Cock said to the Fox, "Thou liest; for I am theirs and not thine." And the Fox began to hit earth with his mouth and head, saying, "Mouth, thou hast spoken too much! Thou shouldest have eaten the Cock had not thy words been over many."

And therefore over much talking harmeth, and too much crowing smarteth. Therefore keep thyself from over many words, to the end that thou repentest not.

THE FISHER

A Fisher sometime touched his bagpipe nigh the river for to make the fish to dance. And when he saw that for no song that he could pipe would the fishes dance, as wroth did he cast his nets into the river and took of fishes great quantity. And when he had drawn out his nets out of the water, the fish began to leap and dance. And then he said to them, "Certainly it appeareth now well that ye be evil beasts. For now when ye be taken ye leap and dance; and when I piped and played of my muse or bagpipe ye deigned ye would not dance." Therefore it appeareth well that the things which be made in season be well made and done by reason.

THE HE-GOAT AND THE WOLF

A Wolf some time ran after a He-goat, and the He-goat, for to save him, leapt upon a rock; and the Wolf besieged him. And after when they had dwelled there two or three days, the Wolf began to wax hungry and the He-goat to have thirst. And thus the Wolf went for to eat, and the He-goat went for to drink. And as the He-goat drank he saw his shadow in the water; and, spying and beholding his shadow, proffered and said such words within himself, "Thou hast so fair legs, so fair a beard, and so fair horns, and hast fear of the Wolf! If it happen that he come again, I shall correct him well and shall keep him well, that he shall have no might over me." And the Wolf, which held his peace and hearkened what was said, took him by the one leg, thus saying, "What words be these which thou profferest and sayest, brother He-goat?" And when the He-goat saw that he was taken, he began to say to the Wolf, "Ha! my lord, I say nothing, and have pity of me! I know well that it is to my blame." And the Wolf took him by the neck and strangled him. And therefore it is great folly when the feeble maketh war against the puissant (powerful) and strong.

THE BALD MAN AND THE FLY

Of a little evil may well come a greater. Whereof Æsop reciteth such a fable of a Fly which pricked a Man upon his bald head. And when he would have smote her she flew away. And thus he smote himself, whereof the Fly began to laugh. And the Bald Man said to her, "Ha, an evil beast! Thou demandest well thy death if I smote myself, whereof thou laughest and mockest me. But if I had hit thee thou haddest been thereof slain." And therefore men say commonly that of the evil of others men ought not to laugh nor scorn. But the injurious mocketh and scorneth the world, and getteth many enemies. For the which cause ofttimes it happeneth that of a few words cometh a great noise and danger.

THE FOX AND THE THORN-BUSH

A Fox, to escape the peril of the chase, leapt into a Thorn-bush, whose thorns hurt him sore. Thereupon the Fox, weeping in his anguish, said to the Thorn-bush, "I am come to thee as to my refuge; and thou hast hurted me to the death." And then the Thorn-bush said to the Fox, "Thou hast erred; and well thou hast beguiled thyself. For thou thought to have taken me as thou art accustomed to take chickens and hens."

II. FABLES FROM JAMES'S ÆSOP

(1848)

THE BOWMAN AND THE LION

A Man who was very skilful with his bow, went up into the mountains to hunt. At his approach there was instantly a great consternation and rout among all the wild beasts, the Lion alone showing any determination to fight. "Stop," said the Bowman to him, "and await my messenger, who has somewhat to say to you." With that he sent an arrow after the Lion, and wounded him in the side. The Lion, smarting with anguish, fled into the depth of the thickets, but a Fox seeing him run, bade him take courage, and face his enemy. "No," said the Lion, "you will not persuade me to that; for if the messenger he sends is so sharp, what must be the power of him who sends it?"

THE WOLF AND THE CRANE

A Wolf had got a bone stuck in his throat, and in the greatest agony ran up and down, beseeching every animal he met to relieve him: at the same time hinting at a very handsome reward to the successful operator. A Crane, moved by his entreaties and promises, ventured her long neck down the Wolf's throat, and drew out the bone. She then modestly asked for the promised reward. To which, the Wolf, grinning and showing his teeth, replied with seeming indignation, "Ungrateful creature! to ask for any other reward than that you have put your head into a Wolf's jaws, and brought it safe out again!"

Those who are charitable only in the hope of a return, must not be surprised if, in their dealings with evil men, they meet with more jeers than thanks.

THE BOY AND THE SCORPION

A Boy was hunting Locusts upon a wall, and had caught a great number of them; when, seeing a Scorpion, he mistook it for another Locust, and was just hollowing his hand to catch it, when the Scorpion, lifting up his sting, said: "I wish you had done it, for I would soon have made you drop me, and the Locusts into the bargain."

THE FOX AND THE GOAT

A Fox had fallen into a well, and had been casting about for a long time how he should get out again; when at length a Goat came to the place, and wanting to drink, asked Reynard whether the water was good, and if there was plenty of it. The Fox, dissembling the real danger of his case, replied, "Come down, my friend; the water is so good that I cannot drink enough of it, and so abundant that it cannot be exhausted." Upon this the Goat without any more ado leaped in; when the Fox, taking advantage of his friend's horns, as nimbly leaped out; and coolly remarked to the poor deluded Goat,—"If you had half as much brains as you have beard, you would have looked before you leaped."

THE WIDOW AND THE HEN

A Widow woman kept a Hen that laid an egg every morning. Thought the woman to herself, "If I double my Hen's allowance of barley, she will lay twice a-day." So she tried her plan, and the Hen became so fat and sleek, that she left off laying at all.

Figures are not always facts.

THE VAIN JACKDAW

A Jackdaw, as vain and conceited as Jackdaw could be, picked up the feathers which some Peacocks had shed, stuck them amongst his own, and despising his old companions, introduced himself with the greatest assurance into a flock of those beautiful birds. They, instantly detecting the intruder, stripped him of his borrowed plumes, and falling upon him with their beaks, sent him about his business. The unlucky Jackdaw, sorely punished and deeply sorrowing, betook himself to his former companions, and would have flocked with them again as if nothing had happened. But they, recollecting what airs he had given himself, drummed him out of their society, while one of those whom he had so lately despised, read him this lecture: "Had you been contented with what nature made you, you would have escaped the chastisement of your betters and also the contempt of your equals."

THE KID AND THE WOLF

A Kid being mounted on the roof of a lofty house, and seeing a Wolf pass below, began to revile him. The Wolf merely stopped to reply, "Coward! it is not you who revile me, but the place on which you are standing."

THE MOUNTAIN IN LABOUR

In days of yore, a mighty rumbling was heard in a Mountain. It was said to be in labour, and multitudes flocked together, from far and near, to see what it would produce. After long expectation and many wise conjectures from the bystanders—out popped a Mouse!

The story applies to those whose magnificent promises end in a paltry performance.

THE KITE AND THE PIGEONS

Some Pigeons had long lived in fear of a Kite, but by being always on the alert, and keeping near their dove-cote, they had contrived hitherto to escape the attacks of the enemy. Finding his sallies unsuccessful, the Kite betook himself to craft: "Why," said he, "do you prefer this life of continual anxiety, when, if you would only make me your king, I would secure you from every attack that could be made upon you?" The Pigeons, trusting to his professions, called him to the throne; but no sooner was he established there than he exercised his prerogative by devouring a pigeon a-day. Whereupon one that yet awaited his turn, said no more than "It serves us right."

They who voluntarily put power into the hand of a tyrant or an enemy, must not wonder if it be at last turned against themselves.

THE OLD HOUND

A Hound, who had been an excellent one in his time, and had done good service to his master in the field, at length became worn out with the weight of years and trouble. One day, when hunting the wild boar, he seized the creature by the ear, but his teeth giving way, he was forced to let go his hold, and the boar escaped. Upon this the huntsman, coming up, severely rated him. But the feeble Dog replied, "Spare your old servant! it was the power not the will that failed me. Remember rather what I was, than abuse me for what I am."

THE ANT AND THE GRASSHOPPER

On a cold frosty day an Ant was dragging out some of the corn which he had laid up in summer time, to dry it. A Grasshopper, half-perished with hunger, besought the Ant to give him a morsel of it to preserve his life. "What were you doing," said the Ant, "this last summer?" "Oh," said the Grasshopper, "I was not idle. I kept singing all the summer long." Said the Ant, laughing and shutting up his granary, "Since you could sing all summer, you may dance all winter."

Winter finds out what Summer lays by.

THE COCK AND THE JEWEL

As a Cock was scratching up the straw in a farm-yard, in search of food for the hens, he hit upon a Jewel that by some chance had found its way there. "Ho!" said he, "you are a very fine thing, no doubt, to those who prize you; but give me a barley-corn before all the pearls in the world."

The Cock was a sensible Cock: but there are many silly people who despise what is precious only because they cannot understand it.

THE FAWN AND HER MOTHER

A Fawn one day said to her mother, "Mother, you are bigger than a dog, and swifter and better winded, and you have horns to defend yourself; how is it that you are so afraid of the hounds?" She smiled and said, "All this, my child, I know full well; but no sooner do I hear a dog bark, than, somehow or other, my heels take me off as fast as they can carry me."

There is no arguing a coward into courage.

THE TWO WALLETS

Every man carries Two Wallets, one before and one behind, and both full of faults. But the one before, is full of his neighbour's faults; the one behind, of his own. Thus it happens that men are blind to their own faults, but never lose sight of their neighbour's.

THE EAGLE AND THE FOX

An Eagle and a Fox had long lived together as good neighbours; the Eagle at the summit of a high tree, the Fox in a hole at the foot of it. One day, however, while the Fox was abroad, the Eagle made a swoop at the Fox's cub, and carried it off to her nest, thinking that her lofty dwelling would secure her from the Fox's revenge. The Fox, on her return home, upbraided the Eagle for this breach of friendship, and begged earnestly to have her young one again; but finding that her entreaties were of no avail, she snatched a torch from an altar-fire that had been lighted hard by, and involving the whole tree in flame and smoke, soon made the Eagle restore, through fear for herself and her own young ones, the cub which she had just now denied to her most earnest prayers.

The tyrant, though he may despise the tears of the oppressed, is never safe from their vengeance.

THE HORSE AND THE GROOM

A Groom who used to steal and sell a Horse's corn, was yet very busy in grooming and wisping him all the day long. "If you really wish me," said the Horse, "to look well, give me less of your currying and more of your corn."

THE COUNTRYMAN AND THE SNAKE

A Countryman returning home one winter's day, found a Snake by the hedge-side, half dead with cold. Taking compassion on the creature, he laid it in his bosom and brought it home to his fire-side to revive it. No sooner had the warmth restored it, than it began to attack the children of the cottage. Upon this the Countryman, whose compassion had saved its life, took up a mattock and laid the Snake dead at his feet.

Those who return evil for good, may expect their neighbour's pity to be worn out at last.

THE MAN AND THE SATYR

A Man and a Satyr having struck up an acquaintance sat down together to eat. The day being wintry and cold, the Man put his fingers to his mouth and blew upon them. "What's that for, my friend?" asked the Satyr. "My hands are so cold," said the Man; "I do it to warm them." In a little while some hot food was placed before them, and the Man, raising the dish to his mouth, again blew upon it. "And what's the meaning of that, now?" said the Satyr. "Oh," replied the Man, "my porridge is so hot, I do it to cool it." "Nay, then," said the Satyr, "from this moment I renounce your friendship, for I will have nothing to do with one who blows hot and cold with the same mouth."

THE FLIES AND THE HONEY-POT

A Pot of Honey having been upset in a grocer's shop, the Flies came around it in swarms to eat it up, nor would they move from the spot while there was a drop left. At length their feet became so clogged that they could not fly away, and stifled in the luscious sweets they exclaimed, "Miserable creatures that we are, who for the sake of an hour's pleasure, have thrown away our lives!"

THE FIGHTING-COCKS AND THE EAGLE

Two young Cocks were fighting as fiercely as if they had been men. At last the one that was beaten crept into a corner of the hen-house, covered with wounds. But the conqueror, straightway flying up to the top of the house, began clapping his wings and crowing, to announce his victory. At this moment an Eagle, sailing by, seized him in his talons and bore him away; while the defeated rival came out from his hiding-place, and took possession of the dunghill for which they had contended.

THE DOG AND THE SHADOW

A Dog had stolen a piece of meat out of a butcher's shop, and was crossing a river on its way home, when he saw his own shadow reflected in the stream below. Thinking that it was another dog with another piece of meat, he resolved to make himself master of that also; but in snapping at the supposed treasure, he dropped the bit he was carrying, and so lost all.

Grasp at the shadow and lose the substance—the common fate of those who hazard a real blessing for some visionary good.

THE FOX AND THE LION

A Fox who had never seen a Lion, when by chance he met him for the first time, was so terrified that he almost died of fright. When he met him the second time, he was still afraid, but managed to disguise his fear. When he saw him the third time, he was so much emboldened that he went up to him and asked him how he did.

Familiarity breeds contempt.

THE CREAKING WHEELS

As some Oxen were dragging a waggon along a heavy road, the Wheels set up a tremendous creaking. "Brute!" cried the driver to the waggon; "why do you groan, when they who are drawing all the weight are silent?"

Those who cry loudest are not always the most hurt.

THE WOLF AND THE LAMB

As a Wolf was lapping at the head of a running brook, he spied a stray Lamb paddling, at some distance, down the stream. Having made up his mind to seize her, he bethought himself how he might justify his violence. "Villain!" said he, running up to her, "how dare you muddle the water that I am drinking?" "Indeed," said the Lamb humbly, "I do not see how I can disturb the water, since it runs from you to me, not from me to you." "Be that as it may," replied the Wolf, "it was but a year ago that you called me many ill names." "Oh, Sir!" said the Lamb, trembling, "a year ago I was not born." "Well," replied the Wolf, "if it was not you, it was your father, and that is all the same; but it is no use trying to argue me out of my supper;"—and without another word he fell upon the poor helpless Lamb and tore her to pieces.

A tyrant never wants a plea. And they have little chance of resisting the injustice of the powerful whose only weapons are innocence and reason.

THE BEAR AND THE FOX

A Bear used to boast of his excessive love for Man, saying that he never worried or mauled him when dead. The Fox observed, with a smile, "I should have thought more of your profession, if you never eat him alive."

Better save a man from dying than salve him when dead.

THE COUNTRY MOUSE AND THE TOWN MOUSE

Once upon a time a Country Mouse who had a friend in town invited him, for old acquaintance sake, to pay him a visit in the country. The invitation being accepted in due form, the Country Mouse, though plain and rough and somewhat frugal in his nature, opened his heart and store, in honour of hospitality and an old friend. There was not a carefully stored up morsel that he did not bring forth out of his larder, peas and barley, cheese-parings and nuts, hoping by quantity to make up what he feared was wanting in quality, to suit the palate of his dainty guest. The Town Mouse, condescending to pick a bit here and a bit there, while the host sat nibbling a blade of barley-straw, at length exclaimed, "How is it, my good friend, that you can endure the dullness of this unpolished life? You are living like a toad in a hole. You can't really prefer these solitary rocks and woods to streets teeming with carriages and men. On my honour, you are wasting your time miserably here. We must make the most of life while it lasts. A mouse, you know, does not live for ever. So come with me and I'll show you life and the town." Overpowered with such fine words and so polished a manner, the Country Mouse assented; and they set out together on their journey to town. It was late in the evening when they crept stealthily into the city, and midnight ere they reached the great house, where the Town Mouse took up his quarters. Here were couches of crimson velvet, carvings in ivory, everything in short that denoted wealth and luxury. On the table were the remains of a splendid banquet, to procure which all the choicest shops in the town had been ransacked the day before. It was now the turn of the courtier to play the host; he places his country friend on purple, runs to and fro to supply all his wants, presses dish upon dish and dainty upon dainty, and as though he were waiting on a king, tastes every course ere he ventures to place it before his rustic cousin. The Country Mouse, for his part, affects to make himself quite at home, and blesses the good fortune that had wrought such a change in his way of life; when, in the midst of his enjoyment, as he is thinking with contempt of the poor fare he has forsaken, on a sudden the door flies open, and a party of revellers returning from a late entertainment, bursts into the room. The affrighted friends jump from the table in the greatest consternation and hide themselves in the first corner they can reach. No sooner do they venture to creep out again than the barking of dogs drives them back in still greater terror than before. At length, when things seemed quiet, the Country Mouse stole out from his hiding place, and bidding his friend good-bye, whispered in his ear, "Oh, my good sir, this fine mode of living may do for those who like it; but give me my barley-bread in peace and security before the daintiest feast where Fear and Care are in waiting."

THE DOG, THE COCK, AND THE FOX

A Dog and a Cock having struck up an acquaintance, went out on their travels together. Nightfall found them in a forest; so the Cock, flying up on a tree,

perched among the branches, while the Dog dozed
below at the foot. As the night passed away and the
day dawned, the Cock, according to his custom, set up
a shrill crowing. A Fox hearing him, and thinking to
make a meal of him, came and stood under the tree,
and thus addressed him :—"Thou art a good little bird,
and most useful to thy fellow-creatures. Come down,
then, that we may sing our matins and rejoice together."
The Cock replied, "Go, my good friend, to the foot of
the tree, and call the sacristan to toll the bell." But
as the Fox went to call him, the Dog jumped out in a
moment, and seized the Fox and made an end of him.

They who lay traps for others are often caught by
their own bait.

THE LION AND THE MOUSE

A Lion was sleeping in his lair, when a Mouse, not
knowing where he was going, ran over the mighty
beast's nose and awakened him. The Lion clapped
his paw upon the frightened little creature, and was
about to make an end of him in a moment, when
the Mouse, in pitiable tone, besought him to spare
one who had so unconsciously offended, and not stain
his honourable paws with so insignificant a prey. The
Lion, smiling at his little prisoner's fright, generously
let him go. Now it happened no long time after, that
the Lion, while ranging the woods for his prey, fell into
the toils of the hunters; and finding himself entangled
without hope of escape, set up a roar that filled the
whole forest with its echo. The Mouse, recognising the
voice of his former preserver, ran to the spot, and without more ado set to work to nibble the knot in the cord
that bound the Lion, and in a short time set the noble
beast at liberty; thus convincing him that kindness is
seldom thrown away, and that there is no creature so
much below another but that he may have it in his
power to return a good office.

THE GULL AND THE KITE

A Gull had pounced upon a fish, and in endeavouring to swallow it got choked, and lay upon the deck for dead. A Kite who was passing by and saw him, gave him no other comfort than—"It serves you right: for what business have the fowls of the air to meddle with the fish of the sea."

THE HOUSE-DOG AND THE WOLF

A lean hungry Wolf chanced one moonshiny night to fall in with a plump well-fed House-Dog. After the first compliments were passed between them, "How is it, my friend," said the Wolf, "that you look so sleek? How well your food agrees with you! and here am I striving for my living night and day, and can hardly save myself from starving." "Well," says the Dog, "if you would fare like me, you have only to do as I do." "Indeed!" says he, "and what is that?" "Why," replies the Dog, "just to guard the master's house and keep off the thieves at night." "With all my heart; for at present I have but a sorry time of it. This woodland life, with its frosts and rains, is sharp work for me. To have a warm roof over my head and a bellyful of victuals always at hand will, methinks, be no bad exchange." "True," says the Dog; "therefore you have nothing to do but to follow me." Now as they were jogging on together, the Wolf spied a mark in the Dog's neck, and having a strange curiosity, could not forbear asking what it meant. "Pooh! nothing at all," says the Dog. "Nay, but pray"— says the Wolf. "Oh! a mere trifle, perhaps the collar to which my chain is fastened——" "Chain!" cries the Wolf in surprise; "you don't mean to say that you cannot rove when and where you please?" "Why, not exactly perhaps; you see I am looked upon as rather fierce, so they sometimes tie me up in the day-time, but I assure you I have perfect liberty at night, and the master feeds me off his own plate, and the servants give me their tit-bits, and I am such a favourite, and —but what is the matter? where are you going?" "Oh, good-night to you," says the Wolf; "you are welcome to your dainties; but for me, a dry crust with liberty against a king's luxury with a chain."

THE FROG AND THE OX

An Ox, grazing in a swampy meadow, chanced to set his foot among a parcel of young Frogs, and crushed nearly the whole brood to death. One that escaped ran off to his mother with the dreadful news; "And, O mother!" said he, "it was a beast—such a big four-footed beast!—that did it." "Big?" quoth the old Frog, "how big? was it as big"—and she puffed herself out to a great degree—"as big as this?" "Oh!" said the little one, "a great deal bigger than that." "Well, was it so big?" and she swelled herself out yet more. "Indeed, mother, but it was; and if you were to burst yourself, you would never reach half its size." Provoked at such a disparagement of her powers, the old Frog made one more trial, and burst herself indeed.

So men are ruined by attempting a greatness to which they have no claim.

THE POMEGRANATE, THE APPLE, AND THE BRAMBLE

The Pomegranate and the Apple had a contest on the score of beauty. When words ran high, and the strife waxed dangerous, a Bramble, thrusting his head from a neighbouring bush, cried out, "We have disputed long enough; let there be no more rivalry betwixt us."

The most insignificant are generally the most presuming.

THE TORTOISE AND THE EAGLE

A Tortoise, dissatisfied with his lowly life, when he beheld so many of the birds, his neighbours, disporting themselves in the clouds, and thinking that, if he could but once get up into the air, he could soar with the best of them, called one day upon an Eagle and offered him all the treasures of Ocean if he could only teach him to fly. The Eagle would have declined the task, assuring him that the thing was not only absurd but impossible, but being further pressed by the entreaties and promises of the Tortoise, he at length consented to do for him the best he could. So taking him up to a great height in the air and loosing his hold upon him, "Now, then!" cried the Eagle; but the Tortoise, before he could answer him a word, fell plump upon a rock, and was dashed to pieces.

Pride shall have a fall.

THE MULE

A Mule that had grown fat and wanton on too great an allowance of corn, was one day jumping and kicking about, and at length, cocking up her tail, exclaimed, "My dam was a Racer, and I am quite as good as ever she was." But being soon knocked up with her galloping and frisking, she remembered all at once that her sire was but an Ass.

Every truth has two sides; it is well to look at both, before we commit ourselves to either.

THE HARE AND THE TORTOISE

A Hare jeered at a Tortoise for the slowness of his pace. But he laughed and said, that he would run against her and beat her any day she would name. "Come on," said the Hare, "you shall soon see what my feet are made of." So it was agreed that they should start at once. The Tortoise went off jogging along, without a moment's stopping, at his usual steady pace. The Hare, treating the whole matter very lightly, said she would first take a little nap, and that she should soon overtake the Tortoise. Meanwhile the Tortoise plodded on, and the Hare oversleeping herself, arrived at the goal, only to see that the Tortoise had got in before her.

Slow and steady wins the race.

THE HEN AND THE CAT

A Cat hearing that a Hen was laid up sick in her nest, paid her a visit of condolence; and creeping up to her said, "How are you, my dear friend? what can I do for you? what are you in want of? only tell me, if there is anything in the world that I can bring you; but keep up your spirits, and don't be alarmed." "Thank you," said the Hen; "do you be good enough to leave me, and I have no fear but I shall soon be well."

Unbidden guests are often welcomest when they are gone.

THE SHEPHERD-BOY AND THE WOLF

A Shepherd-boy, who tended his flock not far from a village, used to amuse himself at times in crying out "Wolf! Wolf!" Twice or thrice his trick succeeded. The whole village came running out to his assistance; when all the return they got was to be laughed at for their pains. At last one day the Wolf came indeed. The Boy cried out in earnest. But his neighbours, supposing him to be at his old sport, paid no heed to his cries, and the Wolf devoured the Sheep. So the Boy learned, when it was too late, that liars are not believed even when they tell the truth.

THE SICK STAG

A Stag that had fallen sick, lay down on the rich herbage of a lawn, close to a wood-side, that she might obtain an easy pasturage. But so many of the beasts came to see her—for she was a good sort of neighbour—that one taking a little, and another a little, they ate up all the grass in the place. So, though recovering from the disease, she pined for want, and in the end lost both her substance and her life.

THE OLD WOMAN AND THE WINE-JAR

An Old Woman saw an empty Wine-jar lying on the ground. Though not a drop of the noble Falernian, with which it had been filled, remained, it still yielded a grateful fragrance to the passers-by. The Old Woman, applying her nose as close as she could and snuffing with all her might and main, exclaimed, "Sweet creature! how charming must your contents once have been, when the very dregs are so delicious!"

THE MOON AND HER MOTHER

The Moon once asked her Mother to make her a little cloak that would fit her well. "How," replied she, "can I make you a cloak to fit you, who are now a New Moon, and then a Full Moon, and then again neither one nor the other?"

THE ASS AND THE GRASSHOPPER

An Ass hearing some Grasshoppers chirping, was delighted with the music, and determining, if he could, to rival them, asked them what it was that they fed upon to make them sing so sweetly? When they told him that they supped upon nothing but dew, the Ass betook himself to the same diet, and soon died of hunger.

One man's meat is another man's poison.

THE FOX AND THE WOODMAN

A Fox, hard pressed by the hounds after a long run, came up to a man who was cutting wood, and begged him to afford him some place where he might hide himself. The man showed him his own hut, and the Fox creeping in, hid himself in a corner. The Hunters presently came up, and asking the man whether he had seen the Fox, "No," said he, but pointed with his finger to the corner. They, however, not understanding the hint, were off again immediately. When the Fox perceived that they were out of sight, he was stealing off without saying a word. But the man upbraided him, saying, "Is this the way you take leave of your host, without a word of thanks for your safety?" "A pretty host!" said the Fox, turning round upon him; "if you had been as honest with your fingers as you were with your tongue, I should not have left your roof without bidding you farewell."

There is as much malice in a wink as in a word.

THE LAMB AND THE WOLF

A Lamb pursued by a Wolf took refuge in a temple. Upon this the Wolf called out to him, and said, that the priest would slay him if he caught him. "Be it so," said the Lamb: "it is better to be sacrificed to God, than to be devoured by you."

THE CROW AND THE PITCHER

A Crow, ready to die with thirst, flew with joy to a Pitcher, which he saw at a distance. But when he came up to it, he found the water so low that with all his stooping and straining he was unable to reach it. Thereupon he tried to break the Pitcher; then to overturn it; but his strength was not sufficient to do either. At last, seeing some small pebbles at hand, he dropped a great many of them, one by one, into the Pitcher, and so raised the water to the brim, and quenched his thirst.

Skill and Patience will succeed where Force fails. Necessity is the Mother of Invention.

THE CRAB AND HER MOTHER

Said an old Crab to a young one, "Why do you walk so crooked, child? walk straight!" "Mother," said the young Crab, "show me the way, will you? and when I see you taking a straight course, I will try and follow."

Example is better than precept.

JUPITER AND THE CAMEL

When the Camel, in days of yore, besought Jupiter to grant him horns, for that it was a great grief to him to see other animals furnished with them, while he had none; Jupiter not only refused to give him the horns he asked for, but cropped his ears short for his importunity.

By asking too much, we may lose the little that we had before.

THE ONE-EYED DOE

A Doe that had but one eye used to graze near the sea, and that she might be the more secure from attack, kept her eye towards the land against the approach of the hunters, and her blind side towards the sea, whence she feared no danger. But some sailors rowing by in a boat and seeing her, aimed at her from the water and shot her. When at her last gasp, she sighed to herself: "Ill-fated creature that I am! I was safe on the land-side whence I expected to be attacked, but find an enemy in the sea to which I most looked for protection."

Our troubles often come from the quarter whence we least expect them.

THE LION AND THE FOX

A Fox agreed to wait upon a Lion in the capacity
of a servant. Each for a time performed the part
belonging to his station; the Fox used to point out
the prey, and the Lion fell upon it and seized it. But
the Fox, beginning to think himself as good a beast
as his master, begged to be allowed to hunt the game
instead of finding it. His request was granted, but as
he was in the act of making a descent upon a herd, the
huntsmen came out upon him, and he was himself made
the prize.

Keep to your place, and your place will keep you.

THE TRAVELLERS AND THE BEAR

Two friends were travelling on the same road
together, when they met with a Bear. The one in
great fear, without a thought of his companion, climbed
up into a tree, and hid himself. The other seeing that
he had no chance, single-handed, against the Bear, had
nothing left but to throw himself on the ground and
feign to be dead; for he had heard that the Bear will
never touch a dead body. As he thus lay, the Bear
came up to his head, muzzling and snuffing at his nose,
and ears, and heart, but the man immovably held his
breath, and the beast supposing him to be dead, walked
away. When the Bear was fairly out of sight, his
companion came down out of the tree, and asked what
it was that the Bear whispered to him,—"for," says he,
"I observed he put his mouth very close to your ear."
"Why," replies the other, "it was no great secret; he
only bade me have a care how I kept company with
those who, when they get into a difficulty, leave their
friends in the lurch."

THE STAG IN THE OX-STALL

A hunted Stag, driven out of covert and distracted
by fear, made for the first farm-house he saw, and

hid himself in an Ox-stall which happened to be open.
As he was trying to conceal himself under the straw,
"What can you mean," said an Ox, "by running into
such certain destruction as to trust yourself to the
haunts of man?" "Only do you not betray me,"
said the Stag, "and I shall be off again on the first
opportunity." Evening came on; the herdsman fod-
dered the cattle, but observed nothing. The other farm-
servants came in and out. The Stag was still safe.
Presently the bailiff passed through; all seemed right.
The Stag now feeling himself quite secure began to
thank the Oxen for their hospitality. "Wait awhile,"
said one of them, "we indeed wish you well, but there
is yet another person, one with a hundred eyes; if he
should happen to come this way I fear your life will
be still in jeopardy." While he was speaking, the
Master, having finished his supper, came round to see
that all was safe for the night, for he thought that his
cattle had not of late looked as well as they ought.
Going up to the rack, "Why so little fodder here?"
says he; "Why is there not more straw?" And "How
long, I wonder, would it take to sweep down these
cobwebs!" Prying and observing, here and there and
everywhere, the Stag's antlers, jutting from out the
straw, caught his eye, and calling in his servants he
instantly made prize of him.

No eye like the Master's eye.

THE COLLIER AND THE FULLER

A Collier, who had more room in his house than he
wanted for himself, proposed to a Fuller to come and
take up his quarters with him. "Thank you," said the
Fuller, "but I must decline your offer; for I fear that
as fast as I whiten my goods you will blacken them
again."

There can be little liking where there is no likeness.

THE LION, THE ASS, AND THE FOX HUNTING

The Lion, the Ass, and the Fox formed a party to go out hunting. They took a large booty, and when the sport was ended bethought themselves of having a hearty meal. The Lion bade the Ass allot the spoil. So dividing it into three equal parts, the Ass begged his friends to make their choice; at which the Lion, in great indignation, fell upon the Ass, and tore him to pieces. He then bade the Fox make a division; who, gathering the whole into one great heap, reserved but the smallest mite for himself. "Ah! friend," says the Lion, "who taught you to make so equitable a division?" "I wanted no other lesson," replied the Fox, "than the Ass's fate."

Better be wise by the misfortunes of others than by your own.

THE ASS AND THE LAP-DOG

There was an Ass and a Lap-dog that belonged to the same master. The Ass was tied up in the stable, and had plenty of corn and hay to eat, and was as well off as Ass could be. The little Dog was always sporting and gambolling about, caressing and fawning upon his master in a thousand amusing ways, so that he became a great favourite, and was permitted to lie in his master's lap. The Ass, indeed, had enough to do; he was drawing wood all day, and had to take his turn at the mill at night. But while he grieved over his own lot, it galled him more to see the Lap-dog living in such ease and luxury; so thinking that if he acted a like part to his master, he should fare the same, he broke one day from his halter, and rushing into the hall began to kick and prance about in the strangest fashion; then swishing his tail and mimicking the frolics of the favourite, he upset the table where his master was at dinner, breaking it in two and smashing all the crockery; nor would he leave off till he jumped upon

his master, and pawed him with his rough-shod feet.
The servants, seeing their master in no little danger,
thought it was now high time to interfere, and having
released him from the Ass's caresses, they so belaboured
the silly creature with sticks and staves, that he never
got up again; and as he breathed his last, exclaimed,
"Why could not I have been satisfied with my natural
position, without attempting, by tricks and grimaces,
to imitate one who was but a puppy after all !"

THE WIND AND THE SUN

A dispute once arose between the Wind and the Sun,
which was the stronger of the two, and they agreed to
put the point upon this issue, that whichever soonest
made a traveller take off his cloak, should be accounted
the more powerful. The Wind began, and blew with
all his might and main a blast, cold and fierce as a
Thracian storm; but the stronger he blew the closer
the traveller wrapped his cloak around him, and the
tighter he grasped it with his hands. Then broke
out the Sun : with his welcome beams he dispersed
the vapour and the cold; the traveller felt the genial
warmth, and as the Sun shone brighter and brighter,
he sat down, overcome with the heat, and cast his cloak
on the ground.

Thus the Sun was declared the conqueror; and it
has ever been deemed that persuasion is better than
force; and that the sunshine of a kind and gentle
manner will sooner lay open a poor man's heart than
all the threatenings and force of blustering authority.

THE TREES AND THE AXE

A Woodman came into a forest to ask the Trees to
give him a handle for his Axe. It seemed so modest
a request that the principal Trees at once agreed to it,
and it was settled among them that the plain homely
Ash should furnish what was wanted. No sooner had
the Woodman fitted the staff to his purpose, than he

began laying about him on all sides, felling the noblest Trees in the wood. The Oak now seeing the whole matter too late, whispered to the Cedar, "The first concession has lost all; if we had not sacrificed our humble neighbour, we might have yet stood for ages ourselves."

When the rich surrender the rights of the poor, they give a handle to be used against their own privileges.

THE HARE AND THE HOUND

A Hound having put up a Hare from a bush, chased her for some distance, but the Hare had the best of it, and got off. A Goatherd who was coming by jeered at the Hound, saying that Puss was the better runner of the two. "You forget," replied the Hound, "that it is one thing to be running for your dinner, and another for your life."

THE LION IN LOVE

It happened in days of old that a Lion fell in love with a Woodman's daughter; and had the folly to ask her of her father in marriage. The Woodman was not much pleased with the offer, and declined the honour of so dangerous an alliance. But upon the Lion threatening him with his royal displeasure, the poor man, seeing that so formidable a creature was not to be denied, hit at length upon this expedient: "I feel greatly flattered," said he, "with your proposal; but, noble sir, what great teeth you have got! and what great claws you have got! where is the damsel that would not be frightened at such weapons as these? You must have your teeth drawn and your claws pared before you can be a suitable bridegroom for my daughter." The Lion straightway submitted (for what will not a body do for love?) and then called upon the father to accept him as a son-in-law. But the Woodman, no longer afraid of the tamed and disarmed bully, seized a stout cudgel and drove the unreasonable suitor from his door.

THE DOLPHINS AND THE SPRAT

The Dolphins and the Whales were at war with one another, and while the battle was at its height, the Sprat stepped in and endeavoured to separate them. But one of the Dolphins cried out, "Let us alone, friend! We had rather perish in the contest, than be reconciled by you."

THE WOLVES AND THE SHEEP

Once on a time, the Wolves sent an embassy to the Sheep, desiring that there might be peace between them for the time to come. "Why," said they, "should we be for ever waging this deadly strife? Those wicked Dogs are the cause of all; they are incessantly barking at us, and provoking us. Send them away, and there will be no longer any obstacle to our eternal friendship and peace." The silly Sheep listened, the Dogs were dismissed, and the flock, thus deprived of their best protectors, became an easy prey to their treacherous enemy.

THE BLIND MAN AND THE WHELP

A Blind Man was wont, on any animal being put into his hands, to say what it was. Once they brought to him a Wolf's whelp. He felt it all over, and being in doubt, said, "I know not whether thy father was a Dog or a Wolf; but this I know, that I would not trust thee among a flock of sheep."

Evil dispositions are early shown.

THE BELLY AND THE MEMBERS

In former days, when all a man's limbs did not work together as amicably as they do now, but each had a will and way of its own, the Members generally began to find fault with the Belly for spending an idle luxurious life, while they were wholly occupied in labouring for its support, and ministering to its wants and pleasures; so they entered into a conspiracy to cut off its supplies for the future. The Hands were no longer to carry food to the Mouth, nor the Mouth to receive the food, nor the Teeth to chew it. They had not long persisted in this course of starving the Belly into subjection, ere they all began, one by one, to fail and flag, and the whole body to pine away. Then the Members were convinced that the Belly also, cumbersome and useless as it seemed, had an important function of its own; that they could no more do without it than it could do without them; and that if they would have the constitution of the body in a healthy state, they must work together, each in his proper sphere, for the common good of all.

THE DOVE AND THE CROW

A Dove that was kept shut up in a cage was congratulating herself upon the number of her family. "Cease, good soul," said a Crow, "to boast on that subject; for the more young ones you have, so many more slaves will you have to groan over."

What are blessings in freedom are curses in slavery.

HERCULES AND THE WAGGONER

As a Countryman was carelessly driving his waggon along a miry lane, his wheels stuck so deep in the clay that the horses came to a stand-still. Upon this the man, without making the least effort of his own, began to call upon Hercules to come and help him out of his trouble. But Hercules bade him lay his shoulder to the wheel, assuring him that Heaven only aided those who endeavoured to help themselves.

It is in vain to expect our prayers to be heard, if we do not strive as well as pray.

THE MONKEY AND THE CAMEL

At a great meeting of the Beasts, the Monkey stood up to dance. Having greatly distinguished himself, and being applauded by all present, it moved the spleen of the Camel, who came forward and began to dance also; but he made himself so utterly absurd, that all the Beasts in indignation set upon him with clubs and drove him out of the ring.

Stretch your arm no further than your sleeve will reach.

THE FOX WITHOUT A TAIL

A Fox being caught in a trap, was glad to compound for his neck by leaving his tail behind him; but upon coming abroad into the world, he began to be so sensible of the disgrace such a defect would bring upon him, that he almost wished he had died rather than come away without it. However, resolving to make the best of a bad matter, he called a meeting of the rest of the Foxes, and proposed that all should follow his example. "You have no notion," said he, "of the ease and comfort with which I now move about : I could never have believed it if I had not tried it myself; but really, when one comes to reason upon it, a tail is such an ugly, inconvenient, unnecessary appendage, that the only wonder is that, as Foxes, we could have put up with it so long. I propose, therefore, my worthy brethren, that you all profit by the experience that I am most willing to afford you, and that all Foxes from this day forward cut off their tails." Upon this one of the oldest stepped forward, and said, "I rather think, my friend, that you would not have advised us to part with our tails, if there were any chance of recovering your own."

THE FARTHING RUSHLIGHT

A Rushlight that had grown fat and saucy with too much grease, boasted one evening before a large company, that it shone brighter than the sun, the moon, and all the stars. At that moment, a puff of wind came and blew it out. One who lighted it again said, "Shine on, friend Rushlight, and hold your tongue; the lights of heaven are never blown out."

THE HARES AND THE FROGS

Once upon a time, the Hares, driven desperate by the many enemies that compassed them about on every side, came to the sad resolution that there was nothing left for them but to make away with themselves, one and all. Off they scudded to a lake hard by, determined to drown themselves as the most miserable of creatures. A shoal of Frogs seated upon the bank, frightened at the approach of the Hares, leaped in the greatest alarm and confusion into the water. "Nay, then, my friends," said a Hare that was foremost, "our case is not so desperate yet; for here are other poor creatures more faint-hearted than ourselves."

Take not comfort, but courage, from another's distress; and be sure, whatever your misery, that there are some whose lot you would not exchange with your own.

THE LIONESS

There was a great stir made among all the Beasts, which could boast of the largest family. So they came to the Lioness. "And how many," said they, "do you have at a birth?" "One," said she, grimly; "but that one is a Lion."

Quality comes before quantity.

THE ANGLER AND THE LITTLE FISH

An Angler, who gained his livelihood by fishing, after a long day's toil, caught nothing but one little fish. "Spare me," said the little creature, "I beseech you; so small as I am, I shall make you but a sorry meal. I am not come to my full size yet; throw me back into the river for the present, and then, when I am grown bigger and worth eating, you may come here and catch me again." "No, no," said the man; "I have got you now, but if you once get back into the water, your tune will be, 'Catch me, if you can.'"

A bird in the hand is worth two in the bush.

THE FARMER AND HIS SONS

A Farmer being on the point of death, and wishing to show his sons the way to success in farming, called them to him, and said, "My children, I am now departing from this life, but all that I have to leave you, you will find in the vineyard." The sons, supposing that he referred to some hidden treasure, as soon as the old man was dead, set to work with their spades and ploughs and every implement that was at hand, and turned up the soil over and over again. They found indeed no treasure; but the vines, strengthened and improved by this thorough tillage, yielded a finer vintage than they had ever yielded before, and more than repaid the young husbandmen for all their trouble. So truly is industry in itself a treasure.

THE HUSBANDMAN AND THE STORK

A Husbandman fixed a net in his field to catch the Cranes that came to feed on his new-sown corn. When he went to examine the net, and see what Cranes he had taken, a Stork was found among the number. "Spare me," cried the Stork, "and let me go. I am no Crane. I have eaten none of your corn.

I am a poor innocent Stork, as you may see—the most pious and dutiful of birds. I honour and succour my father and mother. I——" But the Husbandman cut him short. "All this may be true enough, I dare say, but this I know, that I have caught you with those who were destroying my crops, and you must suffer with the company in which you are taken."

Ill company proves more than fair professions.

THE MOLE AND HER MOTHER

Said a young Mole to her mother, "Mother, I can see." So, in order to try her, her Mother put a lump of frankincense before her, and asked her what it was. "A stone," said the young one. "O, my child!" said the Mother, "not only do you not see, but you cannot even smell."

Brag upon one defect, and betray another.

THE OLD WOMAN AND THE PHYSICIAN

An old Woman, who had become blind, called in a Physician, and promised him, before witnesses, that if he would restore her eyesight, she would give him a most handsome reward, but that if he did not cure her, and her malady remained, he should receive nothing. The agreement being concluded, the Physician tampered from time to time with the old lady's eyes, and meanwhile, bit by bit, carried off her goods. At length after a time he set about the task in earnest and cured her, and thereupon asked for the stipulated fee. But the old Woman, on recovering her sight, saw none of her goods left in the house. When, therefore, the Physician importuned her in vain for payment, and she continually put him off with excuses, he summoned her at last before the Judges. Being now called upon for her defence, she said, "What this man says is true enough; I promised to give him his fee if my sight were restored, and nothing if my eyes continued bad. Now then he says that I am cured, but I say just the contrary; for when my malady first came on, I could see all sorts of furniture and goods in my house; but now, when he says he has restored my sight, I cannot see one jot of either."

He who plays a trick must be prepared to take a joke.

THE SWALLOW AND THE RAVEN

The Swallow and the Raven contended which was the finer bird. The Raven ended by saying, "Your beauty is but for the summer, but mine will stand many winters."

Durability is better than show.

THE NURSE AND THE WOLF

A Wolf, roving about in search of food, passed by a door where a child was crying and its Nurse chiding it. As he stood listening he heard the Nurse say, "Now leave off crying this instant, or I'll throw you out to the Wolf." So thinking that the old woman would be as good as her word, he waited quietly about the house, in expectation of a capital supper. But as it grew dark and the child became quiet, he again heard the Nurse, who was now fondling the child, say, "There's a good dear then; if the naughty Wolf comes for my child, we'll beat him to death, we will." The Wolf, disappointed and mortified, thought it was now high time to be going home, and, hungry as a wolf indeed, muttered as he went along: "This comes of heeding people who say one thing and mean another!"

THE DOG AND HIS MASTER

A certain Man was setting out on a journey, when, seeing his Dog standing at the door, he cried out to him, "What are you gaping about? Get ready to come with me." The Dog, wagging his tail, said, "I am all right, Master; it is you who have to pack up."

THE MONKEY AND THE DOLPHIN

It was an old custom among sailors to carry about with them little Maltese lap-dogs, or Monkeys, to amuse them on the voyage; so it happened once upon a time that a man took with him a Monkey as a companion on board ship. While they were off Sunium, the famous promontory of Attica, the ship was caught in a violent storm, and being capsized, all on board were thrown in the water, and had to swim for land as best they could. And among them was the Monkey. A Dolphin saw him struggling, and, taking him for a man, went to his assistance and bore him on his back straight for shore. When they had just got opposite Piræus, the harbour of Athens, the Dolphin asked the Monkey "If he were an Athenian?" "Yes," answered the Monkey, "assuredly, and of one of the first families in the place." "Then, of course, you know Piræus," said the Dolphin. "Oh, yes," said the Monkey, who thought it was the name of some distinguished citizen, "he is one of my most intimate friends." Indignant at so gross a deceit and falsehood, the Dolphin dived to the bottom, and left the lying Monkey to his fate.

THE WOLF AND THE SHEEP

A Wolf that had been bitten by a dog, and was in a very sad case, being unable to move, called to a Sheep, that was passing by, and begged her to fetch him some water from the neighbouring stream. "For if you," said he, "will bring me drink, I will find meat myself." "Yes," said the Sheep, "I make no doubt of it; for, if I come near enough to give you the drink, you will soon make mince-meat of *me*."

THE BUNDLE OF STICKS

A Husbandman who had a quarrelsome family, after having tried in vain to reconcile them by words, thought he might more readily prevail by an example. So he called his sons and bade them lay a bundle of sticks before him. Then having tied them into a faggot, he told the lads, one after the other, to take it up and break it. They all tried, but tried in vain. Then untying the faggot, he gave them the sticks to break one by one. This they did with the greatest ease. Then said the father, "Thus you, my sons, as long as you remain united, are a match for all your enemies; but differ and separate, and you are undone."

Union is strength.

THE WIDOW AND THE SHEEP

There was a certain Widow who had an only Sheep; and, wishing to make the most of his wool, she sheared him so closely that she cut his skin as well as his fleece. The Sheep, smarting under this treatment, cried out—"Why do you torture me thus? What will my blood add to the weight of the wool? If you want my flesh, Dame, send for the Butcher, who will put me out of my misery at once; but if you want my fleece, send for the Shearer, who will clip my wool without drawing my blood."

Middle measures are often but middling measures.

THE MAN AND THE LION

Once upon a time a Man and a Lion were journeying together, and came at length to high words which was the braver and stronger creature of the two. As the dispute waxed warmer they happened to pass by, on the road-side, a statue of a man strangling a lion. "See there," said the Man; "what more undeniable proof can you have of our superiority than that?" "That," said the Lion, "is your version of the story; let us be the sculptors, and for one lion under the feet of a man, you shall have twenty men under the paw of a lion."

Men are but sorry witnesses in their own cause.

THE MAN BITTEN BY A DOG

A Man who had been bitten by a Dog, was going about asking who could cure him. One that met him said, "Sir, if you would be cured, take a bit of bread and dip it in the blood of the wound, and give it to the dog that bit you." The Man smiled, and said, "If I were to follow your advice, I should be bitten by all the dogs in the city."

He who proclaims himself ready to buy up his enemies will never want a supply of them.

THE HORSE AND THE STAG

A Horse had the whole range of a meadow to himself; but a Stag coming and damaging the pasture, the Horse, anxious to have his revenge, asked a Man if he could not assist him in punishing the Stag. "Yes," said the Man, "only let me put a bit in your mouth, and get upon your back, and I will find the weapons." The Horse agreed, and the Man mounted accordingly; but instead of getting his revenge, the Horse has been from that time forward the slave of Man.

Revenge is too dearly purchased at the price of liberty.

THE BIRDCATCHER AND THE LARK

A Birdcatcher was setting springes upon a common, when a Lark, who saw him at work, asked him from a distance what he was doing. "I am establishing a colony," said he, "and laying the foundations of my first city." Upon that, the man retired to a little distance and hid himself. The Lark, believing his assertion, soon flew down to the place, and swallowing the bait, found himself entangled in the noose; whereupon the Birdcatcher straightway coming up to him, made him his prisoner. "A pretty fellow are you!" said the Lark; "if these are the colonies you found, you will not find many emigrants."

THE MISCHIEVOUS DOG

There was a Dog so wild and mischievous, that his master was obliged to fasten a heavy clog about his neck, to prevent him biting and worrying his neighbours. The Dog, priding himself upon his badge, paraded in the market-place, shaking his clog to attract attention. But a sly friend whispered to him, "The less noise you make, the better; your mark of distinction is no reward of merit, but a badge of disgrace!"

Men often mistake notoriety for fame, and would rather be remarked for their vices or follies than not be noticed at all.

THE TRAVELLERS AND THE PLANE-TREE

Some Travellers, on a hot day in summer, oppressed with the noontide sun, perceiving a Plane-tree near at hand, made straight for it, and throwing themselves on the ground rested under its shade. Looking up, as they lay, towards the tree, they said one to another, "What a useless tree to man is this barren Plane!" But the Plane-tree answered them,— "Ungrateful creatures! at the very moment that you are enjoying benefit from me, you rail at me as being good for nothing."

Ingratitude is as blind as it is base.

THE HERDSMAN AND THE LOST BULL

A Herdsman, who had lost a Bull, went roaming through the forest in search of it. Being unable to find it, he began to vow to all the Nymphs of the forest and the mountain, to Mercury and to Pan, that he would offer up a lamb to them, if he could only discover the thief. At that moment, gaining a high ridge of ground, he sees a Lion standing over the carcase of his beautiful Bull. And now the unhappy man vows the Bull into the bargain, if he may only escape from the thief's clutches.

Were our ill-judged prayers to be always granted, how many would be ruined at their own request!

THE VIPER AND THE FILE

A Viper entering into a smith's shop began looking about for something to eat. At length, seeing a File, he went up to it and commenced biting at it; but the File bade him leave him alone, saying, "You are likely to get little from me, whose business it is to bite others."

JUPITER, NEPTUNE, MINERVA, AND MOMUS

Jupiter, Neptune, and Minerva (as the story goes) once contended which of them should make the most perfect thing. Jupiter made a Man; Pallas made a House; and Neptune made a Bull; and Momus—for he had not yet been turned out of Olympus—was chosen judge to decide which production had the greatest merit. He began by finding fault with the Bull, because his horns were not below his eyes, so that he might see when he butted with them. Next he found fault with the Man, because there was no window in his breast that all might see his inward thoughts and feelings. And lastly he found fault with the House, because it had no wheels to enable its inhabitants to remove from bad neighbours. But Jupiter forthwith drove the critic out of heaven, telling him that a fault-finder could never be pleased, and that it was time to criticise the works of others when he had done some good thing himself.

MERCURY AND THE WOODMAN

A Woodman was felling a tree on the bank of a river, and by chance let slip his axe into the water, when it immediately sunk to the bottom. Being thereupon in great distress, he sat down by the side of the stream and lamented his loss bitterly. But Mercury, whose river it was, taking compassion on him, appeared at the instant before him; and hearing from him the cause of his sorrow, dived to the bottom of the river, and bringing up a golden axe, asked the Woodman if that were his. Upon the man's denying it, Mercury dived a second time, and brought up one of silver. Again the man denied that it was his. So diving a third time, he produced the identical axe which the man had lost. "That is mine!" said the Woodman, delighted to have recovered his own; and so pleased was Mercury with the fellow's truth and honesty, that he at once made him a present of the other two.

The man goes to his companions, and giving them an account of what had happened to him, one of them determined to try whether he might not have the like good fortune. So repairing to the same place, as if for the purpose of cutting wood, he let slip his axe on purpose into the river, and then sat down on the bank, and made a great show of weeping. Mercury appeared as before, and hearing from him that his tears were caused by the loss of his axe, dived once more into the stream; and bringing up a golden axe, asked him if that was the axe he had lost. "Aye, surely," said the man, eagerly; and he was about to grasp the treasure, when Mercury, to punish his impudence and lying, not only refused to give him that, but would not so much as restore him his own axe again.

Honesty is the best policy.

THE GEESE AND THE CRANES

Some Geese and some Cranes fed together in the same field. One day the sportsmen came suddenly down upon them. The Cranes being light of body, flew off in a moment and escaped; but the Geese, weighed down by their fat, were all taken.

In civil commotions, they fare best who have least to fetter them.

JUPITER AND THE BEE

days of yore, when the world was young, a Bee that had stored her combs with a bountiful harvest, flew up to heaven to present as a sacrifice an offering of honey. Jupiter was so delighted with the gift, that he promised to give her whatsoever she should ask for. She therefore besought him, saying, "O glorious Jove, maker and master of me, poor Bee, give thy servant a sting, that when any one approaches my hive to take the honey, I may kill him on the spot." Jupiter, out of love to the man, was angry at her request, and thus answered her: "Your prayer shall not be granted in the way you wish, but the sting which you ask for you shall have; and when any one comes to take away your honey and you attack him, the wound shall be fatal not to him but to you, for your life shall go with your sting."

He that prays harm for his neighbour, begs a curse upon himself.

THE GOATHERD AND THE GOATS

It was a stormy day, and the snow was falling fast, when a Goatherd drove his Goats, all white with snow, into a desert cave for shelter. There he found that a herd of Wild-goats, more numerous and larger than his own, had already taken possession. So, thinking to secure them all, he left his own Goats to take care of themselves, and threw the branches which he had brought for them to the Wild-goats to browse on. But when the weather cleared up, he found his own Goats had perished from hunger, while the Wild-goats were off and away to the hills and woods. So the Goatherd returned a laughing-stock to his neighbours, having failed to gain the Wild-goats, and having lost his own.

They who neglect their old friends for the sake of new, are rightly served if they lose both.

THE COUNTRY MAID AND HER MILK-CAN

A Country Maid was walking along with a can of Milk upon her head, when she fell into the following train of reflections. "The money for which I shall sell this milk will enable me to increase my stock of eggs to three hundred. These eggs, allowing for what may prove addle, and what may be destroyed by vermin, will produce at least two hundred and fifty chickens. The chickens will be fit to carry to market just at the time when poultry is always dear; so that by the new-year I cannot fail of having money enough to purchase a new gown. Green—let me consider—yes, green becomes my complexion best, and green it shall be. In this dress I will go to the fair, where all the young fellows will strive to have me for a partner; but no—I shall refuse every one of them, and with a disdainful toss turn from them." Transported with this idea, she could not forbear acting with her head the thought that thus passed in her mind; when—down came the can of milk! and all her imaginary happiness vanished in a moment.

THE BEEVES AND THE BUTCHERS

The Beeves, once on a time, determined to make an end of the Butchers, whose whole art, they said, was conceived for their destruction. So they assembled together, and had already whetted their horns for the contest, when a very old Ox, who had long worked at the plough, thus addressed them:—"Have a care, my friends, what you do. These men, at least, kill us with decency and skill, but if we fall into the hands of botchers instead of butchers, we shall suffer a double death; for be well assured, men will not go without beef, even though they were without butchers."

Better to bear the ills we have, than fly to others that we know not of.

THE THIEF AND HIS MOTHER

A Schoolboy stole a horn-book from one of his schoolfellows, and brought it home to his mother. Instead of chastising him, she rather encouraged him in the deed. In course of time the boy, now grown into a man, began to steal things of greater value, till at length being caught in the very act, he was bound and led to execution. Perceiving his mother following among the crowd, wailing and beating her breast, he begged the officers to be allowed to speak one word in her ear. When she quickly drew near and applied her ear to her son's mouth, he seized the lobe of it tightly between his teeth and bit it off. Upon this she cried out lustily, and the crowd joined her in upbraiding the unnatural son, as if his former evil ways had not been enough, but that his last act must be a deed of impiety against his mother. But he replied: "It is she who is the cause of my ruin; for if when I stole my schoolfellow's horn-book and brought it to her, she had given me a sound flogging, I should never have so grown in wickedness as to come to this untimely end."

Nip evil in the bud. Spare the rod and spoil the child.

THE CAT AND THE MICE

A Cat, grown feeble with age, and no longer able to hunt the Mice as she was wont to do, bethought herself how she might entice them within reach of her paw. Thinking that she might pass herself off for a bag, or for a dead cat at least, she suspended herself by the hind legs from a peg, in the hope that the Mice would no longer be afraid to come near her. An old Mouse, who was wise enough to keep his distance, whispered to a friend, "Many a bag have I seen in my day, but never one with a cat's head." "Hang there, good Madam," said the other, "as long as you please, but I would not trust myself within reach of you though you were stuffed with straw."

Old birds are not to be caught with chaff.

THE MARRIAGE OF THE SUN

Once upon a time, in a very warm summer, it was currently reported that the Sun was going to be married. All the birds and the beasts were delighted at the thought; and the Frogs, above all others, were determined to have a good holiday. But an old Toad put a stop to their festivities by observing that it was an occasion for sorrow rather than for joy. "For if," said he, "the Sun of himself now parches up the marshes so that we can hardly bear it, what will become of us if he should have half a dozen little Suns in addition?"

THE GNAT AND THE BULL

A Gnat that had been buzzing about the head of a Bull, at length settling himself down upon his horn, begged his pardon for incommoding him : "but if," says he, "my weight at all inconveniences you, pray say so and I will be off in a moment." "Oh, never trouble your head about that," says the Bull, "for 'tis all one to me whether you go or stay; and, to say the truth, I did not know you were there."

The smaller the Mind the greater the Conceit.

THE EAGLE AND THE ARROW

A Bowman took aim at an Eagle and hit him in the heart. As the Eagle turned his head in the agonies of death, he saw that the Arrow was winged with his own feathers. "How much sharper," said he, "are the wounds made by weapons which we ourselves have supplied!"

THE DOG IN THE MANGER

A Dog made his bed in a Manger, and lay snarling and growling to keep the horses from their provender. "See," said one of them, "what a miserable cur! who neither can eat corn himself, nor will allow those to eat it who can."

THE MICE IN COUNCIL

Once upon a time the Mice being sadly distressed by the persecution of the Cat, resolved to call a meeting, to decide upon the best means of getting rid of this continual annoyance. Many plans were discussed and rejected; at last a young Mouse got up and proposed that a Bell should be hung round the Cat's neck, that they might for the future always have notice of her coming, and so be able to escape. This proposition was hailed with the greatest applause, and was agreed to at once unanimously. Upon which an old Mouse, who had sat silent all the while, got up and said that he considered the contrivance most ingenious, and that it would, no doubt, be quite successful; but he had only one short question to put, namely, which of them it was who would Bell the Cat?

It is one thing to propose, another to execute.

THE LION, THE BEAR, AND THE FOX

A Lion and a Bear found the carcase of a Fawn, and had a long fight for it. The contest was so hard and even, that, at last, both of them, half-blinded and half-dead, lay panting on the ground, without strength to touch the prize that was stretched between them. A Fox coming by at the time, and seeing their helpless condition, stepped in between the combatants and carried off the booty. "Poor creatures that we are," cried they, "who have been exhausting all our strength and injuring one another, merely to give a rogue a dinner!"

THE FOX AND THE HEDGEHOG

A Fox, while crossing over a river, was driven by the stream into a narrow gorge, and lay there for a long time unable to get out, covered with myriads of horse-flies that had fastened themselves upon him. A Hedgehog, who was wandering in that direction, saw him, and, taking compassion on him, asked him if he should drive away the flies that were so tormenting him. But the Fox begged him to do nothing of the sort. "Why not?" asked the Hedgehog. "Because," replied the Fox, "these flies that are upon me now, are already full, and draw but little blood, but should you remove them, a swarm of fresh and hungry ones will come, who will not leave a drop of blood in my body."

When we throw off rulers or dependants, who have already made the most of us, we do but, for the most part, lay ourselves open to others who will make us bleed yet more freely.

THE GOOSE WITH THE GOLDEN EGGS

A certain man had the good fortune to possess a Goose that laid him a Golden Egg every day. But dissatisfied with so slow an income, and thinking to seize the whole treasure at once, he killed the Goose; and cutting her open, found her—just what any other goose would be!

Much wants more and loses all.

THE LION AND THE DOLPHIN

A Lion was roaming on the sea-shore, when, seeing a Dolphin basking on the surface of the water, he invited him to form an alliance with him, "for," said he, "as I am the king of the beasts, and you are the king of the fishes, we ought to be the greatest friends and allies possible." The Dolphin gladly assented; and the Lion, not long after, having a fight with a wild bull, called upon the Dolphin for his promised support. But when he, though ready to assist him, found himself unable to come out of the sea for the purpose, the Lion accused him of having betrayed him. "Do not blame me," said the Dolphin in reply, "but blame my nature, which however powerful at sea, is altogether helpless on land."

In choosing allies we must look to their power as well as their will to aid us.

THE TRUMPETER TAKEN PRISONER

A Trumpeter being taken prisoner in a battle, begged hard for quarter. "Spare me, good sirs, I beseech you," said he, "and put me not to death without cause, for I have killed no one myself, nor have I any arms but this trumpet only." "For that very reason," said they who had seized him, "shall you the sooner die, for without the spirit to fight, yourself, you stir up others to warfare and bloodshed."

He who incites to strife is worse than he who takes part in it.

THE MOUNTEBANK AND THE COUNTRYMAN

A certain wealthy patrician, intending to treat the Roman people with some theatrical entertainment, publicly offered a reward to any one who would produce a novel spectacle. Incited by emulation, artists arrived from all parts to contest the prize, among whom a well-known witty Mountebank gave out that he had a new kind of entertainment that had never yet been produced on any stage. This report being spread abroad, brought the whole city together. The theatre could hardly contain the number of spectators. And when the artist appeared alone upon the stage, without any apparatus, or any assistants, curiosity and suspense kept the spectators in profound silence. On a sudden he thrust down his head into his bosom, and mimicked the squeaking of a young pig, so naturally, that the audience insisted upon it that he had one under his cloak, and ordered him to be searched; which being done, and nothing appearing, they loaded him with the most extravagant applause.

A Countryman among the audience observing what passed—"Oh!" says he, "I can do better than this;" and immediately gave out that he would perform the next day. Accordingly, on the morrow, a yet greater crowd was collected. Prepossessed, however, in favour of the Mountebank, they came rather to laugh at the Countryman than to pass a fair judgment on him. They both came out upon the stage. The Mountebank grunts away first, and calls forth the greatest clapping and applause. Then the Countryman, pretending that he concealed a little pig under his garments (and he had, in fact, really got one), pinched its ear till he made it squeak. The people cried out that the Mountebank had imitated the pig much more naturally, and hooted to the Countryman to quit the stage; but he, to convict them to their face, produced the real pig from his bosom. "And now, gentlemen, you may see," said he, "what a pretty sort of judges you are!"

It is easier to convince a man against his senses than against his will.

THE HUNTER AND THE FISHERMAN

A Hunter was returning from the mountains loaded with game, and a Fisherman was at the same time coming home with his creel full of fish, when they chanced to meet by the way. The Hunter took a fancy to a dish of fish: the Fisher preferred a supper of game. So each gave to the other the contents of his own basket. And thus they continued daily to exchange provisions, till one who had observed them said: "Now, by this invariable interchange, will they destroy the zest of their meal; and each will soon wish to return to his own store again."

THE DOG INVITED TO SUPPER

A Gentleman, having prepared a great feast, invited a Friend to supper; and the Gentleman's Dog, meeting the Friend's Dog, "Come," said he, "my good fellow, and sup with us to-night." The Dog was delighted with the invitation, and as he stood by and saw the preparations for the feast, said to himself, "Capital

fare indeed! this is, in truth, good luck. I shall revel
in dainties, and I will take good care to lay in an
ample stock to-night, for I may have nothing to eat
to-morrow." As he said this to himself, he wagged
his tail, and gave a sly look at his friend who had
invited him. But his tail wagging to and fro caught
the cook's eye, who seeing a stranger, straightway
seized him by the legs, and threw him out of the
window. When he reached the ground, he set off
yelping down the street; upon which the neighbours'
Dogs ran up to him, and asked him how he liked his
supper. "I'faith," said he, with a sorry smile, "I
hardly know, for we drank so deep that I can't even
tell you which way I got out of the house."

They who enter by the back-stairs may expect to
be shown out at the window.

THE FROGS ASKING FOR A KING

In the days of old, when the Frogs were all at liberty
in the lakes, and had grown quite weary of following
every one his own devices, they assembled one day
together, and with no little clamour petitioned Jupiter
to let them have a King to keep them in better order,
and make them lead honester lives. Jupiter, knowing
the vanity of their hearts, smiled at their request, and
threw down a Log into the lake, which by the splash
and commotion it made, sent the whole commonwealth
into the greatest terror and amazement. They rushed
under the water and into the mud, and dared not come
within ten leaps' length of the spot where it lay. At
length one Frog bolder than the rest ventured to pop
his head above the water, and take a survey of their
new King at a respectful distance. Presently, when
they perceived the Log lie stock-still, others began to
swim up to it and around it; till by degrees, growing
bolder and bolder, they at last leaped upon it, and
treated it with the greatest contempt. Dissatisfied with
so tame a ruler, they forthwith petitioned Jupiter a

second time for another and more active King. Upon which he sent them a Stork, who no sooner arrived among them than he began laying hold of them and devouring them one by one as fast as he could, and it was in vain that they endeavoured to escape him. Then they sent Mercury with a private message to Jupiter, beseeching him that he would take pity on them once more; but Jupiter replied, that they were only suffering the punishment due to their folly, and that another time they would learn to let well alone, and not be dissatisfied with their natural condition.

THE FIR-TREE AND THE BRAMBLE

A Fir-tree was one day boasting itself to a Bramble. "You are of no use at all; but how could barns and houses be built without me?" "Good sir," said the Bramble, "when the woodmen come here with their axes and saws, what would you give to be a Bramble and not a Fir?"

A humble lot in security is better than the dangers that encompass the high and haughty.

THE LARK AND HER YOUNG ONES

There was a brood of Young Larks in a field of corn, which was just ripe, and the mother, looking every day for the reapers, left word, whenever she went out in search of food, that her young ones should report to her all the news they heard. One day, while she was absent, the master came to look at the state of the crop. "It is full time," said he, "to call in all my neighbours and get my corn reaped." When the old Lark came home, the young ones told their mother what they had heard, and begged her to remove them forthwith. "Time enough," said she; "if he trusts to his neighbours, he will have to wait awhile yet for his harvest." Next day, however, the owner came again, and finding the sun still hotter and the corn more ripe, and nothing done, "There is not a moment to be lost," said he; "we

cannot depend upon our neighbours: we must call in
our relations;" and, turning to his son, "Go call your
uncles and cousins, and see that they begin to-morrow."
In still greater fear, the young ones repeated to their
mother the farmer's words. "If that be all," says she,
"do not be frightened, for the relations have got harvest
work of their own; but take particular notice what you
hear the next time, and be sure you let me know." She
went abroad the next day, and the owner coming as
before, and finding the grain falling to the ground from
over-ripeness, and still no one at work, called to his
son. "We must wait for our neighbours and friends no
longer; do you go and hire some reapers to-night, and
we will set to work ourselves to-morrow." When the
young ones told their mother this—"Then," said she,
"it is time to be off, indeed; for when a man takes up
his business himself, instead of leaving it to others, you
may be sure that he means to set to work in earnest."

THE FISHERMAN

A Fisherman went to a river to fish; and when he
had laid his nets across the stream, he tied a stone
to a long cord, and beat the water on either side of
the net, to drive the fish into the meshes. One of the
neighbours that lived thereabout seeing him thus employed, went up to him and blamed him exceedingly
for disturbing the water, and making it so muddy as to
be unfit to drink. "I am sorry," said the Fisherman,
"that this does not please you, but it is by thus
troubling the waters that I gain my living."

THE THIEF AND THE DOG

A Thief coming to rob a house would have stopped
the barking of a Dog by throwing sops to him. "Away
with you!" said the Dog; "I had my suspicions of
you before, but this excess of civility assures me that
you are a rogue."

A bribe in hand betrays mischief at heart.

THE ASS AND HIS MASTERS

An Ass, that belonged to a Gardener, and had little to eat and much to do, besought Jupiter to release him from the Gardener's service, and give him another master. Jupiter, angry at his discontent, made him over to a Potter. He had now heavier burdens to carry than before, and again appealed to Jupiter to relieve him, who accordingly contrived that he should be sold to a Tanner. The Ass having now fallen into worse hands than ever, and daily observing how his master was employed, exclaimed with a groan, "Alas, wretch that I am! it had been better for me to have remained content with my former masters, for now I see that my present owner not only works me harder while living, but will not even spare my hide when I am dead!"

He that is discontented in one place will seldom be happy in another.

THE OLD MAN AND DEATH

An Old Man that had travelled a long way with a huge bundle of sticks, found himself so weary that he cast it down, and called upon Death to deliver him from his most miserable existence. Death came straightway at his call, and asked him what he wanted. "Pray, good sir," says he, "do me but the favour to help me up with my burden again."

It is one thing to call for Death, and another to see him coming.

THE DOCTOR AND HIS PATIENT

A Doctor had been for some time attending upon a sick man, who, however, died under his hands. At the funeral the Doctor went about among the relations, saying, "Our poor friend, if he had only refrained from wine, and attended to his inside, and used proper

means, would not have been lying there." One of the
mourners answered him, "My good sir, it is of no use
your saying this now; you ought to have prescribed
these things when your Patient was alive to take them."

The best advice may come too late.

THE BIRDS, THE BEASTS, AND THE BAT

Once upon a time there was a fierce war waged
between the Birds and the Beasts. For a long while
the issue of the battle was uncertain, and the Bat, taking
advantage of his ambiguous nature, kept aloof and
remained neutral. At length when the Beasts seemed
to prevail, the Bat joined their forces and appeared
active in the fight; but a rally being made by the
Birds, which proved successful, he was found at the
end of the day among the ranks of the winning party.
A peace being speedily concluded, the Bat's conduct
was condemned alike by both parties, and being acknow-
ledged by neither, and so excluded from the terms of
the truce, he was obliged to skulk off as best he could,
and has ever since lived in holes and corners, never
daring to show his face except in the duskiness of
twilight.

THE TWO POTS

Two Pots, one of earthenware, the other of brass,
were carried down a river in a flood. The Brazen
Pot begged his companion to keep by his side, and he
would protect him. "Thank you for your offer," said
the Earthen Pot, "but that is just what I am afraid of;
if you will only keep at a distance, I may float down
in safety; but should we come in contact, I am sure
to be the sufferer."

Avoid too powerful neighbours; for, should there be
a collision, the weakest goes to the wall.

THE LION AND THE GOAT

On a summer's day, when everything was suffering from extreme heat, a Lion and a Goat came at the same time to quench their thirst at a small fountain. They at once fell to quarrelling which should first drink of the water, till at length it seemed that each was determined to resist the other even to death. But, ceasing from the strife for a moment, to recover breath, they saw a flock of vultures hovering over them, only waiting to pounce upon whichever of them should fall. Whereupon they instantly made up their quarrel, agreeing that it was far better for them both to become friends, than to furnish food for the crows and vultures.

THE ARAB AND THE CAMEL

An Arab having loaded his Camel, asked him whether he preferred to go up hill or down hill. "Pray, Master," said the Camel dryly, "is the straight way across the plain shut up?"

THE WOLF AND THE SHEPHERD

A Wolf had long hung about a flock of sheep, and had done them no harm. The Shepherd, however, had his suspicions, and for a while was always on the look-out against him as an avowed enemy. But when the Wolf continued for a long time following in the train of his flock without the least attempt to annoy them, he began to look upon him more as a friend than a foe; and having one day occasion to go into the city, he intrusted the sheep to his care. The Wolf no sooner saw his opportunity than he forthwith fell upon the sheep and worried them; and the Shepherd, on his return, seeing his flock destroyed, exclaimed, "Fool that I am! yet I deserved no less for trusting my Sheep with a Wolf!"

There is more danger from a pretended friend than from an open enemy.

THE TRAVELLERS AND THE HATCHET

Two men were travelling along the same road, when one of them picking up a hatchet cries, "See what I have found!" "Do not say I," says the other, "but WE have found." After a while, up came the men who had lost the hatchet, and charged the man who had it with the theft. "Alas," says he to his companion, "we are undone!" "Do not say WE," replies the other, "but I am undone; for he that will not allow his friend to share the prize, must not expect him to share the danger."

THE ASS, THE FOX, AND THE LION

An Ass and a Fox having made a compact alliance, went out into the fields to hunt. They met a Lion on the way. The Fox seeing the impending danger, made up to the Lion, and whispered that he would betray the Ass into his power, if he would promise to bear him harmless. The Lion having agreed to do so, the Fox contrived to lead the Ass into a snare. The Lion no sooner saw the Ass secured, than he fell at once upon the Fox, reserving the other for his next meal.

THE BEES, THE DRONES, AND THE WASP

Some Bees had built their comb in the hollow trunk of an oak. The Drones asserted that it was their doing, and belonged to them. The cause was brought into court before Judge Wasp. Knowing something of the parties, he thus addressed them:—"The plaintiffs and defendants are so much alike in shape and colour as to render the ownership a doubtful matter, and the case has very properly been brought before me. The ends of justice, and the object of the court, will best be furthered by the plan which I propose. Let each party take a hive to itself, and build up a

new comb, that from the shape of the cell
taste of the honey, the lawful proprietors of the
in dispute may appear." The Bees readily as
the Wasp's plan. The Drones declined it. Whereupon the Wasp gave judgment :—"It is clear now who
made the comb, and who cannot make it; the Court
adjudges the honey to the Bees."

THE LION AND ASS HUNTING

A Lion and an Ass made an agreement to go out
hunting together. By-and-bye they came to a cave,
where many wild goats abode. The Lion took up his
station at the mouth of the cave, and the Ass, going
within, kicked and brayed and made a mighty fuss to
frighten them out. When the Lion had caught very
many of them, the Ass came out and asked him if he
had not made a noble fight, and routed the goats
properly. "Yes, indeed," said the Lion; "and I assure
you, you would have frightened me too, if I had not
known you to be an Ass."

When braggarts are admitted into the company of
their betters, it is only to be made use of and be
laughed at.

THE ASS AND HIS DRIVER

An Ass that was being driven along the road by his
Master, started on ahead, and, leaving the beaten track,
made as fast as he could for the edge of a precipice.
When he was just on the point of falling over, his
Master ran up, and, seizing him by the tail, endeavoured
to pull him back; but the Ass resisting and pulling
the contrary way, the man let go his hold, saying,
"Well, Jack, if you will be master, I cannot help it.
A wilful beast must go his own way."

THE MICE AND THE WEASELS

The Mice and the Weasels had long been at war with each other, and the Mice being always worsted in battle, at length agreed at a meeting, solemnly called for the occasion, that their defeat was attributable to nothing but their want of discipline, and they determined accordingly to elect regular Commanders for the time to come. So they chose those whose valour and prowess most recommended them to the important post. The new Commanders, proud of their position, and desirous of being as conspicuous as possible, bound horns upon their foreheads as a sort of crest and mark of distinction. Not long after a battle ensued. The Mice, as before, were soon put to flight; the common herd escaped into their holes; but the Commanders, not being able to get in from the length of their horns, were every one caught and devoured.

There is no distinction without its accompanying danger.

THE HART AND THE VINE

A Hart pursued by hunters concealed himself among the branches of a Vine. The hunters passed by without discovering him, and when he thought that all was safe, he began browsing upon the leaves that had concealed him. But one of the hunters, attracted by the rustling, turned round, and guessing that their prey was there, shot into the bush and killed him. As he was dying, he groaned out these words : "I suffer justly for my ingratitude, who could not forbear injuring the Vine that had protected me in time of danger."

THE HEDGE AND THE VINEYARD

A foolish young Heir who had just come into possession of his wise father's estate, caused all the Hedges about his Vineyard to be grubbed up, because they bore no grapes. The throwing down of the fences laid his grounds open to man and beast, and all his vines were presently destroyed. So the simple fellow learnt, when it was too late, that he ought not to expect to gather grapes from brambles, and that it was quite as important to protect his Vineyard as to possess it.

THE FOX AND THE MASK

A Fox had stolen into the house of an actor, and in rummaging among his various properties, laid hold of a highly-finished Mask. "A fine-looking head, indeed!" cried he; "what a pity it is that it wants brains!"

A fair outside is but a poor substitute for inward worth.

THE FATHER AND HIS TWO DAUGHTERS

A Man who had two daughters married one to a Gardener, the other to a Potter. After awhile he paid a visit to the Gardener's, and asked his daughter how she was, and how it fared with her. "Excellently well," said she; "we have everything that we want; I have but one prayer, that we may have a heavy storm of rain to water our plants." Off he set to the Potter's, and asked his other daughter how matters went with her. "There is not a thing we want," she replied; "and I only hope this fine weather and hot sun may continue, to bake our tiles." "Alack," said the Father, "if you wish for fine weather, and your sister for rain, which am I to pray for myself?"

THE HORSE AND THE LOADED ASS

A Man who kept a Horse and an Ass was wont in his journeys to spare the Horse, and put all the burden upon the Ass's back. The Ass, who had been some while ailing, besought the Horse one day to relieve him of part of his load; "For if," said he, "you would take a fair portion, I shall soon get well again; but if you refuse to help me, this weight will kill me." The Horse, however, bade the Ass get on, and not trouble him with his complaints. The Ass jogged on in silence, but presently, overcome with the weight of his burden, dropped down dead, as he had foretold. Upon this, the master coming up, unloosed the load from the dead Ass, and putting it upon the Horse's back, made him carry the Ass's carcase in addition. "Alas, for my ill nature!" said the Horse; "by refusing to bear my just portion of the load, I have now to carry the whole of it, with a dead weight into the bargain."

A disobliging temper carries its own punishment along with it.

THE SICK LION

A Lion, no longer able, from the weakness of old age, to hunt for his prey, laid himself up in his den, and, breathing with great difficulty, and speaking with a low voice, gave out that he was very ill indeed. The report soon spread among the beasts, and there was great lamentation for the sick Lion. One after the other came to see him; but, catching him thus alone, and in his own den, the Lion made an easy prey of them, and grew fat upon his diet. The Fox, suspecting the truth of the matter, came at length to make his visit of inquiry, and standing at some distance, asked his Majesty how he did? "Ah, my dearest friend," said the Lion, "is it you? Why do you stand so far from me? Come, sweet friend, and pour a word of consolation in the poor Lion's ear, who has but a short time to live." "Bless you!" said the Fox, "but excuse me if I cannot stay; for, to tell the truth, I feel quite uneasy at the mark of the footsteps that I see here, all pointing towards your den, and none returning outwards."

Affairs are easier of entrance than of exit; and it is but common prudence to see our way out before we venture in.

THE FARMER AND THE CRANES

Some Cranes settled down in a Farmer's field that was newly sown. For some time the Farmer frightened them away by brandishing an empty sling at them. But when the Cranes found that he was only slinging to the winds, they no longer minded him, nor flew away. Upon this the Farmer slung at them with stones, and killed a great part of them. "Let us be off," said the rest, "to the land of the Pygmies, for this man means to threaten us no longer, but is determined to get rid of us in earnest."

THE EAGLE AND THE JACKDAW

An Eagle made a swoop from a high rock, and carried off a lamb. A Jackdaw, who saw the exploit, thinking that he could do the like, bore down with all the force he could muster upon a ram, intending to bear him off as a prize. But his claws becoming entangled in the wool, he made such a fluttering in his efforts to escape, that the shepherd, seeing through the whole matter, came up and caught him, and having clipped his wings, carried him home to his children at nightfall. "What bird is this, father, that you have brought us?" exclaimed the children. "Why," said he, "if you ask himself, he will tell you that he is an Eagle; but if you will take my word for it, I know him to be but a Jackdaw."

THE THIRSTY PIGEON

A Pigeon severely pressed by thirst, seeing a glass of water painted upon a sign, supposed it to be real; so dashing down at it with all her might, she struck against the board, and, breaking her wing, fell helpless to the ground, where she was quickly captured by one of the passers-by.

Great haste is not always good speed.

THE HEIFER AND THE OX

A Heifer that ran wild in the fields, and had never felt the yoke, upbraided an Ox at plough for submitting to such labour and drudgery. The Ox said nothing, but went on with his work. Not long after, there was a great festival. The Ox got his holiday: but the Heifer was led off to be sacrificed at the altar. "If this be the end of your idleness," said the Ox, "I think that my work is better than your play. I had rather my neck felt the yoke than the axe."

THE BALD KNIGHT

A certain Knight growing old, his hair fell off, and he became bald; to hide which imperfection, he wore a periwig. But as he was riding out with some others a-hunting, a sudden gust of wind blew off the periwig, and exposed his bald pate. The company could not forbear laughing at the accident; and he himself laughed as loud as anybody, saying, "How was it to be expected that I should keep strange hair upon my head, when my own would not stay there?"

THE FOX AND THE STORK

A Fox one day invited a Stork to dinner, and being disposed to divert himself at the expense of his guest, provided nothing for the entertainment but some thin soup in a shallow dish. This the Fox lapped up very readily, while the Stork, unable to gain a mouthful with her long narrow bill, was as hungry at the end of dinner as when she began. The Fox meanwhile professed his regret at seeing her eat so sparingly, and feared that the dish was not seasoned to her mind. The Stork said little, but begged that the Fox would do her the honour of returning her visit; and accordingly he agreed to dine with her on the following day. He arrived true to his appointment, and the dinner was ordered forthwith; but when it was served up, he found to his dismay that it was contained in a narrow-necked vessel, down which the Stork readily thrust her long neck and bill, while he was obliged to content himself with licking the neck of the jar.   Unable to satisfy his hunger, he retired with as good a grace as he could, observing that he could hardly find fault with his entertainer, who had only paid him back in his own coin.

THE FALCONER AND THE PARTRIDGE

A Falconer having taken a Partridge in his net, the bird cried out sorrowfully, "Let me go, good Master Falconer, and I promise you I will decoy other Partridges into your net."   "No," said the man, "whatever I might have done, I am determined now not to spare you ; for there is no death too bad for him who is ready to betray his friends."

THE BULL AND THE GOAT

A Bull being pursued by a Lion, fled into a cave where a wild Goat had taken up his abode.   The Goat upon this began molesting him and butting at him with his horns.   "Don't suppose," said the Bull, "if I suffer this now, that it is you I am afraid of. Let the Lion be once out of sight, and I will soon show you the difference between a Bull and a Goat."

Mean people take advantage of their neighbours' difficulties to annoy them ; but the time will come when they will repent them of their insolence.

THE HUSBANDMAN AND THE SEA

A Husbandman seeing a ship full of sailors tossed about up and down upon the billows, cried out, "O Sea ! deceitful and pitiless element, that destroyest all who venture upon thee ! "   The Sea heard him, and assuming a woman's voice replied, "Do not reproach me ; I am not the cause of this disturbance, but the Winds, that when they fall upon me will give no repose. But should you sail over me when they are away, you will say that I am milder and more tractable than your own mother earth."

THE JACKASS IN OFFICE

An Ass carrying an Image in a religious procession, was driven through a town, and all the people who passed by made a low reverence. Upon this the Ass, supposing that they intended this worship for himself, was mightily puffed up, and would not budge another step. But the driver soon laid the stick across his back, saying at the same time, "You silly dolt! it is not you that they reverence, but the Image which you carry."

Fools take to themselves the respect that is given to their office.

THE PORKER AND THE SHEEP

A young Porker took up his quarters in a fold of Sheep. One day the shepherd laid hold on him, when he squeaked and struggled with all his might and main. The Sheep reproached him for crying out, and said, "The master often lays hold of us, and we do not cry." "Yes," replied he, "but our case is not the same; for he catches you for the sake of your wool, but me for my fry."

THE HOUND AND THE HARE

A Hound after long chasing a Hare at length came up to her, and kept first biting and then licking her. The Hare, not knowing what to make of him, said: "If you are a friend, why do you bite me?—but if a foe, why caress me?"

A doubtful friend is worse than a certain enemy; let a man be one thing or the other, and we then know how to meet him.

THE BOY AND THE FILBERTS

A certain Boy put his hand into a pitcher where great plenty of Figs and Filberts were deposited; he grasped as many as his fist could possibly hold, but when he endeavoured to pull it out, the narrowness of the neck prevented him. Unwilling to lose any of them, but unable to draw out his hand, he burst into tears, and bitterly bemoaned his hard fortune. An honest fellow who stood by, gave him this wise and reasonable advice :—"Grasp only half the quantity, my boy, and you will easily succeed."

THE KID AND THE WOLF

A Kid that had strayed from the herd was pursued by a Wolf. When she saw all other hope of escape cut off, she turned round to the Wolf, and said, "I must allow indeed that I am your victim, but as my life is now but short, let it be a merry one. Do you pipe for awhile, and I will dance." While the Wolf was piping and the Kid was dancing, the Dogs hearing the music ran up to see what was going on, and the Wolf was glad to take himself off as fast as his legs would carry him.

He who steps out of his way to play the fool, must not wonder if he misses the prize.

THE QUACK FROG

A Frog emerging from the mud of a swamp, proclaimed to all the world that he was come to cure all diseases. "Here!" he cried, "come and see a doctor, the proprietor of medicines such as man never heard of before; no, not Æsculapius himself, Jove's court-physician!" "And how," said the Fox, "dare you set up to heal others, who are not able to cure your own limping gait, and blotched and wrinkled skin?"

Test a man's professions by his practice. Physician, heal thyself!

THE ANT AND THE DOVE

An Ant went to a fountain to quench his thirst, and tumbling in, was almost drowned. But a Dove that happened to be sitting on a neighbouring tree saw the Ant's danger, and plucking off a leaf, let it drop into the water before him, and the Ant mounting upon it, was presently wafted safe ashore. Just at that time, a Fowler was spreading his net, and was in the act of ensnaring the Dove, when the Ant, perceiving his object, bit his heel. The start which the man gave made him drop his net, and the Dove, aroused to a sense of her danger, flew safe away.

One good turn deserves another.

THE ASS IN THE LION'S SKIN

An Ass having put on a Lion's skin, roamed about, frightening all the silly animals he met with, and, seeing a Fox, he tried to alarm him also. But Reynard, having heard his voice, said, "Well, to be sure! and I should have been frightened too, if I had not heard you bray."

They who assume a character that does not belong to them generally betray themselves by overacting it.

THE GOAT AND THE GOATHERD

A Goat had strayed from the herd, and the Goatherd was trying all he could to bring him back to his companions. When by calling and whistling he could make no impression on him, at last, taking up a stone, he struck the Goat on the horn and broke it. Alarmed at what he had done, he besought the Goat not to tell his master; but he replied, "O most foolish of Goatherds! my horn will tell the story, though I should not utter a word."

Facts speak plainer than words.

THE BOY BATHING

A Boy was bathing in a river, and, getting out of his depth, was on the point of sinking, when he saw a wayfarer coming by, to whom he called out for help with all his might and main. The Man began to read the Boy a lecture for his foolhardiness; but the urchin cried out, "O, save me now, sir! and read me the lecture afterwards."

THE FARMER AND THE DOGS

A Farmer, during a severe winter, being shut up by the snow in his farm-house, and sharply pressed for food, which he was unable to get about to procure, began consuming his own sheep. As the hard weather continued, he next ate up his goats. And at last—for there was no break in the weather—he betook himself to the plough-oxen. Upon this, the Dogs said to one another, "Let us be off; for since the master, as we see, has had no pity on the working oxen, how is it likely he will spare us?"

When our neighbour's house is on fire, it is time to look to our own.

THE MOUSE AND THE WEASEL

A little starveling Mouse had made his way with some difficulty into a basket of corn, where, finding the entertainment so good, he stuffed and crammed himself to such an extent, that when he would have got out again, he found the hole was too small to allow his puffed-up body to pass. As he sat at the hole groaning over his fate, a Weasel, who was brought to the spot by his cries, thus addressed him :—"Stop there, my friend, and fast till you are thin; for you will never come out till you reduce yourself to the same condition as when you entered."

THE FARMER AND THE LION

A Lion entered one day into a farm-yard, and the Farmer, wishing to catch him, shut the gate. When the Lion found that he could not get out, he began at once to attack the sheep, and then betook himself to the oxen. So the Farmer, afraid for himself, now opened the gate, and the Lion made off as fast as he could. His wife, who had observed it all, when she saw her husband in great trouble at the loss of his cattle, cried out—"You are rightly served; for what could have made you so mad as to wish to detain a creature, whom, if you saw at a distance, you would wish further off."

Better scare a thief than snare him.

THE CHARGER AND THE ASS

A Charger adorned with his fine trappings came thundering along the road, exciting the envy of a poor Ass who was trudging along the same way with a heavy load upon his back. "Get out of my road!" said the proud Horse, "or I shall trample you under my feet." The Ass said nothing, but quietly moved on one side to let the Horse pass. Not long afterwards the Charger was engaged in the wars, and being badly wounded in battle was rendered unfit for military service, and sent to work upon a farm. When the Ass saw him dragging with great labour a heavy waggon, he understood how little reason he had had to envy one who, by his overbearing spirit in the time of his prosperity, had lost those friends who might have succoured him in time of need.

THE BRAZIER AND HIS DOG

There was a certain Brazier who had a little Dog. While he hammered away at his metal, the Dog slept; but whenever he sat down to his dinner the Dog woke up. "Sluggard cur!" said the Brazier, throwing him a bone; "you sleep through the noise of the anvil, but wake up at the first clatter of my teeth."

Men are awake enough to their own interests, who turn a deaf ear to their friend's distress.

VENUS AND THE CAT

A Cat having fallen in love with a young man, besought Venus to change her into a girl, in the hope of gaining his affections. The Goddess, taking compassion on her weakness, metamorphosed her into a fair damsel; and the young man, enamoured of her beauty, led her home as his bride. As they were sitting in their chamber, Venus, wishing to know whether in changing her form she had also changed her nature, set down a Mouse before her. The Girl, forgetful of her new condition, started from her seat, and pounced upon the Mouse as if she would have eaten it on the spot; whereupon the Goddess, provoked at her frivolity, straightway turned her into a Cat again.

What is bred in the bone, will never out of the flesh.

THE WOLF AND THE LION

One day a Wolf had seized a sheep from a fold, and was carrying it home to his own den, when he met a Lion, who straightway laid hold of the sheep and bore it away. The Wolf, standing at a distance, cried out, that it was a great shame, and that the Lion had robbed him of his own. The Lion laughed, and said, "I suppose, then, that it was your good friend the shepherd who gave it to *you*."

THE GREAT AND THE LITTLE FISHES

A Fisherman was drawing up a net which he had cast into the sea, full of all sorts of fish. The Little Fish escaped through the meshes of the net, and got back into the deep, but the Great Fish were all caught and hauled into the ship.

Our insignificance is often the cause of our safety.

THE BOYS AND THE FROGS

A troop of Boys were playing at the edge of a pond, when, perceiving a number of Frogs in the water, they began to pelt at them with stones. They had already killed many of the poor creatures, when one more hardy than the rest putting his head above the water, cried out to them: "Stop your cruel sport, my lads; consider, what is Play to you is Death to us."

THE WOLF AND THE GOAT

A Wolf seeing a Goat feeding on the brow of a high precipice where he could not come at her, besought her to come down lower, for fear she should miss her footing at that dizzy height; "and moreover," said he, "the grass is far sweeter and more abundant here below." But the Goat replied: "Excuse me; it is not for my dinner that you invite me, but for your own."

THE ASS, THE COCK, AND THE LION

An Ass and a Cock lived in a farm-yard together. One day a hungry Lion passing by and seeing the Ass in good condition, resolved to make a meal of him. Now, they say that there is nothing a Lion hates so much as the crowing of a Cock; and at that moment the Cock happening to crow, the Lion straightway made off with all haste from the spot. The Ass, mightily amused to think that a Lion should be frightened at a bird, plucked up courage and galloped after him, delighted with the notion of driving the king of beasts before him. He had, however, gone no great distance, when the Lion turned sharply round upon him, and made an end of him in a trice.

Presumption begins in ignorance and ends in ruin.

TIIE RIVERS AND THE SEA

Once upon a time the Rivers combined against the Sea, and, going in a body, accused her, saying : "Why is it that when we Rivers pour our waters into you so fresh and sweet, you straightway render them salt and unpalatable?" The Sea, observing the temper in which they came, merely answered : "If you do not wish to become salt, please to keep away from me altogether."

Those who are most benefited are often the first to complain.

THE ASS CARRYING SALT

A certain Huckster who kept an Ass, hearing that Salt was to be had cheap at the sea-side, drove down his Ass thither to buy some. Having loaded the beast as much as he could bear, he was driving him home, when, as they were passing a slippery ledge of rock, the Ass fell into the stream below, and the Salt being melted, the Ass was relieved of his burden, and having gained the bank with ease, pursued his journey onward, light in body and in spirit. The Huckster soon afterwards set off for the sea-shore for some more Salt, and loaded the Ass, if possible, yet more heavily than before. On their return, as they crossed the stream into which he had formerly fallen, the Ass fell down on purpose, and by the dissolving of the Salt, was again released from his load. The Master, provoked at the loss, and thinking how he might cure him of this trick, on his next journey to the coast freighted the beast with a load of sponges. When they arrived at the same stream as before, the Ass was at his old tricks again, and rolled himself into the water; but the sponges becoming thoroughly wet, he found to his cost, as he proceeded homewards, that instead of lightening his burden, he had more than doubled its weight.

The same measures will not suit all circumstances; and we may play the same trick once too often.

THE LION AND HIS THREE COUNCILLORS

The Lion called the Sheep to ask her if his breath smelt : she said Ay; he bit off her head for a fool. He called the Wolf, and asked him : he said No; he tore him in pieces for a flatterer. At last he called the Fox, and asked him. Truly he had got a cold, and could not smell.

Wise men say nothing in dangerous times.

THE BLACKAMOOR

A certain man bought a Blackamoor, and thinking that the colour of his skin arose from the neglect of his former master, he no sooner brought him home than he procured all manner of scouring apparatus, scrubbing-brushes, soaps, and sand-paper, and set to work with his servants to wash him white again. They drenched and rubbed him for many an hour, but all in vain; his skin remained as black as ever; while the poor wretch all but died from the cold he caught under the operation.

No human means avail of themselves to change a nature originally evil.

THE SEA-SIDE TRAVELLERS

As some Travellers were making their way along the sea-shore, they came to a high cliff, and looking out upon the sea saw a Faggot floating at a distance, which they thought at first must be a large Ship; so they waited, expecting to see it come into harbour. As the Faggot drifted nearer to the shore, they thought it no longer to be a Ship, but a Boat. But when it was at length thrown on the beach, they saw that it was nothing but a Faggot after all.

Dangers seem greatest at a distance; and coming events are magnified according to the interest or inclination of the beholder.

THE LEOPARD AND THE FOX

A Leopard and a Fox had a contest which was the finer creature of the two. The Leopard put forward the beauty of its numberless spots; but the Fox replied—"It is better to have a versatile mind than a variegated body."

THE MONKEY AND THE FISHERMEN

A Monkey was sitting up in a high tree, when, seeing some Fishermen laying their nets in a river, he watched what they were doing. The Men had no sooner set their nets, and retired a short distance to their dinner, than the Monkey came down from the tree, thinking that he would try his hand at the same sport. But in attempting to lay the nets he got so entangled in them, that being well-nigh choked, he was forced to exclaim: "This serves me right; for what business had I, who know nothing of fishing, to meddle with such tackle as this?"

THE EAGLE AND THE BEETLE

A Hare being pursued by an Eagle, betook himself for refuge to the nest of a Beetle, whom he entreated to save him. The Beetle therefore interceded with the Eagle, begging of him not to kill the poor suppliant, and conjuring him, by mighty Jupiter, not to slight his intercession and break the laws of hospitality because he was so small an animal. But the Eagle, in wrath, gave the Beetle a flap with his wing, and straightway seized upon the Hare and devoured him. When the Eagle flew away, the Beetle flew after him, to learn where his nest was, and getting into it, he rolled the Eagle's eggs out of it one by one, and broke them. The Eagle, grieved and enraged to think that any one should attempt so audacious a thing, built his nest the next time in a higher place; but there too the Beetle got at it again, and served him in the same manner as before. Upon this the Eagle, being at a loss what to do, flew up to Jupiter, his Lord and King, and placed the third brood of eggs, as a sacred deposit, in his lap, begging him to guard them for him. But the Beetle, having made a little ball of dirt, flew up with it and dropped it in Jupiter's lap; who, rising up on a sudden to shake it off, and forgetting the eggs, threw them down, and they were again broken. Jupiter being informed by the Beetle that he had done this to be revenged upon the Eagle, who had not only wronged him, but had acted impiously towards Jove himself, told the Eagle, when he came to him, that the Beetle was the aggrieved party, and that he complained not without reason. But being unwilling that the race of Eagles should be diminished, he advised the Beetle to come to an accommodation with the Eagle. As the Beetle would not agree to this, Jupiter transferred the Eagle's breeding to another season, when there are no Beetles to be seen.

No one can slight the laws of hospitality with impunity; and there is no station or influence, however powerful, that can protect the oppressor, in the end, from the vengeance of the oppressed.

THE MAN AND HIS TWO WIVES

In days when a man was allowed more wives than one, a middle-aged bachelor, who could be called neither young nor old, and whose hair was only just beginning to turn grey, must needs fall in love with two women at once, and marry them both. The one was young and blooming, and wished her husband to appear as youthful as herself; the other was somewhat more advanced in age, and was as anxious that her husband should appear a suitable match for her. So, while the young one seized every opportunity of pulling out the good man's grey hairs, the old one was as industrious in plucking out every black hair she could find. For a while the man was highly gratified by their attention and devotion, till he found one morning that, between the one and the other, he had not a hair left.

He that submits his principles to the influence and caprices of opposite parties will end in having no principles at all.

THE VINE AND THE GOAT

There was a Vine teeming with ripe fruit and tender shoots, when a wanton Goat came up and gnawed the bark, and browsed upon the young leaves. "I will revenge myself on you," said the Vine, "for this insult; for when in a few days you are brought as a victim to the altar, the juice of my grapes shall be the dew of death upon thy forehead."

Retribution though late comes at last.

THE SICK KITE

A Kite, who had been long very ill, said to his mother, "Don't cry, mother; but go and pray to the gods that I may recover from this dreadful disease and pain." "Alas! child," said the mother, "which of the gods can I entreat for one who has robbed all their altars?"

A death-bed repentance is poor amends for the errors of a life-time.

THE BOY AND THE NETTLE

A Boy playing in the fields got stung by a Nettle. He ran home to his mother, telling her that he had but touched that nasty weed, and it had stung him. "It was just your touching it, my boy," said the mother, "that caused it to sting you; the next time you meddle with a Nettle, grasp it tightly, and it will do you no hurt."

Do boldly what you do at all.

THE FOX AND THE CROW

A Crow had snatched a goodly piece of cheese out of a window, and flew with it into a high tree, intent to enjoy her prize. A Fox spied the dainty morsel, and thus he planned his approaches. "O Crow," said he, "how beautiful are thy wings, how bright thine eye! how graceful thy neck! thy breast is the breast of an eagle! thy claws—I beg pardon—thy talons, are a match for all the beasts of the field. O! that such a bird should be dumb, and want only a voice!" The Crow, pleased with the flattery, and chuckling to think how she would surprise the Fox with her caw, opened her mouth:—down dropped the cheese! which the Fox snapping up, observed, as he walked away, "that whatever he had remarked of her beauty, he had said nothing yet of her brains."

Men seldom flatter without some private end in view; and they who listen to such music may expect to have to pay the piper.

THE THREE TRADESMEN

There was a city in expectation of being besieged, and a council was called accordingly to discuss the best means of fortifying it. A Bricklayer gave his opinion that no material was so good as brick for the purpose. A Carpenter begged leave to suggest that timber would be far preferable. Upon which a Currier started up, and said, "Sirs, when you have said all that can be said, there is nothing in the world like leather."

THE ASS'S SHADOW

A Youth, one hot summer's day, hired an Ass to carry him from Athens to Megara. At mid-day the heat of the sun was so scorching, that he dismounted, and would have sat down to repose himself under the shadow of the Ass. But the driver of the Ass dis-

puted the place with him, declaring that he had an
equal right to it with the other. "What!" said the
Youth, "did I not hire the Ass for the whole journey?"
"Yes," said the other, "you hired the Ass, but not the
Ass's Shadow." While they were thus wrangling and
fighting for the place, the Ass took to his heels and
ran away.

THE DOGS AND THE HIDES

Some hungry Dogs, seeing some raw Hides which
a skinner had left in the bottom of a stream, and not
being able to reach them, agreed among themselves to
drink up the river to get at the prize. So they set to
work, but they all burst themselves with drinking before
ever they came near the Hides.

They who aim at an object by unreasonable means,
are apt to ruin themselves in the attempt.

THE LION AND THE BULLS

Three Bulls fed in a field together in the greatest
peace and amity. A Lion had long watched them in
the hope of making a prize of them, but found that there
was little chance for him so long as they kept all
together. He therefore began secretly to spread evil
and slanderous reports of one against the other, till
he had fomented a jealousy and distrust amongst them.
No sooner did the Lion see that they avoided one
another, and fed each by himself apart, than he fell
upon them singly, and so made an easy prey of
them all.

The quarrels of friends are the opportunities of foes.

THE RAVEN AND THE SWAN

A Raven envied a Swan the whiteness of her
plumage; and, thinking that its beauty was owing to
the water in which she lived, he deserted the altars

where he used to find his livelihood, and betook himself to the pools and streams. There he plumed and dressed himself and washed his coat, but all to no purpose, for his plumage remained as black as ever, and he himself soon perished for want of his usual food.

Change of scene is not change of nature.

THE SHEPHERD AND THE SEA

A Shepherd moved down his flock to feed near the shore, and beholding the Sea lying in a smooth and breathless calm, he was seized with a strong desire to sail over it. So he sold all his sheep and bought a cargo of Dates, and loaded a vessel, and set sail. He had not gone far when a storm arose; his ship was wrecked, and his Dates and everything lost, and he himself with difficulty escaped to land. Not long after, when the Sea was again calm, and one of his friends came up to him and was admiring its repose, he said, "Have a care, my good fellow, of that smooth surface; it is only looking out for your Dates."

THE SWALLOW IN CHANCERY

A Swallow had built her nest under the eaves of a Court of Justice. Before her young ones could fly, a Serpent gliding out of his hole ate them all up. When the poor bird returned to her nest and found it empty, she began a pitiable wailing; but a neighbour suggesting, by way of comfort, that she was not the first bird who had lost her young, "True," she replied, "but it is not only my little ones that I mourn, but that I should have been wronged in that very place where the injured fly for justice."

THE OLD WOMAN AND HER MAIDS

A thrifty old Widow kept two Servant-maids, whom she used to call up to their work at cock-crow. The

Maids disliked exceedingly this early rising, and determined between themselves to wring off the Cock's neck,
as he was the cause of all their trouble by waking their
mistress so early. They had no sooner done this, than
the old lady, missing her usual alarum, and afraid of
oversleeping herself, continually mistook the time of
day, and roused them up at midnight.

Too much cunning overreaches itself.

THE MISER

A Miser, to make sure of his property, sold all that
he had and converted it into a great lump of gold,
which he hid in a hole in the ground, and went
continually to visit and inspect it. This roused the
curiosity of one of his workmen, who, suspecting that
there was a treasure, when his master's back was
turned, went to the spot, and stole it away. When
the Miser returned and found the place empty, he
wept and tore his hair. But a neighbour who saw
him in this extravagant grief, and learned the cause
of it, said, "Fret thyself no longer, but take a stone
and put it in the same place, and think that it is your
lump of gold; for, as you never meant to use it, the
one will do you as much good as the other."

The worth of money is not in its possession, but in
its use.

THE WILD BOAR AND THE FOX

A Wild Boar was whetting his tusks against a tree,
when a Fox coming by asked why he did so; "For,"
said he, "I see no reason for it; there is neither
hunter nor hound in sight, nor any other danger that
I can see, at hand." "True," replied the Boar; "but
when that danger does arise, I shall have something
else to do than to sharpen my weapons."

It is too late to whet the sword when the trumpet
sounds to draw it.

THE WOLF IN SHEEP'S CLOTHING

A Wolf, once upon a time, resolved to disguise himself, thinking that he should thus gain an easier livelihood. Having, therefore, clothed himself in a sheep's skin, he contrived to get among a flock of Sheep, and feed along with them, so that even the Shepherd was deceived by the imposture. When night came on and the fold was closed, the Wolf was shut up with the Sheep, and the door made fast. But the Shepherd, wanting something for his supper, and going in to fetch out a sheep, mistook the Wolf for one of them, and killed him on the spot.

THE BOASTING TRAVELLER

A man who had been travelling in foreign parts, on his return home was always bragging and boasting of the great feats he had accomplished in different places. In Rhodes, for instance, he said he had taken such an extraordinary leap, that no man could come near him, and he had witnesses there to prove it. "Possibly," said one of his hearers; "but if this be true, just suppose this to be Rhodes, and then try the leap again."

THE WOLF AND THE HORSE

As a Wolf was roaming over a farm, he came to a field of oats, but not being able to eat them, he left them and went his way. Presently meeting with a Horse, he bade him come with him into the field; "For," says he, "I have found some capital oats; and I have not tasted one, but have kept them all for you, for the very sound of your teeth is music to my ear." But the Horse replied: "A pretty fellow! if Wolves were able to eat oats, I suspect you would not have preferred your ears to your appetite."

Little thanks are due to him who only gives away what is of no use to himself.

THE STAG AT THE POOL

A Stag one summer's day came to a pool to quench his thirst, and as he stood drinking he saw his form reflected in the water. "What beauty and strength," said he, "are in these horns of mine; but how unseemly are these weak and slender feet!" While he was thus criticising, after his own fancies, the form which Nature had given him, the huntsmen and hounds drew that way. The feet, with which he had found so much fault, soon carried him out of the reach of his pursuers; but the horns, of which he was so vain, becoming entangled in a thicket, held him till the hunters again came up to him, and proved the cause of his death.

Look to use before ornament.

THE OLD LION

A Lion worn out with years lay stretched upon the ground, utterly helpless, and drawing his last breath. A Boar came up, and to satisfy an ancient grudge, drove at him with his tusks. Next a Bull, determined to be revenged on an old enemy, gored him with his horns. Upon this an Ass, seeing that the old Lion could thus be treated with impunity, thought that he would show his spite also, and came and threw his heels in the Lion's face. Whereupon the dying beast exclaimed: "The insults of the powerful were bad enough, but those I could have managed to bear; but to be spurned by so base a creature as thou—the disgrace of nature, is to die a double death."

THE HUNTER AND THE WOODMAN

A Man went out Lion-hunting into a forest, where meeting with a Woodman, he asked him if he had seen any tracks of a Lion, and if he knew where his lair was. "Yes," says the Man, "and if you will come with me I will show you the Lion himself." At this

the Hunter, turning ghastly pale, and his teeth chatter-
ing, he said, "Oh! thank you; it was the Lion's track,
not himself, that I was hunting."

A coward can be a hero at a distance; it is presence
of danger that tests presence of mind.

MERCURY AND THE SCULPTOR

Mercury having a mind to know in what estimation
he was held among men, disguised himself as a traveller,
and going into a Sculptor's workshop, began asking the
price of the different statues he saw there. Pointing to
an image of Jupiter, he asked how much he wanted for
that. "A drachma," said the image-maker. Mercury
laughed in his sleeve, and asked, "How much for this
of Juno?" The man wanted a higher price for that.
Mercury's eye now caught his own image. "Now, will
this fellow," thought he, "ask me ten times as much
for this, for I am the messenger of heaven, and the
source of all his gain." So he put the question to him,
what he valued that Mercury at. "Well," says the
Sculptor, "if you will give me my price for the other
two, I will throw you that into the bargain."

They who are over anxious to know how the world
values them, will seldom be set down at their own
price.

THE WOLF AND THE SHEPHERDS

A Wolf looking into a hut and seeing some shepherds
comfortably regaling themselves on a joint of mutton—
"A pretty row," said he, "would these men have made
if they had caught me at such a supper!"

Men are too apt to condemn in others the very things
that they practise themselves.

THE ASTRONOMER

An Astronomer used to walk out every night to gaze
upon the stars. It happened one night that, as he was

The Miller, his Son, and their Ass

wandering in the outskirts of the city, with his whole thoughts rapt up in the skies, he fell into a well. On his holloaing and calling out, one who heard his cries ran up to him, and when he had listened to his story, said, "My good man, while you are trying to pry into the mysteries of heaven, you overlook the common objects that are under your feet."

THE MILLER, HIS SON, AND THEIR ASS

A Miller and his Son were driving their Ass to a neighbouring fair to sell him. They had not gone far when they met with a troop of girls returning from the town, talking and laughing. "Look there!" cried one of them, "did you ever see such fools, to be trudging along the road on foot, when they might be riding!" The old Man, hearing this, quietly bade his Son get on the Ass, and walked along merrily by the side of him. Presently they came up to a group of old men in earnest debate. "There!" said one of them, "it proves what I was a-saying. What respect is shown to old age in these days? Do you see that idle young rogue riding, while his old father has to walk?—Get down, you scapegrace! and let the old Man rest his weary limbs." Upon this the Father made his Son dismount, and got up himself. In this manner they had not proceeded far when they met a company of women and children. "Why, you lazy old fellow!" cried several tongues at once, "how can you ride upon the beast, while that poor little lad there can hardly keep pace by the side of you." The good-natured Miller stood corrected, and immediately took up his Son behind him. They had now almost reached the town. "Pray, honest friend," said a townsman, "is that Ass your own?" "Yes," says the old Man. "Oh! One would not have thought so," said the other, "by the way you load him. Why, you two fellows are better able to carry the poor beast than he you!" "Anything to please you," said the old Man; "we can but try."

So, alighting with his Son, they tied the Ass's legs
together, and by the help of a pole endeavoured to
carry him on their shoulders over a bridge that led
to the town. This was so entertaining a sight that
the people ran out in crowds to laugh at it; till the
Ass, not liking the noise nor his situation, kicked
asunder the cords that bound him, and, tumbling off
the pole, fell into the river. Upon this the old Man,
vexed and ashamed, made the best of his way home
again—convinced that by endeavouring to please every-
body he had pleased nobody, and lost his Ass into the
bargain.

FABLES FROM PHÆDRUS

THE VAIN JACKDAW AND THE PEACOCK

That one ought not to plume oneself on the merits
which belong to another, but ought rather to pass his
life in his own proper guise, Æsop has given us this
illustration :—

A Jackdaw, swelling with empty pride, picked up
some feathers which had fallen from a Peacock, and
decked himself out therewith; upon which, despising
his own kind, he mingled with a beauteous flock of
Peacocks. They tore his feathers from off the impudent
bird, and put him to flight with their beaks. The Jackdaw, thus roughly handled, in grief hastened to return
to his own kind; repulsed by whom, he had to submit
to sad disgrace. Then said one of those whom he had
formerly despised : "If you had been content with our
station, and had been ready to put up with what nature
had given, you would neither have experienced the
former affront, nor would your ill fortune have had to
feel the additional pang of this repulse."

THE COW, THE SHE-GOAT, THE SHEEP, AND THE LION

A Cow, a She-Goat, and a Sheep patient under injuries, were partners in the forests with a Lion. When they had captured a Stag of vast bulk, thus spoke the Lion, after it had been divided into shares: "Because my name is Lion, I take the first; the second you will yield to me because I am courageous; then, because I am the strongest, the third will fall to my lot; if any one touches the fourth, woe betide him."

THE ASS AND THE LION HUNTING

A Lion having resolved to hunt in company with an Ass, concealed him in a thicket, and at the same time enjoined him to frighten the wild beasts with his voice, to which they were unused, while he himself was to catch them as they fled. Upon this, Long-ears, with all his might, suddenly raised a cry, and terrified the beasts with this new cause of astonishment. While, in their alarm, they are flying to the well-known outlets, they are overpowered by the dread onset of the Lion; who, after he was wearied with slaughter, called forth the Ass from his retreat, and bade him cease his clamour. On this the other, in his insolence, inquired: "What think you of the assistance given by my voice?" "Excellent!" said the Lion, "so much so, that if I had not been acquainted with your spirit and your race, I should have fled in alarm like the rest."

THE MAN AND THE WEASEL

A Weasel, on being caught by a Man, wishing to escape impending death: "Pray," said she, "do spare me, for 'tis I who keep your house clear of troublesome mice." The Man made answer: "If you did so for my sake, it would be a reason for thanking you, and I should have granted you the pardon you entreat. But, inasmuch as you do your best that you may enjoy the scraps which they would have gnawed, and devour the mice as well, don't think of placing your pretended services to my account;" and so saying, he put the wicked creature to death.

Those persons ought to recognise this as applicable to themselves, whose object is private advantage, and who boast to the unthinking of an unreal merit.

THE FAITHFUL DOG

A Thief one night threw a crust of bread to a Dog, to try whether he could be gained by the proffered victuals: "Hark you," said the Dog, "do you think to stop my tongue so that I may not bark for my master's property? You are greatly mistaken. For this sudden liberality bids me be on the watch, that you may not profit by my neglect."

THE DOG AND THE CROCODILE

It has been related, that Dogs drink at the river Nile running along, that they may not be seized by the Crocodiles. Accordingly, a Dog having begun to drink while running along, a Crocodile thus addressed him: "Lap as leisurely as you like; drink on; come nearer, and don't be afraid," said he. The other replied: "Egad, I would do so with all my heart, did I not know that you are eager for my flesh."

THE DOG, THE TREASURE, AND THE VULTURE

Grubbing up human bones, a Dog met with a Treasure; and, because he had offended the Gods, a desire for riches was inspired in him, that so he might pay the penalty due to the holy character of the place. Accordingly, while he was watching over the gold, forgetful of food, he was starved to death; on which a Vulture, standing over him, is reported to have said: "O Dog, you justly meet your death, who, begotten at a cross-road, and bred up on a dunghill, have suddenly coveted regal wealth."

THE FROGS FRIGHTENED AT THE BATTLE OF THE BULLS

When the powerful are at variance, the lowly are the sufferers.

A Frog, viewing from a marsh, a combat of some Bulls: "Alas!" said she, "what terrible destruction is threatening us." Being asked by another why she said so, as the Bulls were contending for the sovereignty of the herd, and passed their lives afar from them: "Their habitation is at a distance," said she, "and they are of a different kind; still, he who is expelled from the sovereignty of the meadow, will take to flight, and come to the secret hiding-places in the fens, and trample and crush us with his hard hoof. Thus does their fury concern our safety."

THE KITE AND THE PIGEONS

Some Pigeons, having often escaped from a Kite, and by their swiftness of wing avoided death, the spoiler had recourse to stratagem, and by a crafty device of this nature, deceived the harmless race. "Why do you prefer to live a life of anxiety, rather than conclude a treaty, and make me your king, who can ensure your safety from every injury?" They, putting confidence in him, entrusted themselves to the Kite, who, on obtaining the sovereignty, began to devour them one by one, and to exercise authority with his cruel talons. Then said one of those that were left: "Deservedly are we smitten."

THE LION, THE ROBBER, AND THE TRAVELLER

While a Lion was standing over a Bullock, which he had brought to the ground, a Robber came up, and demanded a share. "I would give it to you," said the Lion, "were you not in the habit of taking without leave;" and so repulsed the rogue. By chance, a harmless Traveller was led to the same spot, and on seeing the wild beast, retraced his steps; on which the Lion kindly said to him: "You have nothing to fear; boldly take the share which is due to your modesty." Then having divided the carcase, he sought the woods, that he might make room for the Man.

THE EAGLE, THE CROW, AND THE TORTOISE

An Eagle carried a Tortoise aloft, who had hidden her body in her horny abode and thought, in her concealment, she could not be injured in any way. A Crow came through the air, and flying near, exclaimed: "You really have carried off a rich prize in your talons; but if I don't instruct you what you must do, in vain will you tire yourself with the heavy weight." So a share of the prey being promised her, the Crow persuades the Eagle to dash the hard shell upon a rock, that, it being broken to pieces, he may easily feed upon the meat. Induced by her words, the Eagle attends to her suggestion, and at the same time gives a large share of the banquet to his instructress, mistress Crow.

SOCRATES TO HIS FRIENDS

Socrates having laid for himself the foundation of a small house, one of the people, no matter who, amongst such passing remarks as are usual in these cases, asked: "Why do you, so famed as you are, build so small a house?"

"I only wish," he replied, "I could fill it with real friends."

THE BEES AND THE DRONES, THE WASP SITTING AS JUDGE

Some Bees had made their combs in a lofty oak. Some lazy Drones asserted that these belonged to them. The cause was brought into court, the Wasp sitting as judge; who, being perfectly acquainted with either race, proposed to the two parties these terms: "Your shape is not unlike, and your colour is similar; so that the affair clearly and fairly becomes a matter of doubt. But that my sacred duty may not be at fault through insufficiency of knowledge, each of you take hives, and pour your productions into the waxen cells; that from the flavour of the honey and the shape of the comb, the maker of them, about which the present dispute exists, may be evident." The Drones decline; the proposal pleases the Bees. Upon this, the Wasp pronounces sentence to the following effect: "It is evident who cannot, and who did, make them; wherefore, to the Bees I restore the fruits of their labours."

ÆSOP AT PLAY

An Athenian seeing Æsop in a crowd of boys at play with nuts, stopped and laughed at him for a madman. As soon as the Sage,—a laugher at others rather than one to be laughed at,—perceived this, he placed an unstrung bow in the middle of the road: "Hark you,

wise man," said he, "unriddle what I have done." The
people gather round. The man torments his invention
a long time, but cannot make out the reason of the
proposed question. At last he gives up. Upon this,
the victorious Philosopher says: "You will soon break
the bow, if you always keep it bent; but if you loosen
it, it will be fit for use when you want it."

THE ASS AND THE PRIESTS OF CYBELE

The Galli, priests of Cybele, were in the habit, on
their begging excursions, of leading about an Ass, to
carry their burdens. When he was dead with fatigue
and blows, his hide being stripped off, they made themselves tambourines therewith. Afterwards, on being
asked by some one what they had done with their
favourite, they answered in these words: "He fancied
that after death he would rest in quiet; but see, dead
as he is, fresh blows are heaped upon him."

THE HORSE AND THE WILD BOAR

While a Wild Boar was wallowing, he muddied the
shallow water, at which a Horse had been in the habit
of quenching his thirst. Upon this, a disagreement
arose. The Horse, enraged with the beast, sought the
aid of man, and, raising him on his back, returned
against the foe. After the Horseman, hurling his
javelins, had slain the Boar, he is said to have spoken
thus: "I am glad that I gave assistance at your entreaties, for I have captured a prey, and have learned
how useful you are;" and so compelled him, unwilling
as he was, to submit to the rein. Then said the Horse,
sorrowing: "Fool that I am! while seeking to revenge
a trifling matter, I have met with slavery."

This Fable will admonish the passionate, that it is
better to be injured with impunity, than to put ourselves
in the power of another.

A THIEF PILLAGING THE ALTAR OF JUPITER

A Thief lighted his Lamp at the altar of Jupiter, and then plundered it by the help of its own light. Just as he was taking his departure, laden with the results of his sacrilege, the Holy Place suddenly sent forth these words: "Although these were the gifts of the wicked, and to me abominable, so much so that I care not to be spoiled of them, still, profane man, thou shalt pay the penalty with thy life, when hereafter, the day of punishment, appointed by fate, arrives. But, that our fire, by means of which piety worships the awful Gods, may not afford its light to crime, I forbid that henceforth there shall be any such interchange of light." Accordingly, to this day, it is neither lawful for a lamp to be lighted at the fire of the Gods, nor yet a sacrifice kindled from a lamp.

THE PILOT AND THE MARINERS

On a certain man complaining of his adverse fortune, Æsop, for the purpose of consoling him, invented this Fable.

A ship which had been tossed by a fierce tempest (while the passengers were all in tears, and filled with apprehensions of death) on the day suddenly changing to a serene aspect, began to be borne along in safety upon the buoyant waves, and to inspire the mariners with an excess of gladness. On this, the Pilot, who had been rendered wise by experience, remarked: "We ought to be moderate in our joy, and to complain with caution; for the whole of life is a mixture of grief and joy."

THE MAN AND THE SNAKE

A Man took up a Snake stiffened with frost, and warmed her in his bosom, being compassionate to his own undoing; for when she had recovered, she instantly killed the Man. On another one asking her the reason of this crime, she made answer: "That people may learn not to assist the wicked."

THE SHIPWRECK OF SIMONIDES

A learned man has always a fund of riches in himself. Simonides, who wrote such excellent lyric poems, the more easily to support his poverty, began to make a tour of the celebrated cities of Asia, singing the praises of victors for such reward as he might receive. After he had become enriched by this kind of gain, he resolved to return to his native land by sea; (for he was born, it is said, in the island of Ceos). Accordingly he embarked in a ship, which a dreadful tempest, together with its own rottenness, caused to founder at sea. Some gathered together their girdles, others their precious effects, which formed the support of their existence. One who was over inquisitive, remarked: "Are you going to save none of your property, Simonides?" He made reply: "All my possessions are about me." A few only made their escape by swimming, for the majority, being weighed down by their burdens, perished. Some thieves too made their appearance, and seized what each person had saved, leaving him naked. Clazomenæ, an ancient city, chanced to be near; to which the shipwrecked persons repaired. Here a person devoted to the pursuits of literature, who had often read the lines of Simonides, and was a very great admirer of him though he had never seen him, knowing from his very language who he was, received him with the greatest pleasure into his house, and furnished him with clothes, money, and attendants. The others meanwhile were carrying about their pictures, begging for victuals. Simonides chanced to meet them; and, as soon as he saw them, remarked: "I told you that all my property was about me; what you have endeavoured to save is lost."

THE ANT AND THE FLY

An Ant and a Fly were contending with great warmth which was of the greater importance. The Fly was the first to begin: "Can you possibly compare with my endowments? When a sacrifice is made, I am the first to taste of the entrails that belong to the Gods. I pass my time among the altars, I wander through all the temples; soon as I have espied it, I seat myself on the head of a king; and I taste of the chaste kisses of matrons. I labour not, and yet enjoy the nicest of things: what like to this, good rustic, falls to your lot?" "Eating with the Gods," said the Ant, "is certainly a thing to be boasted of; but by him who is invited, not him who is loathed as an intruder. You talk about kings and the kisses of matrons. While I am carefully heaping up a stock of grain for winter, I see you feeding on filth about the walls. You frequent the altars; yes, and are driven away as often as you come. You labour not; therefore it is that you have nothing when you stand in need of it. And, further, you boast about what modesty ought to conceal. You tease me in summer; when winter comes you are silent. While the cold is shrivelling you up and putting you to death, a well-stored abode harbours me. Surely I have now pulled down your pride enough."

SIMONIDES PRESERVED BY THE GODS

I have said, above, how greatly learning is esteemed among men: I will now hand down to posterity how great is the honour paid to it by the Gods.

Simonides, the very same of whom I have before made mention, agreed, at a fixed price, to write a panegyric for a certain Pugilist, who had been victorious: accordingly he sought retirement. As the meagreness of his subject cramped his imagination, he used, according to general custom, the license of the Poet, and introduced the twin stars of Leda, citing them as an example of similar honours. He finished the Poem according to contract, but received only a third part of the sum agreed upon. On his demanding the rest: "They," said he, "will give it you whose praises occupy the other two-thirds; but, that I may feel convinced that you have not departed in anger, promise to dine with me, as I intend to-day to invite my kinsmen, in the number of whom I reckon you." Although defrauded, and smarting under the injury, in order that he might not, by parting on bad terms, break off all friendly intercourse, he promised that he would. At the hour named he returned, and took his place at table. The banquet shone joyously with its cups; the house resounded with gladness, amid vast preparations, when, on a sudden, two young men, covered with dust, and dripping with perspiration, their bodies of more than human form, requested one of the servants to call Simonides to them, and say that it was of consequence to him to make no delay. The man, quite confused, called forth Simonides; and hardly had he put one foot out of the banqueting-room, when suddenly the fall of the ceiling crushed the rest, and no young men were to be seen at the gate.

DEMETRIUS AND MENANDER

Demetrius, who was called Phalereus, unjustly took possession of the sovereignty of Athens. The mob, according to their usual practice, rush from all quarters vying with each other, and cheer him, and wish him joy. Even the chief men kiss the hand by which they are oppressed, while they silently lament the sad vicissitudes of fortune. Moreover, those who live in retirement, and take their ease, come creeping in last of all, that their absence may not injure them. Among these Menander, famous for his Comedies (which Demetrius, who did not know him, had read, and had admired the genius of the man), perfumed with unguents, and clad in a flowing robe, came with a mincing and languid step. As soon as the Tyrant caught sight of him at the end of the train : "What effeminate wretch," said he, "is this, who presumes to come into my presence?" Those near him made answer : "This is Menander the Poet." Changed in an instant, he exclaimed : "A more agreeable-looking man could not possibly exist."

THE TRAVELLERS AND THE ROBBER

Two Soldiers having fallen in with a Robber, one fled, while the other stood his ground, and defended himself with a stout right hand. The Robber slain, his cowardly companion comes running up, and draws his sword; then throwing back his travelling cloak, says : "Let's have him;" "I'll take care he shall soon know whom he attacks." On this, he who had vanquished the robber made answer : "I wish you had seconded me just now at least with those words; I should have been still more emboldened, believing them true; now keep your sword quiet, as well as your silly tongue, that you may be able to deceive others who don't know you. I, who have experienced with what speed you take to your heels, know full well that no dependence is to be placed upon your valour."

THE MAN AND THE ASS

A Man having sacrificed a young boar to the god Hercules, to whom he owed performance of a vow made for the preservation of his health, ordered the remains of the barley to be set for the Ass. But he refused to touch it, and said : "I would most willingly accept your food, if he who had been fed upon it had not had his throat cut."

THE TWO BALD MEN

A Bald Man chanced to find a comb in the public road. Another, equally destitute of hair, came up :

"Come," said he, "shares, whatever it is you have found." The other showed the booty, and added withal: "The will of the Gods has favoured us, but through the malignity of fate, we have found, as the saying is, a coal instead of a treasure."

THE HUNTSMAN AND THE DOG

A Dog, who had always given satisfaction to his master by his boldness against swift and savage beasts, began to grow feeble under increasing years. On one occasion, being urged to the combat with a bristling Boar, he seized him by the ear; but, through the rottenness of his teeth, let go his prey. Vexed at this, the Huntsman upbraided the Dog. Old Barker replied: "It is not my courage that disappoints you, but my strength. You commend me for what I have been; and you blame me that I am not what I was."

THE CITY MOUSE AND COUNTRY MOUSE

A City Mouse being once entertained at the table of a Country one, dined on humble acorns in a hole. Afterwards he prevailed upon the Countryman by his entreaties to enter the city and a cellar that abounded with the choicest things. Here, while they were enjoying remnants of various kinds, the door is thrown open, and in comes the Butler; the Mice, terrified at the noise, fly in different directions, and the City one easily hides himself in his well-known holes; while the unfortunate Rustic, all trepidation in that strange house, and dreading death, runs to and fro along the walls. When the Butler had taken what he wanted, and had shut the door, the City Mouse bade the Country one again to take courage. The latter, still in a state of perturbation, replied: "I hardly can take any food for fear. Do you think he will come?" "Why are you in such a fright?" said the City one; "come, let us enjoy dainties which you may seek in vain in the country." The Countryman replied: "You, who don't know what it is to fear, will enjoy all these things; but, free from care and at liberty, may acorns be my food!"

'Tis better to live secure in poverty, than to be consumed by the cares attendant upon riches.

THE CRANE, THE CROW, AND THE COUNTRYMAN

A Crane and a Crow had made a league on oath, that the Crane should protect the Crow against the Birds, and that the Crow should foretell the future, so that the Crane might be on her guard. After this, on their frequently flying into the fields of a certain Countryman, and tearing up by the roots what had been sown, the owner of the field saw it, and being vexed, cried out: "Give me a stone, Boy, that I may hit the Crane." When the Crow heard this, at once she warned the Crane, who took all due precaution. On another day, too, the Crow hearing him ask for a stone, again warned the Crane carefully to avoid the danger. The Countryman, suspecting that the divining Bird heard his commands, said to the Boy: "If I say, give me a cake, do you secretly hand me a stone." The Crane came again; he bade the Boy give him a cake, but the Boy gave him a stone, with which he hit the Crane, and broke her legs. The Crane, on being wounded, said: "Prophetic Crow, where now are your auspices? Why did you not hasten to warn your companion, as you swore you would, that no such evil might befall me?" The Crow made answer: "It is not my art that deserves to be blamed; but the purposes of double-tongued people are so deceiving, who say one thing and do another."

Those who impose upon the inexperienced by deceitful promises, fail not to cajole them by and by with pretended reasons.

THE BIRDS AND THE SWALLOW

The Birds having assembled in one spot, saw a Man sowing flax in a field. When the Swallow found that they thought nothing at all of this, she is reported to have called them together, and thus addressed them: "Danger awaits us all from this, if the seed should come to maturity." The Birds laughed at her. When the crop, however, sprang up, the Swallow again remarked: "Our destruction is impending; come, let us root up the noxious blades, lest, if they shortly grow up, nets may be made thereof, and we may be taken by the contrivances of man." The Birds persist in laughing at the words of the Swallow, and foolishly despise this most prudent advice. But she, in her caution, at once betook herself to Man, that she might suspend her nest in safety under his rafters. The Birds, however, who had disregarded her wholesome advice, being caught in nets made of the flax, came to an untimely end.

THE PARTRIDGE AND THE FOX

Once on a time a Partridge was sitting in a lofty tree. A Fox came up, and began thus to speak: "O Partridge, how beautiful is your aspect! Your beak transcends the coral; your thighs the brightness of purple. And then, if you were to sleep, how much more beauteous you would be." As soon as the silly Bird had closed her eyes, that instant the Fox seized the credulous thing. Suppliantly she uttered these words, mingled with loud cries: "O Fox, I beseech you, by the graceful dexterity of your exquisite skill, utter my name as before, and then you shall devour me." The Fox, willing to speak, opened his mouth, and so the Partridge escaped destruction. Then said the deluded Fox: "What need was there for me to speak?" The Partridge retorted: "And what necessity was there for me to sleep, when my hour for sleep had not come?"

This is for those who speak when there is no occasion, and who sleep when it is requisite to be on the watch.

THE ASS, THE OX, AND THE BIRDS

An Ass and an Ox, fastened to the same yoke, were drawing a waggon. While the Ox was pulling with all his might he broke his horn. The Ass swears that he experiences no help whatever from his weak companion. Exerting himself in the labour, the Ox breaks his other horn, and at length falls dead upon the ground. Presently, the Herdsman loads the Ass with the flesh of the Ox, and he breaks down amid a thousand blows, and stretched in the middle of the road, expires. The Birds flying to the prey, exclaim: "If you had shown yourself compassionate to the Ox when he entreated you, you would not have been food for us through your untimely death."

THE GNAT AND THE BULL

A Gnat having challenged a Bull to a trial of strength, all the People came to see the combat. Then said the Gnat: "'Tis enough that you have come to meet me in combat; for though little in my own idea, I am great in your judgment," and so saying, he took himself off on light wing through the air, and duped the multitude, and eluded the threats of the Bull. Now if the Bull had kept in mind his strength of neck, and had contemned an ignoble foe, the vapouring of the trifler would have been all in vain.

He loses character who puts himself on a level with the undeserving.

THE STORK, THE GOOSE, AND THE HAWK

A Stork, having come to a well-known pool, found a Goose diving frequently beneath the water, and inquired why she did so. The other replied: "This is our custom, and we find our food in the mud; and then, besides, we thus find safety, and escape the attack of the Hawk when he comes against us." "I am much stronger than the Hawk," said the Stork; "if you choose to make an alliance with me, you will be able victoriously to deride him." The Goose believing her, and immediately accepting her aid, goes with her into the fields: forthwith comes the Hawk, and seizes the Goose in his remorseless claws and devours her, while the Stork flies off. The Goose called out after her: "He who trusts himself to so weak a protector, deserves to come to a still worse end."

THE CAMEL AND THE FLY

A Fly, chancing to sit on the back of a Camel who was going along weighed down with heavy burdens, was quite delighted with himself, as he appeared to be so much higher. After they had made a long journey, they came together in the evening to the stable. The Fly immediately exclaimed, skipping lightly to the ground: "See, I have got down directly, that I may not weary you any longer, so galled as you are." The Camel replied: "I thank you; but neither when you were on me did I find myself oppressed by your weight, nor do I feel myself at all lightened now you have dismounted."

He who, while he is of no standing, boasts to be of a lofty one, falls under contempt when he comes to be known.

ENGLISH FOLK TALES

THE WOODMAN'S LUCK

Once a Woodman went to a wood to fell trees. Just as he was laying the axe to the trunk of a great old oak, out jumped a *Dryad*, who begged him to spare the tree. Moved more by fright than anything, he consented, and as a reward was promised his three next wishes should come true. At night, when he and his dame sat by the fire, the old Woodman waxed hungry, and said aloud he wished for a link of hog's pudding. No sooner had he said it than a rustling was heard in the chimney, and down came a bunch of black-puddings and fell at the feet of the Woodman, who, reminded of the *Dryad* and the three wishes, began to tell his wife about them. "Thou art a fool, Jan," said she, angry at his neglecting to make the best of his good luck; "I wish 'em were at thy nose!" Whereupon the black-puddings at once stuck there, so tight that the Woodman, finding no force would remove them from his nose, was obliged to wish them off again. This was the last of his three wishes, and with it all the riches and gold-pieces they might have brought him flew up the chimney.

Good luck is no gain to him that hath not the wit to use it.

THE MOON IN THE POND

Once a merchant went on his travels. And he came to a village, and outside the village there was a Pond, and round the Pond was a crowd of people. And they had got rakes, and brooms, and pikels (pitchforks) reaching into the Pond; and the traveller asked what was the matter? "Why," they says, "matter enough! Moon's tumbled into the Pond, and we can't get her out anyhow!" So the merchant burst out a-laughing, and told them to look up at the Moon in the sky, and said it was only its shadow in the water. But they wouldn't listen to him, and only abused him for his pains.

You cannot teach sense to the silly.

WELSH FABLES

ENVY BURNING ITSELF

Cwta Cyfarwydd, of Glamorgan, had a son named Howel, who was brought up by his father in every honourable acquirement and in all knowledge. When Howel grew up, he wished to follow his fortunes about the world. As he set out, his father gave him this advice : Never to pass by the preaching of God's word without stopping to listen. So Howel departed; and after travelling a long way, he came to the sea-shore, where the road passed over a long, smooth and level beach. And Howel, with the point of his staff, wrote on the sand the following old proverb : "Whoso wishes evil to his neighbour, to himself will it come." And as he was writing it, behold, a powerful nobleman overtook him; and on seeing the beauty of the writing, he knew that Howel was not a common rustic, and he asked him whence he came, and who he was, and whither he was going. And Howel gave him courteous answers to all he had asked him. The nobleman admired him much, and asked him if he would come and live with him as his domestic clerk, in order to manage for him all matters of learning and knowledge; and he promised him a salary suitable to a gentleman. So Howel agreed with him, and went to live with him. And all the noblemen and knights who came to visit this nobleman were amazed at the learning and wisdom

of Howel, and praised him greatly, so that the nobleman became jealous of him for excelling him so vastly
in wisdom, and learning, and good breeding.

Howel's fame increased daily, and in the same
measure did the envy of the nobleman, his master,
increase. And one day he complained to his lady of
the great evil and disrespect that Howel had caused
him, and he counselled with her about slaying him.
And she, in her great affection for him, bethought her
how to do it. The nobleman had on his property lime-
burners, burning lime; and the lady went to them, and
gave them a large sum of gold, upon condition of their
throwing into the kiln the first person who should come
to them with a vessel of mead; and they promised to
do so; and the lady, when she returned home, mentioned
the plan to her husband; and they filled a large vessel
with mead, and ordered Howel to take it to the lime-
burners. Howel took the vessel and carried it towards
the kiln; and on the way he heard in a house an old
and godly man reading the Word of God; and he
turned in to listen to him, and stayed with him a long
time, according to his father's advice. After this delay,
the nobleman concluded that Howel was by this time
burnt in the kiln; so he took another vessel of mead
as a reward to the lime-burners; and when he came to
the kiln, he was seized by the lime-burners, and thrown
into the fire in the kiln, and burnt there.

Thus did envy burn itself.

SIR FOULK AND THE KNIGHTS OF GLAMORGAN

The Castle of Foulk of Glamorgan consisted of one
large and lofty tower, and much higher than any other
tower in the island of Britain. As Sir Foulk, on one
Whitsuntide, speaking of the trials he had endured
when fighting with the Saracens, and of the way in
which he managed to defeat them, whilst knights and
noblemen of high descent were listening: "I could

easily have done that myself," said one Knight. "And I also," said another. "And I also," said a third. And so from "I also" to "I also," until each was heard to boast himself equal to the best, and as good as Sir Foulk himself. "One thing besides I did," said Sir Foulk, "but less wonderful, I confess, than anything else." "What was that?" said one and the other of all that were present. Said Sir Foulk, "I jumped to the top of my own castle, which every one of you acknowledges to be the highest in the kingdom." "This is true as relates to its height," said one and the other and all of them, "but as to jumping to its top, nothing but seeing the exploit with my own eyes will make me believe that." "Very good, truly," said Sir Foulk; "and if I shall have the honour of your company to dine with me some day in my castle, you shall see me jumping to the top of it." Every one promised to come, and the day was named, and all of them came, and they dined, eating and drinking well. "Now," said Sir Foulk, "for jumping to the top of the castle tower; come with me and see every one with his own eyes." They proceeded to the foot of the stairs, and Sir Foulk jumped to the top of the first step, and from that to the second, and then to the third, and thus jumped from step to step till he jumped to the top of the castle. "O!" said one, and after him every one else, "I could have easily jumped to the top of the castle in that way myself." "Yes," said Sir Foulk, "I know you could, and that every one of you easily can, now after seeing me do so, and the way I did it."

From step to step to the top of the castle of knowledge.

HITOPADESA FABLES

THE ASS IN THE TIGER SKIN

Said the King to the Birds : "The Ass, who had been fed on good corn, and fell to braying ignorantly in the hide of a Tiger, was slain for his impertinence."

"How happened that?" said the Birds.

"There is," answered the King, "in a certain town a fuller, whose Ass, weakened by carrying heavy loads, was like an animal wanting to die. The master, therefore, carried him in a Tiger's skin, and left him in a wood in a field of corn. The owners of the field, taking him at a distance for a Tiger, fled; but one of them, covering himself with a piece of cloth of an Ass's colour, stooped down to bend his bow; and the Ass perceiving him, thought he was another Ass, and began braying, and ran towards him. But the keeper of the cornfield knowing, by his voice, that he was only an Ass, killed him with ease."

THE MOUSE AND THE SAINT

A mean person, raised to a high degree, seeks the ruin of his lord : as the Mouse, having attained the form and force of a Tiger, went to kill the Saint. For there is in the sacred grove of the divine philosopher a Saint who is very pious; who seeing a young Mouse fall near his dwelling, from the bill of a Crow, kindly took him up, and fed him with grains of rice. One day when the Mouse was preparing to eat, a Cat appeared, and the kind Saint, by the power of his devotion, changed the Mouse into a Cat. This new animal was soon afterwards terrified by a Dog, and so he, too, was turned by the Saint into a Dog. At length, being in dread of a Tiger, he became a Tiger, through the prayers of the Saint, who then perceived the difference between a

Tiger and a Rat. All the people said: "See how the piety of the Saint has changed yon Rat into a Tiger!" Then the ungrateful beast thought within himself: "As long as the Saint lives, they will say these spiteful things against me." With this thought, he ran towards his protector and attempted to kill him, but was changed, by a short prayer of the heaven-eyed Saint, into a Mouse again. Thus a mean person, raised to a high degree, seeks the ruin of his lord.

THE THREE ROGUES

Once there was a Brahmin who bought a goat in another village, and carrying it home on his shoulder, was seen by three Rogues, who said to one another: "If by some contrivance that goat can be taken from him, it will be great pleasure to us." With this view they severally sat down in the road under three trees, at some distance from each other, by which the Brahmin was to pass. One of the Scoundrels called out, as he was going by: "O Brahmin! why dost thou carry that dog on thy shoulder?" "It is not a dog," answered the Brahmin; "it is a goat for a sacrifice." Then at a certain distance away, the second Knave put the same question to him; which when the Brahmin heard, he threw the goat down on the ground, and looking at it again and again, placed it a second time on his shoulder, and walking on with a mind waving like a swing. The Brahmin heard the same question from the third Villain, was persuaded that the goat was really a dog, and taking it from his back, threw it down, and having washed himself, returned to his home. The three Rogues took the goat to their own house, and feasted on it. Thence he who thinks a knave as honest as himself, is deceived by him, like this Brahmin who was ruined.

THE MONKEYS AND THE BELL

A noise only, when the cause of it is unknown, must not be dreaded. One day a thief, escaping from a house in which he had stolen a Bell, was killed and eaten by a tiger on the top of this mountain; and the Bell, which had dropped from his hand, was taken up by some Monkeys, who from time to time made it sound. The people of the town having discovered that a man had been killed, and hearing continually the noise of the Bell, said that the Cruel Demon had in his rage eaten him, and they all fled from the town. It came into the head of a certain woman that the Bell was only sounded by Monkeys; and she went to the Prince, saying, "If you will advance me a large sum of money, I will make the Demon quiet." The King gave her a treasure, and she, having paid adoration to a certain quarter of the globe, made idols, and formed circles, and acquired great reputation for sanctity, she then took such fruits as Monkeys love, and having entered the forest, scattered them about, which the Monkeys perceiving, quitted the Bell, and eagerly devoured the fruits. The woman took up the Bell, and went with it to the palace of the King, where all the people did her reverence.

Hence a noise only, when the cause of it is unknown, must not be dreaded.

THE ELEPHANT AND THE MOON

By using the great name of a powerful king, prosperity is attained, as the Fawn found security by naming the Moon. For in the forest of Dandaca a herd of Elephants being distressed by a scarcity of rain in winter, thus addressed their king: "O, sir, what remedy has our distress? Yonder is a pool used by little quadrupeds, who are bending their necks to drink it; but we, parched with thirst, whither shall we go? What can we do? " The king of the Elephants hearing this, went to a little distance, and discovered a pond of

clear water, on the borders of which were some little
Antelopes, who were trodden from time to time by the
feet of the Elephants. One of them thus thought
within himself : "If this mighty Elephant bring his herd
hither every day to quench their thirst, our whole race
will be destroyed." An old Antelope guessing the cause
of his melancholy, said : "Be not sorrowful; I will
provide a remedy for this evil." With this promise he
departed, and considered how he should approach the
Elephant near enough to address him without danger.
"I will," said he, "climb up yon mountain and thence
discourse with him." Having done as he had resolved,
he thus began : "O sovereign of Elephants, I come to
thee, by the command of that great monarch the
Moon." "Who art thou?" said the Elephant; "and
what is thy business? " "I am an ambassador," he
answered; "I speak by order of his Lunar Majesty.
In driving away the Antelopes who are appointed
keepers of the pool thou hast acted improperly : we
Antelopes are its guardians." When the pretended
ambassador had said this, the Elephant said with great
fear : "This has been done by me through ignorance;
we will not again come hither." "Come, then," said
the Antelope, "and having saluted the god who dwells
here, and trembles with rage, appease him." The
Elephant went, and as it was night, the Antelope showed
him the reflection of the Moon quivering in the water,
and commanded him to bow down. "Great sir," said
the Elephant, "my offence was through ignorance;
therefore be moved to forgiveness." Saying this and
making profound salutation, he went his way.

THE CAT AND THE VULTURE

The Crow said to the Rat : "To a strange person of
an unknown tribe, or uncertain temper, no one should
give his house : by means of a Cat, the Vulture *Jaradgabah* was slain." "How did it happen?" said the Rat.
The Crow answered : "There stands near the *Gangà*,

on a mountain called 'Vulture-fort,' a large hollow tree; high in whose trunk, his sight dim with the fear of danger, lived a Vulture, named *Jaradgabah;* by little and little he supplied his young with sustenance from his own prey, and thus the other birds of his species were supported. It happened that a Cat, named Long-ears, used to devour the young birds, and then to depart. The young ones saw her coming, and confounded with fear, made a noise. *Jaradgabah* heard it, and said: 'Who is coming?' The Cat seeing the Vulture, was alarmed, and said: 'Alas! I am destroyed. I cannot now escape from this enemy; so, as a last resource, let me boldly go to him.' Having resolved on this, she went near him, and said: 'Great sir, I am thy servant!'

"'Who art thou?' said the Vulture. 'A Cat,' said he. 'Depart far off,' said the other, 'or thou shalt be chastised.' 'Hear me, however,' replied the Cat, 'and if I deserve chastisement, then chastise me.' 'Speak on,' said the Vulture. 'I live here,' said the Cat, 'near the *Gangà*, in which I daily bathe myself; eating neither fish nor flesh, and performing the hard tasks of a holy person: thou, who art well acquainted with justice, art therefore one worthy to be trusted by me. The birds continually pray before me; and I came hither to hear a discourse on justice from thee, who art great in age and wisdom. And now tell me, thou who art so learned, why shouldst thou be prepared to beat me, who am a stranger?'

"'Shall cats,' answered the Vulture, 'who love delicate flesh, dwell here with young birds? On that account I forbid thee.' Then the Cat, stroking her ears and touching the ground with her head, thus spoke: 'I who have learnt the *Dermasastra*, and who have performed all the difficult offices of religion, am without appetite for flesh, and I speak nothing but truth.'

"And so the Vulture trusted him, and he abode in the cavern; but some days having elapsed, he assailed the young birds, carried them off, and devoured them:

during this cruel repast, on their plaintive cries, a question was asked, what he was doing?

"The Cat perceiving the discovery, left the cavern and ran away. The birds having examined the place on all sides, took up the scattered bones of their young, and suspecting that the Vulture had eaten them, united all their force, and by their first onset the Vulture was killed. For this reason I say: To a person of an unknown temper no one should give his house."

THE ELEPHANT AND THE SHAKAL

In the forest of Brahma lives an Elephant, whom when the Shakals saw, they said among themselves: "If this animal can by any stratagem be killed, we shall be supplied with food from his carcase for four months." An old Shakal upon this boldly said: "By my sagacity and courage his death shall be effected." He accordingly went close to the Elephant, and saluting him by bending his whole body, thus addressed him: "Divine beast! grant me the favour of an interview." "Who art thou?" said the Elephant, "and whence dost thou come hither?" "I am," replied he, "a Shakal, surnamed Little and Wise, and am sent into thy presence by the assembled inhabitants of these woods. Since the vast forest cannot subsist without a king, it is therefore determined to perform the ceremony of washing thee, as sovereign of the forest; thee who art possessed of every princely virtue. Lest, therefore, the fortunate time for thy inauguration should slip away, come quickly." So saying, he rose, and erecting his tail, ran on; while the Elephant, conceiving in his mind the desire of royalty, marched in the same road with the Shakal, and stuck in a deep bog. "Friend Shakal," said he, "what can now be contrived for my escape? I am fallen into a quagmire, and cannot rise out of it." The Shakal said, laughing, "Take hold of my tail, my lord, and get out by the help of it." "Such is the fruit," said the Elephant, "of my confidence in your deceitful speech."

THE STAG AND THE LION

He who has knowledge has force. See how a proud Lion was killed by a Stag. In the mountain named Mandara dwells a Lion called Darganta, who hunts the other beasts, and kills great numbers of them for his food. All the beasts being assembled, he was thus addressed by them: "Why are so many beasts killed by thee? We will give you one every day in our turns for your food: so many ought not to be slain by thee." "Be it so," said the Lion; and all of them, one by one, for his food daily gave a beast.

On a certain day, when the lot fell upon an old Stag, he thus thought within himself: "For the sake of our own souls, and in hope of life, homage is paid: but if I must meet this fate, what need have I to respect the Lion?" He moved, therefore, slowly step by step; and the Lion, tormented by hunger, said to him angrily: "Why dost thou come so late?" "It is not my fault," said he, "for in the way I was forcibly seized by another Lion, till I swore to the necessity of my coming to you; and now I approach thee with supplication." The Lion having heard this, passionately said: "Where is that audacious animal?" The Stag led him near a deep well, and said: "Let my lord behold." Then the Lion seeing his own image in the water, proudly roared, and throwing himself down with rage, perished in the well.

III. FABLES FROM L'ÉSTRANGE'S ÆSOP AND OTHER MYTHOLOGISTS
(1692)

BARLANDUS'S FABLES

AN ANT AND A PIGEON

An Ant dropped unluckily into the water as she was drinking at the side of a brook. A Wood-pigeon took pity of her, and threw her a little bough to lay hold on. The Ant saved herself by that bough, and in that very instant spies a fellow with a birding-piece, making a shot at the Pigeon. Upon this discovery, she presently runs up to him and stings him. The fowler starts, and breaks his aim, and away flies the Pigeon.

A PEACOCK AND A PYE

In the days of old, the birds lived at random in a lawless state of anarchy; but in time they began to weary on't, and moved for the setting up of a king. The Peacock valued himself upon his gay feathers, and put in for the office: The pretenders were heard, the question debated; and the choice fell upon the poll to King Peacock: The vote was no sooner passed, but up stands a Pye with a speech in his mouth to this effect: "May it please your Majesty," says he, "we should be glad to know, in case the Eagle should fall upon us in your reign, as she has formerly done, how will you be able to defend us?"

A LION, ASS, AND FOX

There was a hunting-match agreed upon betwixt a Lion, an Ass, and a Fox, and they were to go equal shares in the booty. They ran down a brave stag, and the Ass was to divide the prey; which he did very honestly and innocently into three equal parts, and left the Lion to take his choice: who never minded the dividend; but in a rage worried the Ass, and then bade the Fox divide; who had the wit to make only one share of the whole, saving a miserable pittance that he reserved for himself. The Lion highly approved of his way of distribution; but "Prithee, Reynard," says he, "who taught thee to carve?" "Why, truly," says the Fox, "I had an Ass to my master; and it was his folly made me wise."

A WOMAN AND HER MAIDS

It was the way of a good housewifely Old Woman, to call up her Maids every morning just at the cock-crowing. The Wenches were loth to rise so soon, and so they laid their heads together, and killed the poor cock; "For," say they, "if it were not for his waking our dame, she would not wake us." But when the good Woman's cock was gone, she'd mistake the hour many times, and call them up at midnight: so that instead of mending the matter, they found themselves in a worse condition now than before.

BUSTARDS AND CRANES

Some sportsmen that were abroad upon game, spied a company of Bustards and Cranes a-feeding together, and so made in upon them as fast as their horses could carry them. The Cranes that were light, took wing immediately, and saved themselves, but the Bustards were taken; for they were fat and heavy, and could not shift so well as the other.

JUPITER AND AN APE

Jupiter took a fancy once to summon all the birds and beasts under the canopy of heaven to appear before him with their brats and their little ones, to see which of them had the prettiest children: and who but the Ape to put herself foremost, with a brace of her cubs in her arms, for the greatest beauties in the company.

AN EAGLE AND AN OWL

A certain Eagle that had a mind to be well served, took up a resolution of preferring those that she found most agreeable for person and address; and so there passed an order of council for all her Majesty's subjects to bring their children to court. They came accordingly, and every one in their turn was for advancing their own: till at last the Owl fell a-mopping and twinkling, and told her Majesty, that if a gracious mien and countenance might entitle any of her subjects to a preference, she doubted not but her brood would be looked upon in the first place; for they were as like the mother, as if they had been spit out of her mouth. Upon this the board fell into a fit of laughing, and called another cause.

ANIANUS'S FABLES

AN OAK AND A WILLOW

There happened a controversy betwixt an Oak and a Willow, upon the subject of strength, constancy, and patience, and which of the two should have the preference. The Oak upbraided the Willow, that it was weak and wavering, and gave way to every blast. The Willow made no other reply, than that the next tempest should resolve that question. Some very little while after this dispute, it blew a violent storm. The Willow plied, and gave way to the gust, and still recovered itself again, without receiving any damage : but the Oak was stubborn, and chose rather to break than bend.

A FISHERMAN AND A LITTLE FISH

As an Angler was at his sport, he had the hap to draw up a very little Fish from among the fry. The poor wretch begged heartily to be thrown in again; "For," says he, "I'm not come to my growth yet, and if you'll let me alone till I am bigger, your purchase will turn to a better account." "Well," says the man, "but I'd rather have a little fish in possession, than a great one in reversion."

A BULL AND A GOAT

A Bull that was hard pressed by a Lion, ran directly toward a goat-stall, to save himself. The Goat made good the door, and head to head disputed the passage with him. "Well," says the Bull, with indignation, "if I had not a more dangerous enemy at my heels, than I have before me, I should soon teach you the difference betwixt the force of a Bull and of a Goat."

A NURSE AND A WOLF

As a Wolf was hunting up and down for his supper, he passed by a door where a little child was bawling, and an old woman chiding it. "Leave your vixen-tricks," says the Woman, "or I'll throw you to the Wolf." The Wolf overheard her, and waited a pretty while, in hope the Woman would be as good as her word; but no child coming, away goes the Wolf for that bout. He took his walk the same way again toward the evening, and the Nurse, he found, had changed her note; for she was then soothing and coaxing of it. "That's a good dear," says she, "if the Wolf comes for my child, we'll e'en beat his brains out." The Wolf went muttering away upon it. "There's no meddling with people," says he, "that say one thing and mean another."

AN EAGLE AND A TORTOISE

A Tortoise was thinking with himself, how irksome a sort of life it was to spend all his days in a hole, with a house upon his head, when so many other creatures had the liberty to divert themselves in the free, fresh air, and to ramble about at pleasure. So that the humour took him one day, and he must needs get an Eagle to teach him to fly. The Eagle would fain have put him off, and told him 'twas a thing against nature and common sense; but (according to a freak of the wilful part of the world) the more the one was against it, the more the other was for it: and when the Eagle saw that the Tortoise would not be said "Nay," she took him up a matter of steeple-high into the air, and there turned him loose to shift for himself. That is to say, she dropped him down squab upon a rock, that dashed him to pieces.

AN OLD CRAB AND A YOUNG

"Child," says the Mother, "you must use yourself to walk straight, without skewing and scuffling so every step you set." "Pray, Mother," says the Young Crab, "do but set the example yourself, and I'll follow ye."

THE GOOSE AND THE GOSLING

"Why do you go nodding and waggling so like a fool, as if you were Hipshot?" says the Goose to her Gosling. The young one tried to mend it, but could not; and so the Mother tied little sticks to her legs, to keep her upright: but the little one complained then, that she could neither swim nor dabble with them. "Well," says the Mother, "do but hold up your head at least." The Gosling endeavoured to do that too; but upon the stretching out of her long neck, she complained that she could not see the way before her. "Nay, then," says the Goose, "if it will be no better, e'en carry your head and your feet as your elders have done before ye."

THE DOG AND THE BELL

There was a very good House-Dog, but so dangerous a cur to strangers, that his master put a bell about his neck, to give people notice beforehand when he was a-coming. The Dog took this bell for a particular mark of his master's favour, till one of his companions showed him his mistake. "You are mightily out," says he, "to take this for an ornament or a token of esteem, which is, in truth, no other than a note of infamy set upon you for your ill manners."

THE TWO POTS

There were Two Pots that stood near one another by the side of a river, the one of brass, and the other of clay. The water overflowed the banks, and carried them both away: the Earthen Vessel kept aloof from t'other, as much as possible. "Fear nothing," says the Brass Pot, "I'll do you no hurt." "No, no," says t'other, "not willingly; but if we should happen to knock by chance, 'twould be the same thing to me: so that you and I shall never do well together."

AN OLD WOMAN AND THE DEVIL

'Tis a common practice, when people draw mischiefs upon their own heads, to cry, "The Devil's in it," and

"The Devil's in it." Now the Devil happened to spy an old Woman upon an apple-tree. "Look ye," says he, "you shall see that Beldam catch a fall there by and by, and break her bones, and then say 'twas all long of me. Pray, good people, will you bear me witness, that I was none of her adviser." The Woman got a tumble, as the Devil said she would, and there was she at it. "The Devil ought her a shame, and it was the Devil that put her upon't." But the Devil cleared himself by sufficient evidence that he had no hand in it at all.

A PEACOCK AND A CRANE

As a Peacock and a Crane were in company together, the Peacock spreads his tail, and challenges the other to show him such a fan of feathers. The Crane, upon this, springs up into the air, and calls to the Peacock to follow him if he could. "You brag of your plumes," says he, "that are fair indeed to the eye, but no way useful or fit for any manner of service."

A FIR AND A BRAMBLE

There goes a story of a Fir-tree, that in a vain spiteful humour, was mightily upon the pin of commending itself, and despising the Bramble. "My head," says the Fir, "is advanced among the stars. I furnish beams for palaces, masts for shipping: the very sweat of my body is a sovereign remedy for the sick and wounded: whereas the rascally Bramble runs creeping in the dirt, and serves for nothing in the world but mischief." "Well," says the Bramble (that overheard all this), "you might have said somewhat of your own misfortune, and to my advantage too, if your pride and envy would have suffered you to do it. But pray will you tell me, however, when the Carpenter comes next with his axe into the wood to fell timber, whether you had not rather be a Bramble than a Fir-tree."

A COVETOUS MAN AND AN ENVIOUS

There was a Covetous and an Envious Man, that joined in a petition to Jupiter; who very graciously ordered Apollo to tell them that their desire should be granted at a venture; provided only, that whatever the one asked, should be doubled to the other. The Covetous Man, that thought he could never have enough, was a good while at a stand; considering, that let him ask never so much, the other should have twice as much. But he came, however, by degrees to pitch upon one thing after another, and his companion had it double. It was now the Envious Man's turn to offer up his request, which was, that one of his own eyes might be put out, for his companion was then to lose both.

A CROW AND A PITCHER

A Crow that was extremely thirsty, found a Pitcher with a little water in it, but it lay so low he could not come at it. He tried first to break the pot, and then to overturn it, but it was both too strong and too heavy for him. He bethought himself, however, of a device at last that did his business; which was, by dropping a great many little pebbles into the water, and raising it that way, till he had it within reach.

A MAN AND A SATYR

There was a Man and a Satyr that kept much together. The Man clapped his fingers one day to his mouth, and blew upon them. "What's that for?" says the Satyr. "Why," says he, "my hands are extremely cold, and I do it to warm them." The Satyr, at another time, found this Man blowing his porridge. "And pray," says he, "what's the meaning of that now?" "Oh!" says the Man, "my porridge is hot, and I do it to cool it." "Nay," says the Satyr, "if you have gotten a trick of blowing hot and cold out of the same mouth, I have e'en done with ye."

A BULL AND A MOUSE

A Mouse pinched a Bull by the foot, and then slunk into her hole. The Bull tears up the ground upon it, and tosses his head in the air, looking about, in a rage, for his enemy, but sees none. As he was in the height of his fury, the Mouse puts out her head, and laughs at him. "Your pride," says she, "may be brought down, I see, for all your blustering and your horns; for here's a poor Mouse has got the better of ye, and you do not know how to help yourself."

A COUNTRYMAN AND HERCULES

A Carter that had laid his waggon fast in a slough, stood gaping and bawling to as many of the gods and goddesses as he could muster up, and to Hercules especially, to help him out of the mire. "Why, ye lazy puppy you," says Hercules, "lay your shoulder to the wheel, and prick your oxen first, and then's your time to pray. Are the gods to do your drudgery, d'ye think, and you lie bellowing with your finger in your mouth?"

ABSTEMIUS'S FABLES

A MOUSE IN A CHEST

A Mouse that was bred in a Chest, and had lived all her days there upon what the dame of the house laid up in it, happened one time to drop out over the side, and to stumble upon a very delicious morsel, as she was hunting up and down to find her way in again. She had no sooner the taste of it in her mouth, but she brake out into exclamations, what a fool she had been thus long, to persuade herself that there was no happiness in the world but in that box.

A HUSBANDMAN AND CERES

A certain Farmer complained that the beards of his corn cut the reapers' and the thrashers' fingers sometimes, and therefore he desired Ceres that his corn might grow hereafter without beards. The request was granted, and the little birds ate up all his grain. "Fool that I was," says he, "rather to lose the support of my life, than venture the pricking of my servants' fingers."

A COUNTRYMAN AND A HAWK

A Country Fellow had the fortune to take a Hawk in the hot pursuit of a Pigeon. The Hawk pleaded for herself, that she never did the Countryman any harm, "and therefore I hope," says she, "that you'll do me none." "Well," says the Countryman, "and pray what wrong did the Pigeon ever do you? Now by the reason of your own argument, you must e'en expect to be treated yourself, as you yourself would have treated this Pigeon."

A SWALLOW AND A SPIDER

A Spider that observed a Swallow catching of flies, fell immediately to work upon a net to catch swallows, for she looked upon it as an encroachment upon her right: but the birds, without any difficulty, brake through the work, and flew away with the very net itself. "Well," says the Spider, "bird-catching is none of my talent, I perceive." And so she returned to her old trade of catching flies again.

A COUNTRYMAN AND A RIVER

A Countryman that was to pass a river sounded it up and down to try where it was most fordable; and

upon trial he made this observation on it : "Where the
water ran smooth, he found it deepest; and on the
contrary, shallowest where it made most noise."

CAPONS FAT AND LEAN

There were a great many crammed Capons together
in a coop; some of them very fair and fat, and
others again that did not thrive upon feeding. The
Fat ones would be ever and anon making sport with
the Lean, and calling them starvelings; till in the end,
the cook was ordered to dress so many Capons for
supper, and to be sure to take the best in the pen :
when it came to that once, they that had most flesh
upon their backs wished they had had less, and 'twould
have been better for them.

A SWAN AND A STORK

A Stork that was present at the song of a dying
Swan, told her 'twas contrary to nature to sing so
much out of season; and asked her the reason of it?
"Why," says the Swan, "I am now entering into a
state where I shall be no longer in danger of either
snares, guns, or hunger : and who would not joy at
such a deliverance? "

A FLY UPON A WHEEL

"What a dust do I raise ! " says the Fly, "upon the
Coach-wheel? And what a rate do I drive at," says
the same Fly again, "upon the horse's buttock ! "

THE FISHES AND THE FRYING-PAN

A Cook was frying a dish of live fish, and so soon
as ever they felt the heat of the pan : "There's no

enduring of this," cried one, and so they all leapt into the fire; and instead of mending the matter, they were worse now than before.

A LEAGUE OF BEASTS AND FISHES

The Beasts entered into a league with the Fishes against the Birds. The war was declared; but the Fishes, instead of their quota, sent their excuse, that they were not able to march by land.

A SPANIEL AND A SOW

"I wonder," says a Sow to a Spaniel, "how you can fawn thus upon a master that gives you so many blows and twinges by the ears." "Well," says the Dog, "but then set the good bits and the good words he gives me, against those blows and twinges, and I'm a gainer by the bargain."

WAX AND BRICK

There was a question started once about Wax and Brick, why the one should be so brittle, and liable to be broken with every knock, and the other bear up against all injuries and weathers, so durable and firm. The Wax philosophised upon the matter, and finding out at last, that it was burning made the Brick so hard, cast itself into the fire, upon an opinion that heat would harden the Wax too; but that which consolidated the one, dissolved the other.

V. FABLES FROM PILPAY:

Tales told by the Brahmin Pilpay to the Great King, Dabschelim, whose Grand Vizir he was.

THE TRAVELLING PIGEON

There were once in a certain part of your Majesty's dominions two Pigeons, a male and a female, which had been hatched from the same brood of eggs, and bred up together afterwards in the same nest, under the roof of an old building, in which they lived together in mutual content and perfect happiness, safely sheltered from all the injuries of the weather, and contented with a little water and a few tares. It is a treasure to live in a desert when we enjoy the happiness of a friend; and there is no loss in quitting for the sake of such a one all other company in the world. But it seems too often the peculiar business of destiny to separate friends. Of these Pigeons the one was called the Beloved, the other the Lover. One day the Lover, having an eager desire to travel, imparted his design to his companion. "Must we always," said he, "live confined to a hole? No; be it with you as you please, but for my part I am resolved to take a tour about the world. Travellers every day meet with new things, and acquire experience; and all the great and learned among our ancestors have told us, that travelling is the only means to acquire knowledge. If the sword be never unsheathed, it can never show the valour of the person that wears it; and if the pen takes not its run through the extent of a page, it can never show the eloquence of the author that uses it. The heavens, by reason of their perpetual motion, exceed in glory and delight the regions beneath them; and the dull brute earth is the solid place for all creatures to tread upon, only because it is immovable. If a tree could remove itself from one place to another, it would neither be afraid of the saw nor the wedge, nor exposed to the ill usage of the wood-mongers."

"All this is true," said the Beloved; "but, my dear companion, you know not, nor have you ever yet undergone the fatigues of travel, nor do you understand what it is to live in foreign countries; and believe me, travelling is a tree, the chiefest fruit of which is labour and disquiet."

"If the fatigues of travelling are very great," answered the Lover, "they are abundantly rewarded with the pleasure of seeing a thousand rarities; and when people are once grown accustomed to labour, they look upon it to be no hardship."

"Travelling," replied the Beloved, "my dear companion, is never delightful but when we travel in company of our friends; for when we are at a far distance from them, besides that we are exposed to the injuries of the weather, we are grieved to find ourselves separated from what we love: therefore take, my dearest, the advice which my tenderness suggests to you: never leave the place where you live at ease, nor forsake the object of your dearest affection."

"If I find these hardships insupportable," replied the Lover, "believe me, I will return in a little time. If I do not, be assured that I am happy, and let the consciousness of that make you also so." After they had thus reasoned the case together, they went to their rest, and meeting the next morning, the Lover being immovable in his resolution, took their leaves of each other, and so parted.

The Lover left his hole, like a bird that had made his escape out of a cage; and as he went on his journey, was ravished with delight at the prospect of the mountains, rivers, and gardens which he flew over; and, arriving towards evening at the foot of a little hill,

where several rivulets, shaded with lovely trees, watered
the enamelled meadows, he resolved to spend the night
in a place that so effectually resembled a terrestrial
paradise. But, alas! how soon began he to feel the
vicissitudes of fortune! Hardly had he betaken himself to his repose upon a tree, when the air grew
gloomy, and blazing gleams of lightning began to
flash against his eyes, while the thunder rattled along
the plains, and became doubly terrible by its echoes
from the neighbouring mountains. The rain also and
the hail came down together in whole torrents, and
made the poor Pigeon hop from bough to bough,
beaten, wetted to the skin, and in continual terror of
being consumed in a flash of lightning. In short, he
spent the night so ill, that he already heartily repented
his having left his comrade.

The next morning, the sun having dispersed the
clouds, the Lover was prudent enough to take his leave
of the tree, with a full resolution to make the best of
his way home again; he had not, however, flown fifty
yards, when a Sparrow-hawk, with a keen appetite,
perceiving our traveller, pursued him upon the wing.
The Pigeon, seeing him at a distance, began to
tremble; and, as he approached nearer, utterly despair-
ing ever to see his friend again, and no less sorry that
he had not followed her advice, protested that if ever
he escaped that danger, he would never more think of
travelling. In this time the Sparrow-hawk had overtaken, and was just ready to seize him and tear him
in pieces, when a hungry Eagle, lancing down with a
full swoop upon the Sparrow-hawk, cried out, "Hold,
let me devour that Pigeon to stay my stomach, till I
find something else more solid." The Sparrow-hawk,
however, no less courageous than hungry, would not,
though unequal in strength, give way to the Eagle:
so that the two birds of prey fell to fighting one with
another, and in the meantime the poor Pigeon escaped,
and perceiving a hole so small that it would hardly
give entrance to a Titmouse, yet made shift to squeeze

himself into it, and so spent the night in a world of fear and trouble. By break of day he got out again, but he was now become so weak for want of food that he could hardly fly; add to this, he had not yet half recovered himself from the fear he was in the day before. As he was, however, full of terror, looking round about him to see whether the Sparrow-hawk or the Eagle appeared, he spied a Pigeon in a field at a small distance, with a great deal of corn scattered in the place where he was feeding. The Lover, rejoiced at the sight, drew near this happy Pigeon, as he thought him, and without compliments fell to: but he had hardly pecked three grains before he found himself caught by the legs. The pleasures of this world, indeed, are generally but snares which the devil lays for us.

"Brother," said the Lover to the other Pigeon, "we are both of one and the same species; wherefore, then, did you not inform me of this piece of treachery, that I might not have fallen into these springes they have laid for us?" To which the other answered: "Forbear complaints; nobody can prevent his destiny; nor can all the prudence of man preserve him from inevitable accidents." The Lover, on this, next besought him to teach him some expedient to free himself from the danger that threatened him. "Poor, innocent creature," answered the other, "if I knew any means to do this, dost thou not think I would make use of it to deliver myself, that so I might not be the occasion of surprising others of my fellow-creatures? Alas! unfortunate friend, thou art but like the young Camel, who, weary with travelling, cried to his mother, with tears in his eyes, 'O mother without affection! stop a little, that I may take breath and rest myself.' To whom the mother replied, 'O son without consideration! seest thou not that my bridle is in the hand of another? Were I at liberty, I would gladly both throw down my burden, and give thee my assistance: but, alas! we must both submit to what we cannot avoid or prevent.'" Our traveller perceiving, by this discourse, that all hopes of relief from others were vain, resolved to rely only on himself, and strengthened by his own despair, with much striving and long fluttering, at length broke the snare, and taking the benefit of his unexpected good fortune, bent his flight toward his own country; and such was his joy for having escaped so great a danger, that he even forgot his hunger. However, at length passing through a village, and lighting, merely for a little rest, upon a wall that was over against a field newly sown, a countryman, that was keeping the birds from his corn, perceiving the Pigeon, flung a stone at him, and, while the poor Lover was dreaming of nothing less than of the harm that was so near him, hit him so terrible a blow, that he fell quite stunned into a deep and dry well that was at the foot of the wall. By this, however, he escaped being made the countryman's supper, who, not being able to come at his prey, left it in the well, and never thought more of it. There the Pigeon remained all the night long in the well, with a sad heart, and a wing half broken. During the night his misfortunes would not permit him to sleep, and a thousand times over he wished himself at home with his friend; the next day, however, he so bestirred himself, that he got out of the well, and towards evening arrived at his old habitation.

The Beloved, hearing the fluttering of her companion's wings, flew forth with a more than ordinary joy to meet him; but seeing him so weak and in so bad a condition, asked him tenderly the reason of it: upon which the Lover told her all his adventures, protesting heartily to take her advice for the future, and never to travel more.

"I have recited," concluded the Vizir, "this example to your Majesty, to dissuade you from preferring the inconveniences of travelling, to the repose that you enjoy at home, among the praises and adorations of a loyal and happy people."

"Wise Vizir," said the King, "I acknowledge it a painful thing to travel; but it is no less true that there is great and useful knowledge to be gained by it. Should a man be always tied to his own house or his own country, he would be deprived of the sight and enjoyment of an infinite number of noble things. And to continue your allegoric history of birds, the Falcon is happy in seeing the beauties of the world, while Princes frequently carry them upon their hands, and for that honour and pleasure he quits the inglorious life of the nest. On the other hand, the Owl is contemned, because he always hides himself in ruinous buildings and dark holes, and delights in nothing but retirement. The mind of man ought to fly abroad and soar like the Falcon, not hide itself like the Owl. He that travels renders himself acceptable to all the world, and men of wisdom and learning are pleased with his conversation. Nothing is more clear and limpid than running water, while stagnating puddles grow thick and muddy. Had the famous Falcon, that was bred in the Raven's nest, never flown abroad, he would never have been so highly advanced."

THE FABLE OF THE GREEDY CAT, WHICH THE RAVEN NARRATES TO THE FALCON

There was formerly an old Woman in a village, extremely thin, half-starved, and meagre. She lived in a little cottage as dark and gloomy as a fool's heart, and withal as close shut up as a miser's hand. This miserable creature had for the companion of her wretched retirements a Cat meagre and lean as herself; the poor creature never saw bread, nor beheld the face of a stranger, and was forced to be contented with only smelling the mice in their holes, or seeing the prints of their feet in the dust. If by some extraordinary lucky chance this miserable animal happened to catch a mouse, she was like a beggar that discovers a treasure; her visage and her eyes were inflamed with joy, and that booty served her for a whole week; and out of the excess of her admiration, and distrust of her own happiness, she would cry out to herself, "Heavens! Is this a dream, or is it real?" One day, however, ready to die for hunger, she got upon the ridge of her enchanted castle, which had long been the mansion of famine for cats, and spied from thence another Cat, that was stalking upon a neighbour's wall like a Lion, walking along as if she had been counting her steps, and so fat that she could hardly go. The old Woman's Cat, astonished to see a creature of her own species so plump and so large, with a loud voice, cries out to her pursy neighbour, "In the name of pity, speak to me, thou happiest of the Cat kind! why, you look as if you came from one of the Khan [1] of Kathai's feasts; I conjure ye, to tell me how or in what region it is that you get your skin so well stuffed?"

"Where?" replied the fat one; "why, where should one feed well but at a King's table? I go to the house," continued she, "every day about dinner-time, and there I lay my paws upon some delicious morsel or other, which serves me till the next, and then leave enough for an army of mice, which under me live in peace and tranquillity; for why should I commit murder for a piece of tough and skinny mouse-flesh, when I can live on venison at a much easier rate?" The lean Cat, on this, eagerly inquired the way to this house of plenty, and entreated her plump neighbour to carry her one day along with her.

"Most willingly," said the fat Puss; "for thou seest I am naturally charitable, and thou art so lean that I heartily pity thy condition." On this promise they parted; and the lean Cat returned to the old Woman's chamber, where she told her dame the story of what had befallen her.

The old Woman prudently endeavoured to dissuade

[1] A Nobleman of the East, famous for his hospitality.

her Cat from prosecuting her design, admonishing her withal to have a care of being deceived; "for, believe me," said she, "the desires of the ambitious are never to be satiated, but when their mouths are stuffed with the dirt of their graves. Sobriety and temperance are the only things that truly enrich people. I must tell thee, poor silly Cat, that they who travel to satisfy their ambition, have no knowledge of the good things they possess, nor are they truly thankful to Heaven for what they enjoy, who are not contented with their fortune."

The poor starved Cat, however, had conceived so fair an idea of the King's table, that the old Woman's good morals and judicious remonstrances entered in at one ear and went out at the other; in short, she departed the next day with the fat Puss to go to the King's house; but, alas! before she got thither, her destiny had laid a snare for her. For being a house of good cheer, it was so haunted with cats, that the servants had, just at this time, orders to kill all the cats that came near it, by reason of a great robbery committed the night before in the King's larder by several grimalkins. The old Woman's Cat, however, pushed on by hunger, entered the house, and no sooner saw a dish of meat unobserved by the cooks, than she made a seizure of it, and was doing what for many years she had not done before, that is, heartily filling her belly; but as she was enjoying herself under the dresser-board, and feeding heartily upon her stolen morsels, one of the testy officers of the kitchen, missing his breakfast, and seeing where the poor Cat was solacing herself with it, threw his knife at her with such an unlucky hand, that it struck her full in the breast. However, as it has been the providence of Nature to give this creature nine lives instead of one, poor Puss made a shift to crawl away, after she had for some time shammed dead: but, in her flight, observing the blood come streaming from her wound, "Well," said she, "let me but escape this accident, and if ever I quit my old hold and my own mice for all the rarities in the King's kitchen, may I lose all my nine lives at once."

"I cite you this example, to show you, that it is better to be contented with what one has than to travel in search of what ambition prompts us to seek for."

"What you say," said the Falcon, "is true, and it is a very wholesome advice; but it is for mean and low spirits only to confine themselves always to a little hole. He that aspires to be a King, must begin with the conquest of a kingdom, and he that would meet a crown must go in search of it. An effeminate and lazy life can never agree with a great soul."

"You are very magnanimous, Son," replied the Raven, "and I perceive design great conquests; but let me tell you, your enterprise cannot so soon be put in execution: before you can conquer a kingdom, you must get together arms and armies, and make great preparations."

"My talons," replied the Falcon, "are instruments sufficient to bring about my design, and myself am equal to the undertaking. Sure you never heard the story of the warrior, who by his single valour became a King?"

"No," replied the Raven; "therefore let me hear it from you." On which the Falcon related it in this manner.

THE POOR MAN WHO BECAME A GREAT KING

It being the pleasure of Heaven to rescue from misery a Man who lived in extreme poverty, Providence gave him a Son, who from his infancy showed signal signs that he would one day come to be a great man. This infant became an immediate blessing to the old Man's house, for his wealth increased from day to day, from the time that the child was born. So soon as this

young one could speak, he talked of nothing but
swords, and bows and arrows. The Father sent him
to school, and did all he could to infuse into him a
good relish of learning; but he neglected his book,
and devoted his thoughts to nothing but running at
the ring, and other warlike exercises with the other
children.

When he came to the years of discretion, "Son,"
said his Father to him, "thou art now past the age of
childhood, and art in the greatest danger to fall into
disorder and irregularity, if thou givest thyself over
to thy passions. I therefore intend to prevent that
accident by marrying thee betimes."

"Dear Father," replied the stripling, "for Heaven's
sake, refuse me not the mistress which my youthful
years have already made choice of."

"Who is that mistress?" presently replied the old
Man, with great earnestness and uneasiness (for he
had already looked out for him the daughter of a neighbouring hind, and agreed the matter with her father),
"and what is her condition?"

"This is she," the lad made answer, showing his
Father a very noble sword; "and by virtue of this I
expect to become master of a throne."

The Father gave him many reasons to imagine he
disapproved his intentions, and looked on them as little
better than madness: many a good lecture followed
during the remainder of the day; to avoid which for
the future, the young hero the next morning quitted
his Father's house, and travelled in search of opportunities to signalise his courage: many years he warred
under the command of different Monarchs: at length,
after he had everywhere signalised himself, not only
by his conduct, but by his personal courage, a neighbouring Monarch, who, with his whole family, lay
besieged in a small fortress, sent to him to beseech
him to accept of the command of all his forces, to get
them together, and endeavour to raise the siege, and
relieve them; in which, if he succeeded, he would make

him his adopted son, and the heir of his vast empire : our young warrior engaged in this, raised a vast army, fought the besiegers in their trenches, entirely conquered them, and was the gainer of a glorious victory : but, alas ! the heat of the action made him not perceive that the fortress in which the King was, was in flames ; some treacherous person had fired it, at the instigation of the general of the besieger's army, and the King and his whole family perished in the flames ; the old Monarch just lived, however, to see his deliverer, and to settle on him the inheritance of his crown. The Royal Family being all extinct by this fatal calamity, the nobles ratified the grant, and our illustrious hero lived many years a great and glorious monarch.

"I have recited this example," said the Falcon to the Raven, "that you may understand that I also find myself born to undertake great enterprises : I have a strange foreboding within me, that I shall prove no less fortunate than this famous warrior ; and for this reason can never quit my design." When the Raven perceived him so fixed in his resolution, he consented to his putting it in execution : persuaded that so noble a courage would never be guilty of idle or unworthy actions.

The Falcon having taken his leave of the Raven, and bid farewell to all his pretended brethren, left the nest and flew away ; long he continued flying, and in love with liberty, and at length stopped upon a high mountain ; here, looking round about him, he spied a Partridge in the fallow grounds that made all the neighbouring hills resound with her note. Presently the Falcon lanced himself upon her, and having got her in his pounce, began to tear and eat her. "This is no bad beginning," said he to himself ; "though it were for nothing but to taste such delicate food ; 'tis better travelling than to lie sleeping in a nasty nest, and feed upon carrion, as my brothers do." Thus he spent three days in caressing himself with delicate morsels ; but on the fourth, being on the top of another

mountain, he saw a company of men that were hawk-
ing; these happened to be the King of the country
with all his court; and while he was gazing upon them,
he saw their Falcon in pursuit of a Heron. Upon that,
pricked forward by a noble emulation, he flies with all
his force, gets before the King's Falcon, and overtakes
the Heron. The King, admiring this agility, commands
his Falconers to make use of all their cunning to catch
this noble bird, which by good luck they did. And in
a little time he so entirely won the affection of the
King, that he did him the honour to carry him usually
upon his own hand.

"Had he always stayed in his nest," concluded the
Monarch, "this good fortune had never befallen him.
And you see by this Fable, that it is no unprofitable
thing to travel. It rouses the genius of people, and
renders them capable of noble achievements." Dabschelim having ended his discourse, the Vizir, after he
had made his submissions, and paid his duty according
to custom, came forward, and addressing himself to
the King, said, "Sir, what your Majesty has said is
most true, but I cannot but think yet that it is not
advisable that a great, a glorious, and happy King
should quit his repose for the hardship and danger of
travelling."

"Men of courage," answered the King, "delight in
labour, fatigue, and danger. If Kings, who have
power, strip not the thorns from the rose-bushes, the
poor can never gather the roses; and till Princes have
endured the inconveniences of campaigns, the people
can never sleep in peace. Nobody can be safe in these
dominions, while thou seekest nothing but my ease."

THE DERVISE, THE FALCON, AND THE RAVEN

A certain Dervise used to relate, that, in his youth,
once passing through a wood and admiring the works

of the great Author of Nature, he spied a Falcon that held a piece of flesh in his beak; and hovering about a tree, tore the flesh into bits, and gave it to a young Raven that lay bald and featherless in its nest. The Dervise admiring the bounty of Providence, in a rapture of admiration, cried out, "Behold this poor bird, that is not able to seek out sustenance for himself, is not, however, forsaken of its Crëator, who spreads the whole world like a table, where all creatures have their food ready provided for them! He extends His liberality so far, that the serpent finds wherewith to live upon the mountain of Gahen.[1] Why, then, am I so greedy, and wherefore do I run to the ends of the earth, and plough up the ocean for bread? Is it not better that I should henceforward confine myself in repose to some little corner, and abandon myself to fortune." Upon this he retired to his cell, where, without putting himself to any farther trouble for anything in the world, he remained three days and three nights without victuals.

At last, "Servant of mine," said the Creator to him in a dream, "know thou that all things in this world have their causes; and though my providence can never be limited, my wisdom requires that men shall make use of the means that I have ordained them. If thou wouldst imitate any one of the birds thou hast seen to my glory, use the talents I have given thee, and imitate the Falcon that feeds the Raven, and not the Raven that lies a sluggard in his nest, and expects his food from another."

"This example shows us that we are not to lead idle and lazy lives upon the pretence of depending upon Providence."

On this the elder son was silenced, but the second son, taking upon him to speak, said to his Father, "You advise us, sir, to labour, and get estates and

[1] A Mountain in the East, famous for a vast number of venomous animals.

riches; but when we have heaped up a great deal of wealth, is it not also necessary that you inform us what we shall do with it?"

"'Tis easy to acquire wealth," replied the Father, "but a difficult thing to expend it well. Riches many times prove very fatal."

THE FABLE OF THE FOX AND THE HEN, WHICH DAMNA THE FOX TOLD TO THE LION

"There was once upon a time a certain hungry Fox, who eagerly searching about for something to appease his hunger, at length spied a Hen, that was busy scratching the earth and picking up worms at the foot of a tree. Upon the same tree there also hung a drum, which made a noise every now and then, the branches being moved by the violence of the wind, and beating upon it. The Fox was just going to fling himself upon the Hen, and make amends for a long fast, when he first heard the noise of the drum. 'O ho,' quoth he, looking up, 'are you there? I will be with ye by and by: that body, whatever it be, I promise myself must certainly have more flesh upon it than a sorry Hen;' so saying, he clambered up the tree, and in the meanwhile the Hen made her escape. The greedy and famished Fox seized his prey, and fell to work with teeth and claws upon it. But when he had torn off the head of the drum, and found there was nothing within but an empty cavity,—air instead of flesh and gristles, and a mere hollowness instead of good guts and garbage,—fetching a deep sigh, 'Unfortunate wretch that I am,' cried he, 'what a delicate morsel have I lost, only for the show of a large bellyful!'

"I have recited this example," concluded he, "to the end your Majesty may not be terrified with the sound of the bellowing noise you hear, because loud and strenuous, for there is no certainty from that of its coming from a terrible beast; and if you please, I will go and see what sort of creature it is." To which the Lion consented; nevertheless, when Damna was gone, he repented his having sent him. "For," said the Monarch to himself, "I should have remembered my father's excellent rule, that it is a great error in a Prince to discover his secrets to any, but especially that there are ten sorts of people who are never to be intrusted with them. These are, 1. Those whom he has used ill without a cause. 2. Those who have lost their estates or their honour at court. 3. Those who have been degraded from their employments without any hopes of ever being restored to them again. 4. Those that love nothing but sedition and disturbance. 5. Those that see their kindred or acquaintance in preferments from whence themselves have been excluded. 6. Such as, having committed any crime, have been more severely punished than others who have transgressed in the same manner. 7. Such as have done good service, and have been but ill rewarded for it. 8. Enemies reconciled by constraint. 9. Those who believe the ruin of the Prince will turn to their advantage. 10. And lastly, those who believe themselves less obliged to their Sovereign than to his enemy. And as these are together so numerous a class of persons, I hope I have not done imprudently in discovering my secrets to Damna."

While the Lion was making these reflections to himself, Damna returned, and told him, with a smiling countenance, that the beast which made such a noise was no other than an Ox, that was feeding in a meadow, without any other design than to spend his days lazily in eating and sleeping. "And," added Damna, "if your Majesty thinks it convenient, I will so order the matter, that he shall be glad to come and enroll himself in the number of your servants." The Lion was extremely pleased with Damna's proposals, and made him a sign to go and fetch the Ox into his presence. On this, Damna went to Cohotorbe, the Ox, and asked him from whence he came, and what accident had brought him into those quarters? In answer to which, when Cohotorbe had related his history at large, Damna said, "Friend, I am very glad I have happened to see thee, for it may be in my power to do thee a singular service, by acquainting thee with the state of the place thou hast accidentally wandered into: know, then, that here lives a Lion not far off, who is the king of all the beasts of this country, and that he is, though a terrible enemy, yet a most kind and tender friend to all the beasts who put themselves under his protection. When I first saw you here, I acquainted his Majesty with it, and he has graciously desired to see thee, and given me orders to conduct thee to his palace. If thou wilt follow me, I promise thee the favour of being admitted into his service and protection; but if thou refusest to go along with me, know that thou hast not many days to live in this place."

So soon as the Ox but heard the word Lion pronounced, he trembled for fear; but, recovering himself a little as Damna continued his speech, he at length made answer, "If thou wilt assure me that he shall do me no harm, I will follow him." Damna, at that, immediately swore to him; and Cohotorbe, upon the faith of his oaths, consented to go and wait upon the Lion. Damna, on this, ran before to give the King notice of Cohotorbe's coming; and our Ox, arriving soon after, made a profound reverence to the King, who received him with great kindness, and asked him what occasion had brought him into his dominions?

In answer to which, when the Ox had recounted to him all his adventures, "Remain here," said the Lion, "with us, and live in peace; for I permit all my subjects to live within my dominions in repose and tranquillity." The Ox, having returned his Majesty thanks for his kind reception, promised to serve him with a real fidelity; and at length insinuated himself in such a manner into the Lion's favour, that he gained his Majesty's confidence, and became his most intimate favourite.

This, however, was matter of great affliction to poor Damna, who, when he saw that Cohotorbe was in greater esteem at court than himself, and that he was the only depository of the King's secrets, it wrought in him so desperate a jealousy, that he could not rest, but was ready to hang himself for vexation: in the fullness of his heart he flew to make his moan to his wife Kalila. "O wife," said he, "I have taken a world of care and pains to gain the King's favour, and all to no purpose: I brought, you may remember, into his presence the object that occasioned all his disturbances, and that very Ox is now become the sole cause of my disquiet."

To which Kalila answered, "Spouse, you ought not to compalin of what you have done, or at least you have nobody to blame but yourself."

"It is true," said Damna, "that I am the cause of all my troubles; this I am too sensible of, but what I desire of you is, to prescribe me the remedy."

"I told you from the beginning," replied Kalila, "that for my part I would never meddle with your affairs, and now do not intend to trouble myself with the cure of your disturbances. Mind your own business yourself, and consider what course you have to take, and take it; for, as to me, I have plagues enough of my own, without making myself unhappy about the misfortunes which your own follies have brought upon you."

"Well then," replied Damna, "what I shall do is this: I will use all my endeavours to ruin this Ox which occasions me all my misery, and shall be contented if I but find I have as much wit as the Sparrow that revenged himself upon the Hawk." Kalila, upon this, desired him to recite that Fable, and Damna gave it to her in the following manner.

THE SPARROW AND THE SPARROW-HAWK

Two Sparrows had once built their nests under the same hovel, where they had also laid up some small provision for their young ones; but a Sparrow-hawk, who had built his nest upon the top of a mountain, at the foot of which this hovel stood, came continually to watch at what time their eggs would be hatched; and when they were, immediately ate up the young sparrows. This was a most sensible affliction to both the parents. However, they had afterwards another brood, which they hid so among the thatch of the hovel, that the Hawk was never able to find them; these, therefore, they bred up so well, and in so much safety, that they had both of them the pleasure to see them ready to fly. The father and the mother, by their continual chirping, testified for a long time their joy for such a happiness; but all of a sudden, as the young ones began to be fledged, they fell into a profound melancholy, which was caused through extremity of fear lest the Sparrow-hawk should devour these young ones as he had done the others, as soon as they found their way out of the nest. The eldest of these young sparrows one day, perceiving this, desired to know of the father the reason of his affliction, which the father having discovered to him, he made answer, that instead of breaking his heart with sorrow, it much better became him to seek out some way, if possible, to remove so dangerous a neighbour. All the sparrows approved this advice of the young one; and while the mother flew to get food, the father went another way in search of some cure for his sorrows. After he had flown about for some time, said he to himself, "I know not, alas! what it is I am seeking. Whither shall I fly? and to whom shall I discover my troubles?"

At length he resolved, not knowing what course to take, to address himself to the first creature he met, and to consult him about his business. This first creature chanced to be a Salamander, whose extraordinary shape at first affrighted him: however, the Sparrow would not alter his resolution, but accosted and saluted him. The Salamander, who was very civil, gave him an obliging reception; and looking upon him with a fixed eye, "Friend," said he, "I discover much trouble in thy countenance; if it proceed from weariness, sit down and rest thyself; if from any other cause, let me know it; and if it be in my power to serve thee, command me." With that the Sparrow told his misfortunes in such moving language as raised compassion in the Salamander. "Well," said he, "be of courage, let not these troubles any more perplex thee; I will deliver thee from this wicked neighbour this very night; only show me his nest, and then go peaceably to roost with thy young ones." This the Sparrow accordingly punctually did, and returned the Salamander many thanks for being so much concerned for his misfortunes.

No sooner was the night come, but the Salamander, determined to make good his promise, collected together a number of his fellows, and away they went in a body, with every one a bit of lighted sulphur in their mouths to the Sparrow-hawk's nest, who, not dreaming of any such thing, was surprised by the Salamanders, who threw the sulphur into the nest, and burnt the old Hawk, with all the young ones.

"This Fable teaches ye, that whoever has a design to ruin his enemy, may possibly bring it about, let him be never so weak."

"But consider, spouse," replied Kalila, "Cohotorbe is the King's chief favourite, and it will be a difficult thing, believe me, to ruin him; where prudent princes have once placed their confidence, they seldom withdraw it because of bare report. And I presume you will not be able to use any other means on this occasion."

"I will take care, however," replied Damna, "of this, at least, that it shall be represented to the Lion, that one of the six great things which cause the ruin of kingdoms, and which is indeed the principal, is to neglect and contemn men of wit and courage."

"That, indeed," replied Kalila, "is one very great one; but what, I pray, are the other five?"

"The second," continued Damna, "is not to punish the seditious; the third is to be too much given to women, to play, and divertisements; the fourth, the accidents attending a pestilence, a famine, or an earthquake; the fifth is being too rash and violent; and the sixth is the preferring war before peace."

"You are wise and prudent, spouse," replied Kalila; "but let me, though more simple, advise thee in this matter: be not the carver or your own revenge; but consider that whoever meditates mischief, commonly brings it at last upon his own head. On the other side, he that studies his neighbour's welfare, prospers in everything he undertakes, as you may see by the ensuing Fable."

THE KING WHO FROM A SAVAGE TYRANT
BECAME A BENIGN RULER

There was once in the eastern part of Egypt a King, whose reign had long been a course of savage tyranny; long had he ruined the rich and distressed the poor; so that all his subjects, day and night, implored of heaven to be delivered from him. One day, as he returned from hunting, after he had summoned his people together, "Unhappy subjects," says he to them, "my conduct has been long unjustifiable in regard to you; but that tyranny, with which I have governed hitherto, is at an end, and I assure you from henceforward you shall live in peace and at ease, and nobody shall dare to oppress you." The people were extremely overjoyed at this good news, and forbore praying against the King.

In a word, this Prince made from this time such an

alteration in his conduct, that he acquired the title of
the Just, and every one began to bless the felicity of
his reign.   One day, when his subjects were thus settled
in happiness, one of his favourites presuming to ask
him the reason of so sudden and so remarkable a
change, the King gave him this answer : "As I rode
a-hunting the other day," said he, "I saw a series of
accidents which threw me into a turn of mind that has
produced this happy change, which, believe me, cannot
give my people more real satisfaction than it does
myself.   The things that made this change in me were
these : I saw a dog in pursuit of a fox, who, after he
had overtaken him, bit off the lower part of his leg ;
however, the fox, lame as he was, made a shift to
escape and get into a hole, and the dog, not able to
get him out, left him there : hardly had he gone,
however, a hundred paces, when a man threw a great
stone at him and cracked his skull ; at the same instant
the man ran in the way of a horse, that trod upon his
foot and lamed him for ever ; and soon after the horse's
foot stuck so fast between two stones, that he broke
his ankle-bone in striving to get it out.   On seeing the
sudden misfortunes befall those who had engaged in
doing ill to others, I could not help saying to myself,
Men are used as they use others : whoever does that
which he ought not to do, receives what he is not
willing to receive."

"This example shows you, my dear spouse, that
they who do mischief to others, are generally punished
themselves for it, when they least expect it : believe
me, if you attempt to ruin Cohotorbe, you will repent
of it ; he is stronger than you, and has more friends."

"No matter for that, dear spouse," replied Damna,
"wit is always beyond strength, as the following Fable
will convince you."

A RAVEN, A FOX, AND A SERPENT

A Raven had once built her nest for many seasons together in a convenient cleft of a mountain, but however pleasing the place was to her, she had always reason enough to resolve to lay there no more; for every time she hatched, a Serpent came and devoured her young ones. The Raven complaining to a Fox that was one of her friends, said to him, "Pray tell me, what would you advise me to do to be rid of this Serpent?"

"What do you think to do?" asked the Fox.

"Why, my present intent is," replied the Raven, "to go and peck out his eyes when he is asleep, that so he may no longer find the way to my nest." The Fox disapproved this design, and told the Raven, that it became a prudent person to manage his revenge in such a manner that no mischief might befall himself in taking it: "Never run yourself," says he, "into the misfortune that once befell the Crane, of which I will tell you the Fable."

THE CRANE AND THE CRAW-FISH

A Crane had once settled her habitation by the side of a broad and deep lake, and lived upon such fish as she could catch in it; these she got in plenty enough for many years; but at length having become old and feeble, she could fish no longer. In this afflicting circumstance she began to reflect, with sorrow, on the carelessness of her past years: "I did ill," said she to herself, "in not making in my youth necessary provision to support me in my old age; but, as it is, I must now make the best of a bad market, and use cunning to get a livelihood as I can." With this resolution she placed herself by the water-side, and began to sigh and look mighty melancholy. A Craw-fish, perceiving her at a distance, accosted her, and asked her why she appeared so sad? "Alas," said she, "how can I otherwise

choose but grieve, seeing my daily nourishment is like
to be taken from me? for I just now heard this talk
between two fishermen passing this way: said the one
to the other, 'Here is great store of fish, what think
you of clearing this pond?' to whom his companion
answered, 'No; there is more in such a lake: let us
go thither first, and then come hither the day afterwards.' This they will certainly perform; and then,"
added the Crane, "I must soon prepare for death."

The Craw-fish, on this, went to the fish, and told
them what she had heard: upon which the poor fish,
in great perplexity, swam immediately to the Crane,
and addressing themselves to her, told her what they
had heard, and added, "We are now in so great a
consternation, that we are come to desire your protection. Though you are our enemy, yet the wise tell us,
that they who make their enemy their sanctuary, may
be assured of being well received: you know full well
that we are your daily food; and if we are destroyed,
you, who are now too old to travel in search of food,
must also perish; we pray you, therefore, for your own
sake, as well as ours, to consider, and tell us what
you think is the best course for us to take."

To which the Crane replied, "That which you
acquaint me with, I heard myself from the mouths of
the fishermen; we have no power sufficient to withstand
them; nor do I know any other way to secure you, but
this: it will be many months before they can clear the
other pond they are to go about first; and, in the
meantime, I can at times, and as my strength will
permit me, remove you one after another into a little
pond here hard by, where there is very good water,
and where the fishermen can never catch you, by reason
of the extraordinary depth." The fish approved this
counsel, and desired the Crane to carry them one by
one into this pond. Nor did she fail to fish up three
or four every morning, but she carried them no farther
than to the top of a small hill, where she ate them:
and thus she feasted herself for a while.

But one day, the Craw-fish, having a desire to see this delicate pond, made known her curiosity to the Crane, who, bethinking herself that the Craw-fish was her most mortal enemy, resolved to get rid of her at once, and murder her as she had done the rest; with this design she flung the Craw-fish upon her neck, and flew towards the hill. But when they came near the place, the Craw-fish, spying at a distance the small bones of her slaughtered companions, mistrusted the Crane's intention, and laying hold of a fair opportunity, got her neck in her claw, and grasped it so hard, that she fairly saved herself, and strangled the Crane.

"This example," said the Fox, "shows you that crafty, tricking people often become victims to their own cunning."

The Raven, returning thanks to the Fox for his good advice, said, "I shall not by any means neglect your wholesome instructions; but what shall I do?"

"Why," replied the Fox, "you must snatch up something that belongs to some stout man or other, and let him see what you do, to the end he may follow you. Which that he may easily do, do you fly slowly; and when you are just over the Serpent's hole, let fall the thing that you hold in your beak or talons, whatever it be, for then the person that follows you, seeing the Serpent come forth, will not fail to knock him on the head." The Raven did as the Fox advised him, and by that means was delivered from the Serpent.

"What cannot be done by strength," said Damna, "is to be performed by policy."

"It is very true," replied Kalila; "but the mischief here is, that the Ox has more policy than you. He will, by his prudence, frustrate all your projects, and before you can pluck one hair from his tail, will flay off your skin. I know not whether you have ever heard of the Fable of the Rabbit, the Fox, and the Wolf; if not, I will tell it you, that you may make your advantage of it in the present case."

THE RABBIT, THE FOX, AND THE WOLF

A hungry Wolf once spied a Rabbit feeding at the foot of a tree, and was soon preparing to seize him. The Rabbit, perceiving him, would have saved his life by flight, but the Wolf threw himself in his way, and stopped his escape: so that seeing himself in the power of the Wolf, submissive and prostrate at his feet, he gave him all the good words he could think of. "I know," said he, "that the king of all creatures wants a supply to appease his hunger, and that he is now ranging the fields in search of food; but I am but an insignificant morsel for his royal stomach: therefore let him be pleased to take my information. About a furlong from hence lives a Fox that is fat and plump, and whose flesh is as white as a capon's: such a prey will do your Majesty's business. If you please, I will go and give him a visit, and engage him to come forth out of his hole: then, if he prove to your liking, you may devour him; if not, it will be my glory that I had the honour of dying not in vain, but being a small breakfast for your Majesty."

Thus over-persuaded, the Wolf gave the Rabbit leave to seek out the Fox, and followed him at the heels. The Rabbit left the Wolf at the entrance of the hole, and crept in himself, overjoyed that he had such an opportunity to revenge himself on the Fox, from whom he had received an affront which he had for a long time pretended to have forgot. He made him a low congé, and gave him great protestations of his friendship. On the other side, the Fox was no less obliging in his answers to the Rabbit's civilities, and asked him what good wind had blown him thither.

"Only the great desire I had to see your worship," replied the Rabbit; "and there is one of my relations at the door, who is no less ambitious to kiss your hands, but he dares not enter without your permission."

The Fox on this, mistrusting there was something

more than ordinary in all this civility, said to himself, "I shall find the bottom of all this presently, and then, if it proves as I suspect, I will take care to pay this pretended friend of mine in his own coin." However, not seeming to take any notice of what he suspected, "Sir," said he to the Rabbit, "your friend shall be most welcome; he does me too much honour; but," added he, "I must entreat you to let me put my chamber in a little better order to receive him."

The Rabbit, too much persuaded of the good success of his enterprise, "Poh, poh," said he, "my relation is one that never stands upon ceremony," and so went out to give the Wolf notice that the Fox was fallen into the snare. The Wolf thought he had the Fox fast already, and the Rabbit believed himself quite out of danger, as having done the Wolf such a piece of good service. But the Fox was too sharp-sighted to be thus trepanned out of his life. He had, at the entrance of his hole, a very deep trench, which he had digged on purpose to guard him against surprises of this nature. Presently, therefore, he took away the planks, which he had laid for the convenience of those that came to visit him, covered the trench with a little earth and straw, and set open a back door in case of necessity; and having thus prepared all things, he desired the Rabbit and his friend to walk in. But instead of the success of their plot, the two visitors found themselves, before they expected it, in the bottom of a very deep pit; and the Wolf, imagining that the Rabbit had a hand in the contrivance, in the heat of his fury, tore him to pieces.

"By this you see that finesse and policy signify nothing, where you have persons of wit and prudence to deal with."

"It is very true," said Damna; "but the Ox is now proud of his preferment, and thoughtless of danger, at least from me; for he has not the least suspicion of my hatred."

THE TWO FISHERMEN AND THE THREE FISHES: BEING THE FABLE TOLD BY DAMNA, THE FOX, TO THE LION, IN ORDER TO WARN HIM AGAINST THE OX, COHOTORBE

There was once in your Majesty's dominions a certain pond, the water of which was very clear, and emptied itself into a neighbouring river. This pond was in a quiet place; it was remote from the highway, and there were in it three Fishes; the one of which was prudent, the second had but little wit, and the third was a mere fool. One day, by chance, two Fishermen, in their walks, perceiving this pond, made up to it, and no sooner observed these three Fishes, which were large and fat, but they went and fetched their nets to take them. The Fishes suspecting, by what they saw of the Fishermen, that they intended no less than their destruction, began to be in a world of terror. The prudent Fish immediately resolved what course to take: he threw himself out of the pond, through the little channel that opened into the river, and so made his escape. The next morning the two Fishermen returned: they made it their first business to stop up all the passages, to prevent the Fishes from getting out, and were making preparations for taking them. The half-witted Fish now heartily repented that he had not followed his companion: at length, however, he bethought himself of a stratagem; he appeared upon the surface of the water with his belly upward, and feigned to be dead. The Fishermen also, having taken him up, thought him really what he counterfeited himself to be, so threw him again into the water. And the last, which was the foolish Fish, seeing himself pressed by the Fishermen, sunk down to the bottom of the pond, shifted up and down from place to place, but could not avoid at last falling into their hands, and was that day made part of a public entertainment.

"This example," continued Damna, "shows you that

you ought to prevent Cohotorbe, who is a traitor to your Majesty, and has, I believe, some design on your sacred person, from doing the mischief he intends, by making yourself master of his life, before he have yours at his command."

"What you say is very agreeable to reason," said the King, "but I cannot believe that Cohotorbe, upon whom I have heaped so many favours, should be so perfidious as you say."

"Why, it is most true," replied Damna, "that he never received anything but kindness from your Majesty; but what is bred in the bone will never come out of the flesh; neither can anything come out of a vessel but what is put into it: of which the following Fable is a sufficient proof."

THE FALCON AND THE HEN: Being the Fable told by Damna, the Fox, to the Ox, Cohotorbe, in order to warn him against the Lion

"Of all the animals I was ever acquainted with," said a Falcon once to a Hen, "you are the most unmindful of benefits, and the most ungrateful."

"Why, what ingratitude," replied the Hen, "have you ever observed in me?"

"Can there be a greater piece of ingratitude," replied the Falcon, "than that which you commit in regard to men? By day they seek out every nourishment to fat you; and in the night you have a place always ready to roost in, where they take care that your chamber be close barred up, that nothing may trouble your repose: nevertheless, when they would catch you, you forget all their goodness to you, and basely endeavour to escape their hands; which is what I never do, I that am a wild creature, no way obliged to them, and a bird of prey. Upon the meanest of their caresses I grow tame; suffer myself to be taken, and never eat but upon their fists."

"All this is very true," replied the Hen; "but I find you know not the reason of my flight: you never saw a Falcon upon the spit; but I have seen a thousand Hens dressed with all manner of sauces."

"I have recited this Fable to show you that often they who are ambitious of a court-life, know not the inconveniences of it."

"I believe, friend," said Damna, "that the Lion seeks your life for no other reason than that he is jealous of your virtues."

"The fruit-trees only," replied Cohotorbe, "are subject to have their branches broken; Nightingales are caged because they sing more pleasantly than other birds; and we pluck the Peacocks' feathers from their tails for no other reason but because they are beautiful. Merit alone is, therefore, too often the source and origin of our misfortunes. However, I am not afraid of whatever contrivances the malice of wicked people can make to my prejudice; but shall endeavour to submit to what I cannot prevent, and imitate the Nightingale in the following Fable."

THE NIGHTINGALE AND THE COUNTRYMAN

A certain Countryman had a rose-bush in his garden, which he made his sole pleasure and delight. Every morning he went to look upon it, in the season of its flowering, and see his roses ready to blow. One day as he was admiring, according to his custom, the beauty of the flowers, he spied a Nightingale perched upon one of the branches near a very fine flower, and plucking off the leaves of it one after another. This put him into so great a passion, that the next day he laid a snare for the Nightingale, in revenge of the wrong; in which he succeeded so well, that he took the bird, and immediately put her in a cage. The Nightingale, very melancholy to see herself in that condition, with a mournful voice asked the Countryman the reason of her slavery. To whom he replied, "Knowest thou not that my whole delight was in those flowers, which thou wast wantonly destroying? every leaf that thou pluckedst from that rose was as a drop of blood from my heart."

"Alas!" replied the Nightingale, "you use me very severely for having cropped a few leaves from a rose; but expect to be used harshly in the other world, for afflicting me in this manner; for there all people are used after the same manner as they here use the other animals."

The Countryman, moved with these words, gave the Nightingale her liberty again; for which she, willing to thank him, said, "Since you have had compassion in your nature, and have done me this favour, I will repay your kindness in the manner it deserves. Know therefore," continued she, "that, at the foot of yonder tree, there lies buried a pot full of gold; go and take it, and Heaven bless you with it."

The Countryman digged about the tree, and, finding the pot, astonished at the Nightingale's sagacity in discovering it, "I wonder," said he to her, "that, being able to see this pot, which was buried under ground, you could not discover the net that was spread for your captivity."

"Know you not," replied the Nightingale, "that, however sharp-sighted or prudent we are, we can never escape our destiny?"

"By this example you see that, when we are conscious of our own innocence, we are wholly to resign ourselves up to our fate."

"It is very true," replied Damna; "the Lion, however, according to the most just observation of the captive Nightingale in your Fable, in seeking your destruction, cannot but incur divine punishment; and, desirous as he is to augment his grandeur by your fall, I am apt to think that what once befell the Hunter will be his destiny."

THE HUNTER, THE FOX, AND THE LEOPARD

"A certain Hunter once," said Damna, pursuing his discourse, "espied, in the middle of a field, a Fox, who looked with so engaging an aspect, and had on a skin so fair and lovely, that he had a great desire to take him alive. With this intent he found out his hole, and just before the entrance into it dug a very deep trench, which he covered with slender twigs and straw, and, having laid on it a piece of smoking lamb's flesh, just cut up, went and hid himself in a corner out of sight. The Fox, returning to his hole, and observing at a distance what the Hunter had left for his breakfast, presently ran to see what dainty morsel it was. When he came to the trench, he would fain have been tasting the delicate entertainment; but the fear of some treachery would not permit him to fall to: and, in short, finding he had strong reasons to suspect some ill design towards him, he was cunning enough to remove his lodging, and take up other quarters. In a moment after he was gone, as fortune would have it, came a hungry Leopard, who, being tempted by the savoury odour of the yet warm and smoking flesh, made such haste to fall to, that he tumbled into the trench. The Hunter, hearing the noise of the falling Leopard, immediately threw himself into the trench, without looking into it, never questioning but that it was the Fox he had taken; but there found, instead of him, the Leopard, who tore him in pieces, and devoured him."

"This Fable teaches us, that, however earnestly we may wish for any event, providence and wisdom ought to regulate our desires."

"I did very ill, indeed," replied Cohotorbe, "to accept the Lion's offer of favour and friendship, and now heartily wish I had been content with an humbler fortune."

"It is not enough," replied Damna, interrupting him, "to repent and bewail your past life; your business is now to endeavour to moderate the Lion's passion."

"I am assured of his natural good will to me," replied Cohotorbe; "but traitors and flatterers will do their utmost to change his favour into hatred, and I am afraid they will bring about their designs."

"You are perfectly in the right," said Damna; "but, for my part, were I in your condition, I would defend my life; and, if I must perish, fall like a warrior, not like a victim of justice at the gallows. He that dies with his sword in his hand, renders himself famous. It is not good to begin a war; but, when we are attacked, it is ignominious to surrender ourselves like cowards into the enemy's hand."

"This is right and proper counsel," replied Cohotorbe; "but we ought to know our strength before we engage in a combat and attack our enemy."

"An enemy," said Damna, "I very well know, is at no time to be despised."

"However," replied Cohotorbe, "I will not begin the combat; but if the Lion attacks me, I will endeavour to defend myself."

"Well," answered Damna, "that you may know when to be upon your guard, let me give you this caution: when you see him lash the ground with his tail, and roll his eyes angrily about, you may be sure he will immediately be upon you."

"I thank you for your advice," replied Cohotorbe; "and when I observe the signs which you have, so like a friend, informed me of, I shall prepare myself to receive him."

Here they parted; and Damna, overjoyed at the success of his enterprise, ran to Kalila, who asked him how his design went forward. "I thank my fates," cried Damna, "I am just going to triumph over my enemy." After this short confabulation, the two Foxes went to court, where soon after Cohotorbe arrived.

The Lion no sooner beheld him, but he thought him guilty; and Cohotorbe, casting his eyes upon the Lion, made no question, from what he saw, but that his Majesty had resolved his ruin: so that both the one and the other manifesting those signs which Damna had described to each, there began a most terrible combat, wherein the Lion killed the Ox, but not, however, without a great deal of trouble and hazard.

When all was over, "O! what a wicked creature thou art!" cried Kalila to Damna; "thou hast here, for thine own sake, endangered the King's life: thy end will be miserable for contriving such pernicious designs; and that which happened to a cheat, who was the cully of his own knaveries, will one day befall thee."

THE GARDENER AND THE BEAR: Being the Fable told to Damna, the Fox, by his Wife Kalila, to show him his Knavery

There was once, in the eastern parts of our country, a Gardener, who loved gardening to that degree that he wholly absented himself from the company of men, to the end he might give himself up entirely to the care of his flowers and plants. He had neither wife nor children; and from morning till night he did nothing but work in his garden, so that it lay like a terrestrial paradise. At length, however, the good man grew weary of being alone, and took a resolution to leave his garden in search of good company.

As he was, soon after, walking at the foot of a mountain, he spied a Bear, whose looks had in them nothing of a savage fierceness natural to that animal, but were mild and gentle. This Bear was also weary of being alone, and came down from the mountain, for no other reason but to see whether he could meet with any one that would join society with him. So soon, therefore, as these two saw each other, they began to have a friendship one for another; and the Gardener first accosted the Bear, who, in return, made him a profound reverence. After some compliments passed between them, the Gardener made the Bear a sign to follow him, and carrying him into his garden, regaled him with a world of very delicious fruit, which he had carefully preserved; so that at length they entered into a very strict friendship together; insomuch that when the Gardener was weary of working, and lay down to take a little nap, the Bear, out of affection, stayed all the while by him, and kept off the flies from his face. One day as the Gardener lay down to sleep at the foot of a tree, and the Bear stood by, according to his custom, to drive away the flies, it happened that one of those insects did light upon the Gardener's mouth, and still as the Bear drove it away from one side, it would light on the other; which put the Bear into such a passion, that he took up a great stone to kill it. It is true he did kill the fly; but at the same time he broke out two or three of the Gardener's teeth. From whence men of judgment observe, that it is better to have a prudent enemy than an ignorant friend.

"This example shows that we should take care whom we are concerned with; and I am of opinion that your society is no less dangerous than the company of the Bear."

"This is an ill comparison," replied Damna; "I hope I am not so ignorant, but that I am able to distinguish between what is baneful and what is beneficial to my friend."

"Why, I know very well indeed," replied Kalila, "that your transgressions are not the failings of ignorance; but I know, too, that you can betray your friends, and that when you do so, it is not without long premeditation; witness the contrivances you made use of to set the Lion and the poor Ox together by the ears: but after this I cannot endure to hear you pretend to innocence. In short, you are like the man that would make his friend believe that rats eat iron."

THE MERCHANT AND HIS FRIEND

"A certain Merchant," said Kalila, pursuing her discourse, "had once a great desire to make a long journey. Now in regard that he was not very wealthy, 'It is requisite,' said he to himself, 'that before my departure I should leave some part of my estate in the city, to the end that if I meet with ill luck in my travels, I may have wherewithal to keep me at my return.' To this purpose he delivered a great number of bars of iron, which were a principal part of his wealth, in trust to one of his friends, desiring him to keep them during his absence; and then, taking his leave, away he went. Some time after, having had but ill luck in his travels, he returned home; and the first thing he did was to go to his Friend, and demand his iron: but his Friend, who owed several sums of money, having sold the iron to pay his own debts, made him this answer: 'Truly, friend,' said he, 'I put your iron into a room that was close locked, imagining it would have been there as secure as my own gold; but an accident has happened which nobody could have suspected, for there was a rat in the room which ate it all up.'

"The Merchant, pretending ignorance, replied, 'It is a terrible misfortune to me indeed; but I know of old that rats love iron extremely; I have suffered by them many times before in the same manner, and therefore can the better bear my present affliction.' This answer extremely pleased the Friend, who was glad to hear the Merchant so well inclined to believe that a rat had eaten his iron; and to remove all suspicions, desired him to dine with him the next day. The Merchant promised he would, but in the meantime he met in the middle of the city one of his Friend's children; the child he carried home, and locked up in a room. The next day he went to his Friend, who seemed to be in great affliction, which he asked him the cause of, as if he had been perfectly ignorant of what had happened.

"'O, my dear friend,' answered the other, 'I beg you to excuse me, if you do not see me so cheerful as otherwise I would be; I have lost one of my children; I have had him cried by sound of trumpet, but I know not what is become of him.'

"'O!' replied the Merchant, 'I am grieved to hear this; for yesterday in the evening, as I parted from hence, I saw an owl in the air with a child in his claws; but whether it were yours I cannot tell.'

"'Why, you most foolish and absurd creature!' replied the Friend, 'are you not ashamed to tell such an egregious lie? An owl, that weighs at most not above two or three pounds, can he carry a boy that weighs above fifty?'

"'Why,' replied the Merchant, 'do you make such a wonder at that? as if in a country where one rat can eat an hundred tons' weight of iron, it were such a wonder for an owl to carry a child that weighs not over fifty pounds in all!' The Friend, upon this, found that the Merchant was no such fool as he took him to be, begged his pardon for the cheat which he designed to have put upon him, restored him the value of his iron, and so had his son again.

"This Fable shows," continued Kalila, "that these fine-spun deceits are not always successful; but as to your principles, I can easily see that if you could be so unjust as to deceive the Lion, to whom you were so much indebted for a thousand kindnesses, you will with much more confidence put your tricks upon those to whom you are less obliged. This is the reason why I think your company is dangerous."

While Damna and Kalila were thus confabulating together, the Lion, whose passion was now over, made great lamentations for Cohotorbe, saying that he began to be sensible of his loss, because of his extraordinary endowments. "I know not," added he, "whether I did ill or well in destroying him, or whether what was reported of him was true or false." Thus musing for a while in a studious melancholy, at length he repented of having punished a subject who might, for aught he knew, be innocent. Damna, observing that the Lion was seized with remorse of conscience, left Kalila, and accosted the King with a most respectful humility:—

"Sir," said he, "what makes your Majesty so pensive? Consider that here your enemy lies at your feet; and fix your eyes upon such an object with delight."

"When I think upon Cohotorbe's virtues," said the Lion, "I cannot but bemoan his loss. He was my support and my comfort, and it was by his prudent counsel that my people lived in repose."

"This indeed was once the case," replied Damna; "but his revolt was therefore the more dangerous; and I am grieved to see your Majesty bewail the death of an unfaithful subject. It is true he was profitable to the public; but in regard he had a design upon your person, you have done no more than what the wisest have already advised, which is to cut off a member that would prove the destruction of the whole body." These admonitions of Damna's for the present gave the Lion a little comfort; but notwithstanding all, Cohotorbe's innocence crying continually afterwards in the Monarch's breast for vengeance, roused at last some thoughts in him, by which he found means to discover the long chain of villainies Damna had been guilty of. He that will reap wheat must never sow barley. He only that does good actions, and thinks just thoughts, will be happy in this world, and cannot fail of rewards and blessings in the other.

THE PRINCE AND HIS MINISTER: The Fable which the Lion's Mother told to him

There was once a Prince who was very much famed throughout all these countries; he was a great conqueror, and was potent, rich, and just. One day as he rode a-hunting, said he to his Minister, "Put on thy best speed; I will run my horse against thine, that we may see which is the swiftest: I have a long time had a strange desire to make this trial." The Minister, in obedience to his master, spurred his horse, and rode full speed, and the King followed him. But when they were got at a great distance from the grandees and nobles that accompanied them, the King, stopping his horse, said to the Minister, "I had no other design in this but to bring thee to a place where we might be alone; for I have a secret to impart to thee, having found thee more faithful than any other of my servants. I have a jealousy that the Prince, my brother, is framing some contrivance against my person, and for that reason I have made choice of thee to prevent him; but be discreet." The Minister on this swore he would be true to him; and when they had thus agreed, they stayed till the company overtook them, who were in great trouble for the King's person. The Minister, however, notwithstanding his promises to the King, upon the first opportunity he had to speak with the King's brother, disclosed to him the design that was brewing to take away his life. And this obliged the young Prince to thank him for his information, promise him great rewards, and take some precautions in regard to his own safety.

Some few days after, the King died, and his brother succeeded him: but when the Minister who had done him this signal service expected now some great preferment, the first thing he did, after he was advanced to the throne, was to order him to be put to death. The poor wretch immediately upbraided him with the service he had done him. "Is this," said he, "the recompense for my friendship to you? this the reward which you promised me?"

"Yes," answered the new King; "whoever reveals the secrets of his prince deserves no less than death; and since thou hast committed so foul a crime, thou deservest to die. Thou betrayedst a king who put his confidence in thee, and who loved thee above all his court; how is it possible, therefore, for me to trust thee in my service?" It was in vain for the Minister to allege any reasons in his own justification; they would not be heard, nor could he escape the stroke of the executioner.

"You see by this Fable, son," continued the old Lioness, "that secrets are not to be disclosed."

"But, my dear mother," answered the King, "he that intrusted you with this secret desires it should be made known, seeing he is the first that makes the discovery; for if he could not keep it himself, how could he desire another to be more reserved? Let me conjure you," continued he, "if what you have to say be true, put me out of my pain."

The mother seeing herself so hardly pressed, "Then," said she, "I must inform you of a criminal unworthy of pardon; for though it be the saying of wise men that a king ought to be merciful, yet there are certain crimes that ought never to be forgiven. It is Damna I mean," pursued the matron Lioness, "who, by his false insinuations, wrought Cohotorbe's fall." And having so said, she retired, leaving the Lion in a deep astonishment. Some time he pondered with himself on this discovery, and afterwards summoned an assembly of the whole court. Damna, taking umbrage at this (as guilty consciences always make people cowards), comes to one of the King's favourites, and asks him if he knew the reason of the Lion's calling such an assembly; which the Lion's mother overhearing, "Yes," said she, "it is to pronounce thy death; for thy artifice and juggling politics are now, though too late, discovered."

"Madam," answered Damna, "they who render themselves worthy of esteem and honour at court by their virtues, never fail of enemies. O! that we," added he, "would act no otherwise than as the Almighty acts in regard to us; for He gives to every one according to his desert: but we, on the other side, frequently punish those who are worthy of reward, and as often cherish those that deserve our indignation. How much was I to blame to quit my solitude, merely to consecrate my life to the King's service, to meet with this reward! Whoever," continued he, "dissatisfied with what he has, prefers the service of princes before his duty to his Creator, will be sure, I find, early or late, to repent in vain."

THE BLIND MAN WHO TRAVELLED WITH ONE OF HIS FRIENDS: BEING THE FABLE WHICH THE TRUE HERMIT TOLD THE COURT HERMIT

"There were once," says the fable, "two Men that travelled together, one of whom was blind. These two companions being, in the course of their journey, one time, surprised by night upon the road, entered into a meadow, there to rest themselves till morning; and as soon as day appeared, they rose, got on horseback, and continued their journey. Now, the blind Man, instead of his whip, as ill fate would have it, had picked up a Serpent that was stiff with cold; but having it in his hand, as it grew a little warm, he felt it somewhat softer than his whip, which pleased him very much; he thought he had gained by the change, and therefore never minded the loss. In this manner he travelled some time; but when the sun began to appear and illuminate the world, his Companion perceived the Serpent, and with loud cries, ' Friend,' said he, ' you have taken up a Serpent instead of your whip; throw it out of your hand, before you feel the mortal caresses of the venomous animal!'

"But the blind Man, no less blind in his intellects than in his body, believing that his friend had only jested with him to get away his whip, ' What!' said he, 'do you envy my good luck? I lost my whip that was worth nothing, and here my kind fortune has sent me a new one. Pray do not take me for such a simpleton but that I can distinguish a Serpent from a whip.'

"With that his friend replied, ' Companion, I am obliged by the laws of friendship and humanity to inform you of your danger; and therefore let me again assure you of your error, and conjure you, if you love your life throw away the Serpent.'

"To which the blind Man, more exasperated than persuaded; ' Why do you take all this pains to cheat me, and press me thus to throw away a thing which you intend, as soon as I have done so, to pick up yourself?' His Companion, grieved at his obstinacy, entreated him to be persuaded of the truth, swore he had no such design, and protested to him that what he held in his hand was a real and poisonous Serpent. But neither oaths nor protestations would prevail; the blind Man would not alter his resolution. The sun by this time began to grow high, and his beams having warmed the Serpent by degrees, he began to crawl up the blind Man's arm, which he immediately after bit in such a venomous manner, that he gave him his death wound.

"This example teaches us, brother," continued the pious Hermit, "that we ought to distrust our senses; and that it is a difficult task to master them, when we are in possession of the thing that flatters our fancy."

This apposite Fable, and judicious admonition, awakened the Court-Hermit from his pleasing dream : he opened his eyes, and surveyed the hazards that he ran at court; and bewailing the time which he had vainly spent in the service of the world, he passed the night in sighs and tears. His friend constantly attended him, and rejoiced at making him a convert; but, alas ! day being come, the new honours that were done him destroyed all his repentance. At this melancholy sight, the pious stranger, with tears in his eyes, and many prayers for his lost brother, as he accounted him, took his leave of the court, and retired to his cell. On the other hand, the courtier began to thrust himself into all manner of business, and soon became unjust, like the people of the world. One day, in the hurry of his affairs, he rashly and inconsiderately condemned to death a person, who, according to the laws and customs of the country, ought not to have suffered capital punishment. After the execution of the sentence, his conscience teased him with reproaches that troubled his repose for some time : and, at length, the heirs of the person whom he had unjustly condemned, with great difficulty, obtained leave of the King to inform against the Hermit, whom they accused of injustice and oppression; and the council, after mature debate upon the informations, ordered that the Hermit should suffer the same punishment which he had inflicted upon the person deceased. The Hermit made use of all his credit and his riches to save his life. But all availed not, and the decree of the council was executed.

"I must confess," said Damna, "that, according to this example, I ought long since to have been punished for having quitted my solitude to serve the Lion; notwithstanding that, I can safely appeal to Heaven, that I am guilty of no crime against any person yet."

Damna here gave over speaking, and his eloquence was admired by all the court : different opinions were formed of him by the different persons present; and as for the Lion, he held down his head, turmoiled with so many various thoughts, that he knew not what to resolve, nor what answer to give. While the Lion, however, was in this dilemma, and all the courtiers kept silence, a certain creature, called Siagousch, who was one of the most faithful servants the King had, stepped forward, and spoke to this effect :—

"O thou most wicked wretch ! all the reproaches which thou throwest upon those that serve kings, turn only to thy own shame; for besides that it does no way belong to thee to enter into these affairs, know that an hour of service done to the King is worth a hundred years of prayers. Many persons of merit have we seen, that have quitted their little cells to go to court, where, serving princes, they have eased the people, and secured them from tyrannical oppressions."

THREE ENVIOUS PERSONS THAT FOUND MONEY: BEING THE FABLE TOLD BY THE LION TO HIS MOTHER

Three Men once were travelling the same road, and soon by that means became acquainted. As they were journeying on, said the eldest to the rest, "Pray tell me, fellow-travellers, why you leave your settled homes to wander in foreign countries?"

"I have quitted my native soil," answered one, "because I could not endure the sight of some people whom I hated worse than death: and this hatred of mine, I must confess, was not founded on any injury done me by them; but arose from my own temper, which, I own it, cannot endure to see another happy." "Few words will give you my answer," replied the second; "for the same distemper torments my breast, and sends me a-rambling about the world." "Friends," replied the eldest, "then let us all embrace; for I find we are all three troubled with the same disease." On these reciprocal confessions they soon became acquainted, and, being of the same humour, immediately closed in an union together. One day, as they travelled through a certain deep hollow way, they spied a bag of money, which some traveller had dropped in the road. Presently they all three alighted, and cried one to another, "Let us share this money and return home again, where we may be merry and enjoy ourselves." But this they only said in dissimulation; for every one being unwilling that his companion should have the least benefit, they were truly each of them at a stand,

whether it were not best to go on without meddling
with the bag, to the end the rest might do the same;
being well contented not to be happy themselves, lest
another should be so also. In conclusion, they stopped
a whole day and night in the same place to consider
what they should do. At the end of which time, the
King of the country riding a-hunting with all his court,
the chase led him to this place. He rode up to the
three men, and asked them what they did with the
money that lay on the ground. And being thus
surprised, and dreading some ill consequence if they
equivocated, they all frankly told the truth.

"Sir," said they, "we are all three turmoiled with
the same passion, which is envy. This passion has
forced us to quit our native country, and still keeps
us company wherever we go; and a great act of kindness would it be in any one, if it were possible, that
he would cure us of this accursed passion, which,
though we cannot but carry in our bosoms, yet we
hate and abhor."

"Well," said the King, "I will be your doctor; but
before I can do anything, it is requisite that every one
of you should inform me truly in what degree this
passion prevails over him, to the end that I may apply
a remedy in proper proportion of strength."

"My envy, alas!" said the first, "has got such a
head, that I cannot endure to do good to any man
living." "You are an honest man in comparison with
me," cried the second; "for I am so far from doing
good to another myself, that I mortally hate that
anybody else should do another man good." Said the
third, "You both are children in this passion to me;
neither of you possess the quality of envy in a degree
to be compared with me; for I not only cannot endure
to oblige, nor to see any other person obliged, but I
even hate that anybody should do myself a kindness."

The King was so astonished to hear them talk at
this rate, that he knew not what to answer. At length,
after he had considered some time, "Monsters, and not

men, that ye are," said he; "you deserve, not that I should let you have the money, but punishment, if that can be adequate to your tempers." At the same time he commanded the bag to be taken from them, and condemned them to punishments they justly merited. He that could not endure to do good, was sent into the desert barefoot and without provision; he that could not endure to see good done to another, had his head chopped off, because he was unworthy to live, as being one that loved nothing but mischief; and lastly, as for him that could not endure any good to be done to himself, his life was spared, in regard his torment was only to himself; and he was put into a quarter of the kingdom where the people were of all others famous for being the best-natured, and the most addicted to the performance of good deeds and charitable actions. The goodness of these people, and the favours they conferred upon him from day to day, soon became such torment to his soul, that he died in the utmost anguish.

"By this history," continued the Lion, "you see what envy is; that it is of all vices the most abominable, and most to be expelled out of all human society." "Most true," replied the Mother; "and it is for that very reason that Damna ought to be put to death, since he is attainted of so dangerous a vice." "If he be guilty," replied the Lion, "he shall perish; but that I am not well assured of; but am resolved to be, before he is condemned."

While matters were thus carrying on at court, however, Damna's wife, moved with compassion, went to see him in his prison, and read him this curtain-lecture: "Did I not tell you," said she, "that it behoved you to take care of going on with the execution of your enterprise; and that people of judgment and discretion never begin a business till they have warily considered what will be the issue of it? A tree is never to be planted, spouse," continued she, "before we know what fruit it will produce." While Kalila was thus upbraiding Damna, there was in the prison a Bear, of whom they were not aware, and who, having overheard them, resolved to make use of what his ears had furnished him withal, as occasion should direct him.

The next day, betimes in the morning, the council met again, where, after every one had taken his place, the Mother of the Lion thus began: "Let us remind your Majesty," said she, "that we ought no more to delay the punishment of a capital offender than to hurry on the condemnation of the innocent; and that a King that forbears the punishment of a malefactor is guilty of no less a crime than if he had been a confederate with him." The old lady spoke this with much earnestness; and the Lion, considering that she spoke nothing but reason, commanded that Damna should be immediately brought to his trial. On this, the chief justice, rising from his seat, made the accustomed speech on such occasions, and desired the several members of the council to speak, and give their opinion freely, boldly, and honestly, in this matter; saying, withal, that it would produce three great advantages: first, that truth would be found out, and justice done; secondly, that wicked men and traitors would be punished; and thirdly, that the kingdom would be cleared of knaves and impostors, who by their artifices troubled the repose of it. But, notwithstanding the eloquence of the judge, as nobody then present knew the depth of the business, none opened their mouths to speak.

This gave Damna an occasion to defend himself with so much the greater confidence and intrepidity.

"Sir," said he, rising slowly from his seat, and making a profound reverence to his Majesty and the court, "had I committed the crime of which I stand accused, I might draw some colour of advantage from the general silence; but I find myself so innocent, that I wait with indifference the end of this assembly. Nevertheless, I must needs say this, that seeing nobody has been pleased to deliver his sentiments upon this affair, it is a certain sign that all believe me innocent.

Let me not, sacred sir, be blamed for speaking in my own justification : I am to be excused in that, since it is lawful for every one to defend himself. Therefore," said he, pursuing his discourse, "I beseech all this illustrious company to say in the King's presence whatever they know concerning me; but let me caution them at the same time to have a care of affirming anything but what is true, lest they find themselves involved in what befell the ignorant Physician; of whom, with your Majesty's permission, I will relate the Fable."

THE IGNORANT PHYSICIAN

There was once, in a remote part of the East, a man who was altogether void of knowledge, yet presumed to call himself a Physician. He was so ignorant that he knew not the colic from the dropsy, nor could he distinguish rhubarb from bezoar. He never visited a patient twice; for his first coming always killed him. On the other hand, there was in the same province another Physician, of such art that he cured the most desperate diseases by the virtue of the several herbs of the country, of which he had a perfect knowledge. Now this learned man became blind, and not being able to visit his patients, at length retired into a desert, there to live at his ease. The ignorant Physician no sooner understood that the only man he looked upon with an envious eye was retired out of the way, but he began boldly to display his ignorance under the opinion of manifesting his knowledge. One day the King's daughter fell sick, upon which the wise Physician was sent for; because, that besides he had already served the court, people knew that he was much more able than his pompous successor. The wise Physician being in the Princess's chamber, and understanding the nature of her disease, ordered her to take a certain pill composed of such ingredients as he prescribed. Presently they asked him where the drugs were to be had.

"Formerly," answered the Physician, "I have seen them in such and such boxes in the King's cabinet; but what confusion there may have been since among those boxes I know not." Upon this the ignorant Physician pretended that he knew the drugs very well, and that he also knew where to find and how to make use of them. "Go then," said the King, "to my cabinet, and take what is requisite." Away went the ignorant Physician, and fell to searching for the box; but as many of the boxes were alike, and because he knew not the drugs when he saw them, he was not able to find the right ones. He rather chose, in the puzzle of his judgment, to take a box at a venture than to acknowledge his ignorance. But he never considered that they who meddle with what they understand not are likely to repent it; for in the box which he had picked out there was a most deadly poison. Of this he made up the pills, which he caused the Princess to take, who died immediately after : on which the King commanded the foolish Physician to be apprehended and condemned to death.

"This example," pursued Damna, "teaches us that no man ought to say or do a thing which he understands not."

"A man may, however, perceive by your physiognomy," said one of the assistants, interrupting him, "notwithstanding these fine speeches, that you are a sly companion, one that can talk better than you can act; and therefore I pronounce that there is little heed to be given to what you say."

The judge on this asked him that spoke last what proof he could produce of the certainty of what he averred. "Physiognomists," answered he, "observe, that they who have their eyebrows parted, their left eye bleared, and bigger than the right, the nose turned towards the left side, and who, counterfeiting your hypocrites, cast their eyes always toward the ground, are generally traitors and sycophants; and therefore, Damna having all these marks, from what I know of the art, I thought I might safely give that character of him which I have done, without injury to truth."

"Your art may fail you," replied Damna; "for it is our Creator alone who forms us as He pleases, and gives us such a physiognomy as He thinks fitting, and for what purposes He best knows. And permit me to add, that, if what you say were true, and every man carried written in his forehead what he had in his heart, the wicked might certainly be distinguished from the righteous at sight, and there would be no need of judges and witnesses to determine the disputes and differences that arise in civil society. In like manner it would be unjust to put some to their oaths and others to the rack, to discover the truth, because it might be evidently seen. And if the marks you have mentioned impose a necessity upon those that bear them to act amiss, would it not be palpable injustice to punish the wicked, since they are not free in their own actions? We must then conclude, according to this maxim, that if I were the cause of Cohotorbe's death, I am not to be punished for it, since I am not master of my actions, but was forced to it by the marks which I bear. You see, by this way of arguing, therefore, that your inferences are false." Damna, having thus stopped the assistant's mouth, nobody durst venture to say anything more; which forced the judge to send him back to prison, and left the King yet undetermined what to think of him.

Damna, being returned to his prison, was about to have sent a messenger to Kalila to come to him, when a brother Fox that was in the room by accident spared him that trouble, by informing him of Kalila's death, who died the day before of grief at seeing her husband entangled in such an unfortunate affair.

The news of Kalila's death touched Damna so to the quick, that, like one who cared not to live any longer, he seemed to be altogether comfortless. Upon which the Fox endeavoured to cheer him up, telling him, that if he had lost a dear and loving wife, he might, however, if he pleased to try him, find him a zealous and a faithful friend. Damna, on this, knowing he had no friend left that he could trust, and for that the Fox so frankly proffered him his service, accepted his kindness.

"I beseech you then," said Damna, "go to the court, and give me a faithful account of what people say of me: this is the first proof of friendship which I desire of you."

"Most willingly," answered the Fox; and immediately taking his leave, he went to the court to see what observations he could make, but further report of his doing there is none.

The next morning, by the break of day, the Lion's mother went to her son, and asked him what he had determined to do with Damna. "He is still in prison," answered the King; "and I can find nothing proved upon him yet, nor know I what to do about him."

"What a deal of difficulty is here," replied the Mother, "to condemn a traitor and a villain, who deserves more punishments than you can inflict; and yet I am afraid, when all is done, will escape by his dexterity and cunning."

"I cannot blame you for being discontented with these delays," replied the King; "for I also am so, but know not how to help myself; and if you please to be present at his next examination yourself, I will order it immediately, and you shall see what will be resolved upon." Which said, he ordered Damna to be sent for, that the business might be brought to a conclusion. The King's orders were obeyed, and the prisoner being brought to the bar, the chief justice put the same question as the day before, Whether anybody had anything to say against Damna? But nobody said a word; which Damna observing, "I am glad to see," said he, "that in your Majesty's court there is not a single villain; few sovereign princes can say as much: but here is a proof of the truth of it before us, in that there is nobody here who will bear false witness, though it be wished by every one that something were said : and in other courts it were well if the same honour and honesty were kept up."

After Damna had done speaking, the Lion, looking upon his Mother, asked her opinion. "I find," answered she, "that you have a kindness for this most cunning villain; but believe me, he will, if you pardon him, cause nothing but faction and disorder in your court."

"I beseech you," replied the Lion, "to tell me who has so strongly prepossessed you against Damna."

"It is but too true," replied the Queen-mother, "that he has committed the crime that is laid to his charge. I know him to be guilty; but I shall not now discover the person who intrusted me with this secret. However, I will go to him, and ask him whether he will be willing that I should bring him in for a witness : " and so saying, she went home immediately, and sent for the Leopard.

When he was come, "This villain whom you have accused to me," said she, "will escape the hands of justice, unless you appear yourself against him. Go, therefore," continued she, "at my request, and boldly declare what thou knowest concerning Damna. Fear no danger in so honest a cause; for no ill shall befall thee."

"Madam," answered the Leopard, "you know that I could wish to be excused from this; but you also know that I am ready to sacrifice my life to your Majesty's commands; dispose of me, therefore, as you please; I am ready to go wherever you command." With that she carried the Leopard to the King; to whom, "Sir," said she, "here is an undeniable witness which I have to produce against Damna." Then the Lion, addressing himself to the Leopard, asked him what proof he had of the delinquent's treason.

"Sir," answered the Leopard, "I was willing to conceal this truth, on purpose, for some time, to see what reasons the cunning traitor would bring to justify

himself; but now it is time your Majesty knew all."
On this the Leopard made a long recital of what had
passed between Kalila and her husband: which deposi-
tion being made in the hearing of several beasts, was
soon divulged far and near, and presently afterwards
confirmed by a second testimony, which was the Bear's,
of whom I made mention before. After this the delinquent was asked what he had now to say for himself;
but he had not a word to answer. This at length
determined the Lion to sentence that Damna, as a
traitor, should be shut up between four walls, and there
starved to death.

THE MAN AND THE ADDER: BEING THE FABLE WHICH THE RAT TOLD TO THE RAVEN

A Man mounted upon a Camel once rode into a
thicket, and went to rest himself in that part of it
from whence a caravan was just departed, and where
the people having left a fire, some sparks of it, being
driven by the wind, had set a bush, wherein lay an
Adder, all in a flame. The fire environed the Adder
in such a manner that he knew not how to escape,
and was just giving himself over to destruction, when
he perceived the Man already mentioned, and with a
thousand mournful conjurations begged of him to save
his life. The Man, on this, being naturally compassionate, said to himself, "It is true these creatures
are enemies to mankind; however, good actions are of
great value, even of the very greatest when done to
our enemies; and whoever sows the seed of good
works, shall reap the fruit of blessings." After he
had made this reflection, he took a sack, and tying it
to the end of his lance, reached it over the flame to
the Adder, who flung himself into it; and when he was
safe in, the traveller pulled back the bag, and gave
the Adder leave to come forth, telling him he might

go about his business; but hoped he would have the gratitude to make him a promise, never to do any more harm to men, since a man had done him so great a piece of service.

To this the ungrateful creature answered, "You much mistake both yourself and me: think not that I intend to be gone so calmly; no, my design is first to leave thee a parting blessing, and throw my venom upon thee and thy Camel."

"Monster of ingratitude!" replied the Traveller, "desist a moment at least, and tell me whether it be lawful to recompense good with evil."

"No," replied the Adder, "it certainly is not; but in acting in that manner I shall do no more than what yourselves do every day; that is to say, retaliate good deeds with wicked actions, and requite benefits with ingratitude."

"You cannot prove this slanderous and wicked aspersion," replied the Traveller: "nay, I will venture to say, that if you can show me any one other creature in the world that is of your opinion, I will consent to whatever punishment you think fit to inflict on me for the faults of my fellow-creatures."

"I agree to this willingly," answered the Adder; and at the same time spying a Cow, "let us propound our question," said he, "to this creature before us, and we shall see what answer she will make." The Man consented; and so both of them accosting the Cow, the Adder put the question to her, how a good turn was to be requited. "By its contrary," replied the Cow, "if you mean according to the custom of men; and this I know by sad experience. I belong," said she, "to a man, to whom I have long been several ways extremely beneficial: I have been used to bring him a calf every year, and to supply his house with milk, butter, and cheese; but now I am grown old, and no longer in a condition to serve him as formerly I did, he has put me in this pasture to fat me, with a design to sell me to a butcher, who is to cut my throat, and he and his friends are to eat my flesh: and is not this requiting good with evil?"

On this, the Adder taking upon him to speak, said to the Man, "What say you now? are not your own customs a sufficient warrant for me to treat you as I intend to do?"

The Traveller, not a little confounded at this ill-timed story, was cunning enough, however, to answer, "This is a particular case only, and give me leave to say, one witness is not sufficient to convict me; therefore pray let me have another."

"With all my heart," replied the Adder; "let us address ourselves to this Tree that stands here before us." The Tree, having heard the subject of their dispute, gave his opinion in the following words: "Among men, benefits are never requited but with ungrateful actions. I protect travellers from the heat of the sun, and yield them fruit to eat, and a delightful liquor to drink; nevertheless, forgetting the delight and benefit of my shade, they barbarously cut down my branches to make sticks, and handles for hatchets, and saw my body to make planks and rafters. Is not this requiting good with evil?"

The Adder, on this, looking upon the Traveller, asked if he was satisfied. But he was in such a confusion that he knew not what to answer. However, in hopes to free himself from the danger that threatened him, he said to the Adder, "I desire only one favour more; let us be judged by the next beast we meet; give me but that satisfaction, it is all I crave: you know life is sweet; suffer me therefore to beg for the means of continuing it." While they were thus parleying together, a Fox passing by was stopped by the Adder, who conjured him to put an end to their controversy.

The Fox, upon this, desiring to know the subject of their dispute, said the Traveller, "I have done this Adder a signal piece of service, and he would fain persuade me that, for my reward, he ought to do me a mischief." "If he means to act by you as you men do by others, he speaks nothing but what is true," replied the Fox; "but, that I may be better able to judge between you, let me understand what service it is that you have done him."

The Traveller was very glad of this opportunity of speaking for himself, and recounted the whole affair to him: he told him after what manner he had rescued him out of the flames with that little sack, which he showed him.

"How!" said the Fox, laughing outright, "would you pretend to make me believe that so large an Adder as this could get into such a little sack? It is impossible!" Both the Man and the Adder, on this, assured him of the truth of that part of the story; but the Fox positively refused to believe it. At length said he, "Words will never convince me of this monstrous improbability; but if the Adder will go into it again, to convince me of the truth of what you say, I shall then be able to judge of the rest of this affair."

"That I will do most willingly," replied the Adder; and, at the same time, put himself into the sack.

Then said the Fox to the Traveller, "Now you are the master of your enemy's life: and, I believe, you need not be long in resolving what treatment such a monster of ingratitude deserves of you." With that the Traveller tied up the mouth of the sack, and with a great stone, never left off beating it till he had pounded the Adder to death; and, by that means, put an end to his fears and the dispute at once.

"This Fable," pursued the Rat, "informs us, that there is no trusting to the fair words of an enemy, for fear of falling into the like misfortunes."

VI. FABLES FROM LOKMAN

THE GNAT AND THE BULL

A Gnat full of manners, the Bull would address,
And thus in fine language his fancy express:
"I crave your diversion and humbly beg pardon,
If the weight of my body your horn presses hard on,
But if I offend you I'll quickly be gone;"
"E'en go, sir, or stay," says the Bull, "'tis all one."

THE OLD MAN AND DEATH

Quite spent with a burthen of sticks, an old Clown,
To take breath a while, on a bank sat him down:
He called upon Death, and wished he would please
To shorten his life, and so give him some ease.
Straight all of a sudden, pale Death did appear,
Which made the old grumbler's teeth chatter wi' fear.
"I called you," said he, "Mr. Death, in a maggot,
But now you are here, help me up with faggot."
> Men at a distance Death defie
> Who quake like cowards when they die.

THE DOG AND THE WOLF

A Dog once chased a Wolf, and boasted of his force
and the lightness of his course, and the flight of the
Wolf at his presence. And the Wolf returned towards
him, saying to him, "Do not think my fear was of
thee, for certainly my fear is of him who was hunting
with you."

THE WEASEL AND THE CHICKENS

A Weasel heard that the Chickens were sick; the Weasel arose and donned the skin of a Peacock, and went to visit them, and said to them, "Health to you, O Chickens! How are you and how is your state?" And the Chickens said to him, "We are always ill until we see your face."

THE STOMACH AND THE FEET

The Stomach and the Feet disputed between themselves which of them supported the body. The Feet said, "We by our strength carry the body entirely." And the Stomach said, "If I took not some nourishment, surely you could not march far or support anything."

THE DOGS AND THE FOX

The Dogs once found the skin of a Lion, and began to mangle it. A Fox saw them, and said to them, "Surely, if he were alive you would find that his claws are sharper and longer than your teeth."

THE WOMAN AND THE HEN

A Woman had with her a Hen that laid a silver egg every day. The Woman said to herself, "If I increase her food she will lay two eggs." Then the Hen got too much food, and died therefrom.

THE DOE AND THE LIONESS

A Doe once passed near a Lioness, saying, "I have many children in a year, and thou only hast in all thy life but one or two." And the Lioness said to her, "It is true; nevertheless, if it be but one, yet he is a Lion."

VII. FABLES FROM FLORIAN

THE YOUTH AND THE OLD MAN

"My dear father," said an ambitious youth, "have the goodness to tell me how to make a fortune." "It is," said the Old Man, "a glorious pursuit; in order to acquire a fortune, one must labour in the common cause, devote his days, his nights, his talents to the service of his country." "Ah! that would be too wearisome a life; I wish for some less brilliant means." "There is a more certain method, intrigue." "That were disgraceful; I would enrich myself without vice and without labour." "Well, then, be a fool, I have known many a one succeed."

THE SQUIRREL AND THE LION

A Squirrel, merrily leaping on the branches of an oak tree, accidently missed its hold and fell upon a Lion who lay at the trunk, basking in the shade. His Majesty awoke in anger, and, raising his shaggy mane, displayed his terrific teeth to the trembling Squirrel, who, in the most abject manner, begged forgiveness for the intrusion. "I grant you your life," said the Lion; "but on condition that you tell me the reason why you little beings are always so lively and happy, while my time passes so irksomely." "Yes, sire," replied the Squirrel, "I will, in return for your mercy, comply with your request: but he who speaks the truth ought to stand higher than he who hears it; permit me, therefore, to ascend the tree."

The Lion consented to this; and when the Squirrel was out of his reach he thus addressed him : "You seek to know how I am always merry. Conscience gives me a joyous mind, and learn, sire, that the infallible recipe for happiness—a good conscience—you are in want of. You are day and night oppressed with the sting of iniquity for the crimes and wanton cruelties you have committed. How many animals have you devoured, while I have been employed in carrying nuts to alleviate the distresses of my poor brethren! You hate, and I love! Believe me, there is great meaning and truth in these words, and often have I heard my father observe when young : ' Son, let your happiness be founded in virtue, and hilarity will be the constant inmate of your bosom.' "

THE TWO PEASANTS AND THE CLOUD

Two Peasants walking together, one of them remarked to the other, in a piteous tone, that he was sure yonder black Cloud would be the harbinger of misfortune. "How so?" replied William, pleasantly. "How so?" retorted John : "I will wager that it is charged with hailstones; the harvest will be destroyed; not an ear of wheat will be left standing, and famine must ensue."—"What is the man dreaming of?" said William, good-humouredly; "I see nothing in that leaden Cloud but an abundance of rain, which has been so long ardently prayed for. Instead of injury, the rain will enrich us, and ensure a plentiful year; let us, therefore, rejoice, and take a cup of ale upon the strength of it."—"How can you talk at this rate?" exclaimed John, angrily; to which William retorted : "Your eyes serve you to but little purpose." In this manner the quarrel proceeded to such a height, that they were about to proceed to blows; when a brisk wind arose, the Cloud was dispersed, and both were deceived.

THE OLD TREE AND THE GARDENER

A Man had an old, barren Tree in his garden; it was a large pear-tree, which had formerly been very fruitful, but had grown old; such is the fate of all. The ungrateful Gardener resolved to remove it; and one morning took his axe for the purpose. At the first blow, the Tree said to him: "Have some regard for my great age, and recollect the fruit that I have borne for you every year. My death is at hand, I have but a moment to live; do not assassinate a dying Tree, which has so often been your benefactor."—"I regret being compelled to cut you down," replied the Gardener, "but I have need of wood." All at once, a hundred nightingales exclaimed: "Oh! spare it! we have but this one left; when your wife seats herself beneath its shade, we rejoice her with our merry songs; she is often alone, we beguile her solitude."

The Gardener drives them away, laughing at their request, and makes a second stroke. A swarm of bees immediately issued from the trunk, saying to him: "Stay your hand, inhuman man, and listen to us; if you leave us this asylum, we will give you every day a delicious honey-comb, which you can carry to the market for sale." Does this appeal affect him?

"I weep with tenderness," replied the avaricious Gardener: "what am I not indebted to this unhappy pear-tree, which has nourished me in its youth? My wife often comes to listen to these birds; it is enough for me: let them continue their songs unmolested; and for you, who condescend to augment my wealth, I will sow the whole province with flowers." Thus speaking, he departed, and left the old trunk to repose in peace.

THE MOLE AND THE RABBITS

Most of us are aware of some of our defects, but to avow them is quite another matter; we prefer the endurance of real evils, rather than confess that we are afflicted with them. I recollect to have been witness to a fact very difficult of belief, but not the less applicable to what has just been asserted.

One fine moonlight evening, several Rabbits were amusing themselves on the turf with playing at blind-man's buff. Rabbits! you exclaim, the thing is impossible. Nothing, however, is more true; a pliant leaf was placed over the eyes of one, like a bandage, and then tied under the neck; it was done in an instant. He whom the riband deprived of light placed himself in the centre; the others leapt and danced round him, performing miracles; now running away, then coming close, and pulling his ears or his tail. The poor blind Rabbit, turning suddenly round, throws out his paws hap-hazard; but the flock quickly get out of his reach, and he seizes nothing but air; in vain does he torment himself, he would remain there till to-morrow. A stupid Mole, who had heard the noise in her earthy dwelling, coming out of her hole, joined the party. You may imagine that being blind she was immediately caught.

"Gentlemen," said the Rabbit, "it would not be fair play to blindfold our sister; we must let her off, she has no eyes and cannot help herself." "By no means," sharply replied the Mole, "I am caught fairly; put on the bandage." "Willingly, my dear, here it is; but I think it will be unnecessary to tie the knot tightly." "Excuse me, sir," replied the Mole angrily, "tie it very tightly, I can see.—That is not tight enough, I can still see."

THE KING AND THE TWO SHEPHERDS

A certain Monarch was one day regretting the misfortune of being king: "What a wearisome occupation?" said he; "is there any mortal on the earth more annoyed than I am? I wish to live in peace, and am forced to go to war; I cherish my subjects and impose few taxes on them; I am a lover of truth, and yet am incessantly deceived; my people is oppressed with ills, and I am consumed with grief. I seek advice everywhere, use all means; but my trouble is only thrown away; the more I exert myself, the less do I succeed."

At this moment a flock of lean sheep caught his eye in the plain. They were almost without fleece; ewes without lambs, lambs without their mothers; dispersed, bleating, scattered; and the powerless rams wandering among the bushes. Their pastor Lubin was running here and there, now after this sheep, which was at the entrance of the forest, now after yonder, which was lagging behind, then after his pet lambs. While he is in one quarter, a wolf seizes one of the flock and makes off with it. Away posts the Shepherd, and another wolf carries off the lamb he has just quitted. Lubin stops quite out of breath, and tears his hair, not knowing which way to run, and frantically beating his breast, calls on death for relief.

"Here is a faithful representation of me," cried the Monarch; "these poor Shepherds endure a slavery no milder than we Kings, constantly surrounded by danger. That's some consolation."

As he uttered these words, he perceived in a meadow another flock of sheep, all fat and scarcely able to walk from the weight of their fleece; the rams strutted proudly about, and the ewes with their dugs full, made the bounding lambs hasten to share the sweet nourishment. Their Shepherd luxuriously stretched beneath a hedge was composing verses in praise of his mistress, sweetly singing them to the listening echoes; and then repeating the plaintive air on his flute.

The King was astonished, and said : "This beautiful flock will soon be destroyed; the wolves will scarcely be afraid of amorous swains, singing to their shepherdesses; a flute is a sorry weapon wherewith to repel them. Oh ! how I should laugh !——" At that moment, as if to please him, a wolf came in sight; but scarcely had he appeared, when a watchful dog sprung upon and throttled him. Two sheep, frightened at the noise of the combat, quitted the flock and ran about the plain. Another dog sets off, brings them back, and order is restored in an instant. The Shepherd views all, seated on the turf, without ceasing to play.

Hereupon the King said to him half angrily : "How do you manage? The woods are filled with wolves; your sheep, fat and beautiful, are almost countless; and with the utmost tranquillity you take care of the whole flock yourself ! "

"Sire," replied the Shepherd, "the thing is perfectly easy; my whole secret consists in making choice of good dogs."

THE HUSBANDMAN OF CASTILE

The Grandson of a king, rendered great by his very misfortunes, Philip of Spain, without money, troops, or credit, being driven by the English from Madrid, fancied his diadem was lost. He fled almost alone, deploring his misery. Suddenly an old Husbandman presents himself to his view, a frank, simple, straightforward man, loving his children and his king, his wife and his country, better than his life; speaking little of virtue, but extensively practising it; rich but beloved : held up as an example for every family in Castile. His coat, made by his daughters, was girded by the skin of a wolf. Under a large hat, his intelligent head displayed a pair of sparkling eyes, and comely features, and his moustachios depended from his upper lip, reaching down to his ruff. A dozen sons followed him, all tall, handsome and vigorous; a mule laden with gold was in the midst of them.

This Man with his strange equipage stopped before the King, and said: "Where art thou going? Art thou cast down with a single reverse? Of what use is the advantage the arch-duke has gained over thee? it is thou who wilt reign, for thou art cherished by us. What matters it that Madrid has been retaken from thee? Our love still remains, our bodies shall be thy bucklers; we will perish for thee in the field of honour. Battles are gained by chance; but virtue is necessary to gain our hearts. Thou art in possession of it, and wilt reign. Our money, our lives are thine, take all; thanks to forty years of labour and economy, I am enabled to offer thee this gold. Here are my twelve children, behold in them twelve soldiers, despite my grey hairs I will make the thirteenth; and the war being finished, when thy generals, officers, and great men come to demand of thee, wealth, honour, riband, as the price of their services, we will ask but for repose and justice; it is all that we require. We poor people furnish the King with blood and treasure, but, far from revelling in his bounty, the less he gives, the more we love him. When thou shalt be happy, we will fly thy presence, we will bless thee in silence; thou art conquered and we seek thee."

Having so said, he fell on his knees; with a paternal hand, Philip raised him, sobbing audibly; he presses this faithful subject in his arms, wishes to speak, but tears interrupt his words.

Soon, according to the prophecy of the good old Man, Philip became the conqueror; and, seated on the throne of Iberia, did not forget the Husbandman.

The Monarch most beloved is always the most powerful. Fortune in vain endeavours to overwhelm him; in vain do a thousand enemies, leagued against him, seem to presage his destruction as inevitable; the love of his subjects renders their efforts useless.

THE HOUSE OF CARDS

A kind husband, his wife, and two pretty children, lived peacefully in the village where their parents had resided before them. This couple sharing the care of the little household, cultivated their garden, and gathered in their harvests; on summer evenings, supping beneath the green foliage, and in winter before their hearth, they talked to their sons of virtue, wisdom, and of the happiness which these would always procure. The father enlivened his discourse by a story, the mother by a kiss.

The elder of these children, naturally grave and studious, read and reflected incessantly; the younger, merry and active, was always jumping and laughing, and never happy but at play. One evening, according to custom, seated at a table beside their parents, the elder was reading Rollin, the younger, careless about being acquainted with the grand achievements of the Romans and Parthians, was employing all his ingenuity, all his skill, in erecting a fragile House of Cards; he scarcely breathed for fear of demolishing it.

The student leaving off for a moment, said, "Father, be so good as to inform me, why certain warriors are called conquerors, and others founders of empires; have these two names a different meaning?" The father was thinking of a proper answer, when his younger son, transported with pleasure at having, after so much trouble, succeeded in building a second story, cried out: "I have done it!" His brother, angry at the noise, with a single blow, destroyed that which it had taken him so long to erect, and made him burst into tears.

"My son," then replied the father, "the founder is your brother, and you are the conqueror."

THE HORSE AND THE COLT

Unacquainted with the iron sway of tyrant man, lived a venerable Horse, who had been left a widower, with an only son; he reared him in a meadow, where the streams, the flowers, and the inviting shade offered at once all that was requisite for happiness. Abusing these enjoyments, as is customary with youth, the Colt stuffed himself every day with clover, fooled away the time on the flowery plain, galloped about without an object, bathed without requiring it, or rested himself without being fatigued. Lazy and fat, the young hermit grew weary, and became tired of wanting for nothing; disgust soon followed; and, seeking his father, he said to him—"For some time I have been unwell; this grass is unwholesome, and kills me; this clover is without smell; this water is muddy; the air we breathe here attacks my lungs; in short, I shall die unless we leave it." "Since it concerns your life, my dear son," replied his parent, "we will instantly take our departure." No sooner said than done—the two immediately set off in search of a new home.

The young traveller neighed for joy; the old one, less merry, went at a sedate pace, taking the lead, and made his child clamber up steep and arid mountains without a tuft of herbage, and where there was nothing which could afford them the least nourishment.

Evening came, but there was no pasturage; and our travellers were fain to go to bed supperless. The next day, when nearly exhausted by hunger, they were glad of a few stunted briars. This time there was no galloping on the part of the Colt; and after two days, he could scarcely drag one leg after the other.

Considering the lesson sufficient, the father returned by a road unknown to his son, and reconducted him to his meadow in the middle of the night. As soon as our Colt discovered a little fresh grass, he attacked it with avidity. "Oh! what a delicious banquet! What beautiful grass!" he exclaimed: "was there ever anything so sweet and tender? My father, we will seek no further, let us take up our abode for ever in this lovely spot: what country can equal this rural asylum!"

As he thus spoke, day began to break; and the Colt recognising the meadow he had so lately quitted, cast down his eyes in the greatest confusion.

His father mildly said to him: "My dear child, in future remember this maxim; 'he who enjoys too much, is soon disgusted with pleasure; to be happy, one must be moderate.'"

VIII. FABLES FROM LA FONTAINE

THE TWO MULES

Two Mules were bearing on their backs,
One, oats; the other, silver of the tax.
   The latter glorying in his load,
   March'd proudly forward on the road;
And, from the jingle of his bell,
'Twas plain he liked his burden well.
    But in a wild-wood glen
    A band of robber men
Rush'd forth upon the twain.
    Well with the silver pleased,
    They by the bridle seized
The treasure-mule so vain.
Poor Mule! in struggling to repel
His ruthless foes, he fell
Stabb'd through; and with a bitter sighing,
He cried, "Is this the lot they promised me?
My humble friend from danger free,
While, weltering in my gore, I'm dying?"

"My friend," his fellow-mule replied,
"It is not well to have one's work too high.
If thou hadst been a miller's drudge, as I,
Thou wouldst not thus have died."

THE COUNCIL HELD BY THE RATS

Old Rodilard, a certain Cat,
Such havoc of the Rats had made,
'Twas difficult to find a Rat
With nature's debt unpaid.
The few that did remain,
To leave their holes afraid,
From usual food abstain,
Not eating half their fill.
And wonder no one will
That one who made of Rats his revel,
With Rats pass'd not for Cat, but Devil.
Now, on a day, this dread Rat-eater,
Who had a wife, went out to meet her;
And while he held his caterwauling,
The unkill'd Rats, their chapter calling,
Discuss'd the point, in grave debate,
How they might shun impending fate.
Their dean, a prudent Rat,
Thought best, and better soon than late,
To bell the fatal Cat;
That, when he took his hunting round,
The Rats, well caution'd by the sound,
Might hide in safety under ground;
Indeed he knew no other means.
And all the rest
At once confess'd
Their minds were with the dean's.
No better plan, they all believed,
Could possibly have been conceived,
No doubt the thing would work right well,
If any one would hang the bell.

But, one by one, said every Rat,
"I'm not so big a fool as that."
The plan, knock'd up in this respect,
The council closed without effect.
    To argue or refute
      Wise counsellors abound;
    The man to execute
      Is harder to be found.

THE WOLF ACCUSING THE FOX BEFORE THE MONKEY

A Wolf, affirming his belief
That he had suffer'd by a thief,
    Brought up his neighbour Fox—
Of whom it was by all confess'd,
His character was not the best—
    To fill the prisoner's box.
As judge between these vermin,
A Monkey graced the ermine;
And truly other gifts of Themis
    Did scarcely seem his;
For while each party plead his cause,
Appealing boldly to the laws,
And much the question vex'd,
Our Monkey sat perplex'd.
    Their words and wrath expended,
    Their strife at length was ended;
When, by their malice taught,
The judge this judgment brought:
"Your characters, my friends, I long have known,
    As on this trial clearly shown;
And hence I fine you both—the grounds at large
    To state would little profit—
You Wolf, in short, as bringing groundless charge,
    You Fox, as guilty of it."
  Come at it right or wrong, the judge opined
  No other than a villain could be fined.

THE WOLF TURNED SHEPHERD

A Wolf, whose gettings from the flocks
   Began to be but few,
Bethought himself to play the Fox
   In character quite new.
A Shepherd's hat and coat he took,
    A cudgel for a crook,
    Nor e'en the pipe forgot:
And more to seem what he was not,
Himself upon his hat he wrote,
"I'm Willie, Shepherd of these sheep."
   His person thus complete,
   His crook in upraised feet,
The impostor Willie stole upon the keep.
The real Willie, on the grass asleep,
   Slept there, indeed, profoundly,
His dog and pipe slept, also soundly;
   His drowsy sheep around lay.
   As for the greatest number,
Much bless'd the hypocrite their slumber,
And hoped to drive away the flock,
Could he the Shepherd's voice but mock.
   He thought undoubtedly he could.
He tried: the tone in which he spoke,
   Loud echoing from the wood,
   The plot and slumber broke;
   Sheep, dog, and man awoke.
   The Wolf, in sorry plight,
   In hampering coat bedight,
   Could neither run nor fight.
There's always leakage of deceit
Which makes it never safe to cheat.
   Whoever is a Wolf had better
   Keep clear of hypocritic fetter.

THE LION GOING TO WAR

The Lion had an enterprise in hand;
   Held a war-council, sent his provost-marshal,
   And gave the animals a call impartial—
Each, in his way, to serve his high command.
The Elephant should carry on his back
The tools of war, the mighty public pack,
And fight in elephantine way and form;
The Bear should hold himself prepared to storm;
The Fox all secret stratagems should fix;
The Monkey should amuse the foe by tricks.
"Dismiss," said one, "the blockhead Asses,
   And Hares, too cowardly and fleet."
"No," said the King; "I use all classes;
   Without their aid my force were incomplete.
The Ass shall be our trumpeter, to scare
Our enemy.   And then the nimble hare
Our royal bulletins shall homeward bear."
   A monarch provident and wise
Will hold his subjects all of consequence,
   And know in each what talent lies.
There's nothing useless to a man of sense.

THE COBBLER AND THE RICH MAN

A Cobbler sang from morn till night;
   'Twas sweet and marvellous to hear,
   His trills and quavers told the ear
Of more contentment and delight,
   Enjoy'd by that laborious wight
Than e'er enjoy'd the sages seven,
Or any mortals short of heaven.
His neighbour, on the other hand,
With gold in plenty at command,
But little sang, and slumber'd less—
A Financier of great success.

If e'er he dozed, at break of day,
The Cobbler's song drove sleep away;
And much he wish'd that Heaven had made
Sleep a commodity of trade,
In market sold, like food and drink,
So much an hour, so much a wink.
At last, our songster did he call
To meet him in his princely hall.
Said he, "Now, honest Gregory,
What may your yearly earnings be?"
"My yearly earnings! faith, good sir,
I never go, at once, so far,"
The cheerful Cobbler said,
And queerly scratched his head,—
    "I never reckon in that way,
    But cobble on from day to day,
Content with daily bread."
"Indeed!   Well, Gregory, pray,
What may your earnings be per day?"
"Why, sometimes more and sometimes less.
The worst of all, I must confess,
(And but for which our gains would be
A pretty sight, indeed, to see,)
Is that the days are made so many
In which we cannot earn a penny—
The sorest ill the poor man feels:
They tread upon each other's heels,
Those idle days of holy saints!
    And though the year is shingled o'er,
    The parson keeps a-finding more!"
With smiles provoked by these complaints,
Replied the lordly Financier,
    "I'll give you better cause to sing.
These hundred pounds I hand you here
Will make you happy as a king.
Go, spend them with a frugal heed;
They'll long supply your every need."
The Cobbler thought the silver more
Than he had ever dream'd before,

The mines for ages could produce,
Or world, with all its people, use.
He took it home, and there did hide—
And with it laid his joy aside.
No more of song, no more of sleep,
  But cares, suspicions in their stead,
    And false alarms, by fancy fed.
His eyes and ears their vigils keep,
And not a cat can tread the floor
But seems a thief slipp'd through the door.
    At last, poor man!
    Up to the Financier he ran,—
Then in his morning nap profound:
  "O, give me back my songs," cried he,
"And sleep, that used so sweet to be,
And take the money, every pound!"

THE SCULPTOR AND THE STATUE OF JUPITER

A block of marble was so fine,
  To buy it did a Sculptor hasten.
"What shall my chisel, now 'tis mine—
  A god, a table, or a basin?"

"A god," said he, "the thing shall be;
  I'll arm it, too, with thunder.
Let people quake, and bow the knee
  With reverential wonder."

So well the cunning Artist wrought
  All things within a mortal's reach,
That soon the marble wanted nought
  Of being Jupiter, but speech.

Indeed, the Man whose skill did make
  Had scarcely laid his chisel down,
Before himself began to quake,
  And fear his manufacture's frown.

Imagination rules the heart:
 And here we find the fountain head
From whence the pagan error start,
 That o'er the teeming nations spread.

All men, as far as in them lies,
 Create realities of dreams.
To truth our nature proves but ice;
 To falsehood, fire it seems.

THE FISHES AND THE SHEPHERD WHO
PLAYED THE FLUTE

Thyrsis—who for his Annette dear
 Made music with his flute and voice,
Which might have roused the dead to hear,
 And in their silent graves rejoice—
  Sang once the livelong day,
  In the flowery month of May,
Up and down a meadow brook,
While Annette fish'd with line and hook.
  But ne'er a Fish would bite;
   So the Shepherdess's bait
   Drew not a Fish to its fate,
  From morning dawn till night.
The Shepherd, who, by his charming songs,
Had drawn savage beasts to him in throngs,
 And done with them as he pleased to,
 Thought that he could serve the Fish so.
"O citizens," he sang, "of this water,
Leave your Naiad in her grot profound;
Come and see the blue sky's lovely daughter,
 Who a thousand times more will charm you;
 Fear not that her prison will harm you,
Though there you should chance to get bound.
'Tis only to us men she is cruel:
  You she will treat kindly;
  A snug little pond she'll find ye,
Clearer than a crystal jewel,

Where you may all live and do well;
 Or, if by chance some few
  Should find their fate
  Conceal'd in the bait,
 The happier still are you;
For envied is the death that's met
At the hands of sweet Annette."
 This eloquence not effecting
  The object of his wishes,
 Since it failed in collecting
  The deaf and dumb Fishes,—
  His sweet preaching wasted,
  His honey'd talk untasted,
A net the Shepherd seized, and, pouncing
With a fell scoop at the scaly fry,
He caught them; and now, madly flouncing,
 At the feet of his Annette they lie!
O ye shepherds, whose sheep men are,
To trust in reason never dare.
The arts of eloquence sublime
 Are not within your calling;
Your fish were caught, from oldest time,
 By dint of nets and hauling.

THE FOUR FRIENDS

Rat, Raven, Tortoise, and Gazelle,
Once into firmest friendship fell.
'Twas in a home unknown to Man
That they their happiness began.
 But safe from Man there's no retreat:
Pierce you the loneliest wood,
Or dive beneath the deepest flood,
Or mount you where the eagles brood,—
 His secret ambuscade you meet.
The light Gazelle, in harmless play,
Amused herself abroad one day,

When, by mischance, her track was found
And follow'd by the baying Hound—
That barbarous tool of barbarous Man—
From which far, far away she ran.
  At meal-time to the others
  The Rat observed,—"My brothers,
  How happens it that we
  Are met to-day but three?
Is Miss Gazelle so little steady?
Hath she forgotten us already?"
Out cried the Tortoise at the word,—
"Were I, as Raven is, a bird,
  I'd fly this instant from my seat,
And learn what accident, and where,
Hath kept away our sister fair,—
  Our sister of the flying feet;
For of her heart, dear Rat,
It were a shame to doubt of that."
    The raven flew;
He spied afar,—the face he knew,—
The poor Gazelle entangled in a snare,
In anguish vainly floundering there.
Straight back he turn'd, and gave the alarm;
For to have ask'd the sufferer now,
The why and wherefore, when and how,
She had incurr'd so great a harm,—
    And lose in vain debate
    The turning-point of fate,
As would the master of a school,—
He was by no means such a fool.
On tidings of so sad a pith,
The three their council held forthwith.
  By two it was the vote
  To hasten to the spot
  Where lay the poor Gazelle.
  "Our friend here in his shell,
  I think, will do as well
To guard the house," the Raven said;
  "For, with his creeping pace,

When would he reach the place?
Not till the Deer were dead."
Eschewing more debate,
They flew to aid their mate,
That luckless mountain Roe.
The Tortoise, too, resolved to go.
Behold him plodding on behind,
And plainly cursing in his mind,
The fate that left his legs to lack,
And glued his dwelling to his back.
The snare was cut by Rongemail,
(For so the Rat they rightly hail).
Conceive their joy yourself you may.
Just then the Hunter came that way,
And, "Who hath filch'd my prey?"
    Cried he, upon the spot
    Where now his prey was not.—
    A hole did Rongemail;
    A tree the Bird as well;
    The woods, the free Gazelle.
    The Hunter, well nigh mad,
To find no inkling could be had,
Espied the Tortoise in his path,
And straightway check'd his wrath.
    "Why let my courage flag,
Because my snare has chanced to miss?
I'll have a supper out of this,"
    He said, and put it in his bag.
And it had paid the forfeit so,
Had not the Raven told the Roe,
    Who from her covert came,
    Pretending to be lame.
The Man, right eager to pursue,
Aside his wallet threw,
Which Rongemail took care
To serve as he had done the snare;
    Thus putting to an end
The Hunter's supper on his friend.

THE ACORN AND THE PUMPKIN

God's works are good. This truth to prove
Around the world I need not move;
  I do it by the nearest pumpkin.
"This fruit so large, on vine so small,"
  Surveying once, exclaim'd a Bumpkin—
"What could He mean who made us all?
He's left this Pumpkin out of place.
If I had order'd in the case,
Upon that Oak it should have hung—
A noble fruit as ever swung
To grace a tree so firm and strong.
Indeed, it was a great mistake,
  As this discovery teaches,
That I myself did not partake
His counsels whom my curate preaches.
All things had then in order come;
  This Acorn, for example,
    Not bigger than my thumb,
Had not disgraced a tree so ample.
The more I think, the more I wonder
To see outraged proportion's laws,
And that without the slightest cause;
God surely made an awkward blunder."
With such reflections proudly fraught,
Our sage grew tired of mighty thought.
And threw himself on Nature's lap,
Beneath an Oak, to take his nap.
Plump on his nose, by lucky hap,
An Acorn fell: he waked, and in
The matted beard that graced his chin,
He found the cause of such a bruise
As made him different language use.
"O! O!" he cried; "I bleed! I bleed!
And this is what has done the deed!
But, truly, what had been my fate,
Had this had half a Pumpkin's weight!

I see that God had reasons good,
And all His works well understood."
Thus home he went in humbler mood.

IX. FABLES BY JOHN GAY

THE WILD BOAR AND THE RAM

Against an elm a sheep was tied,
The butcher's knife in blood was dyed:
The patient flock, in silent fright,
From far beheld the horrid sight.
A savage Boar, who near them stood,
Thus mock'd to scorn the fleecy brood:
   "All cowards should be serv'd like you
See, see! your murd'rer is in view;
With purple hands, and reeking knife,
He strips the skin yet warm with life:
Your quarter'd sires, your bleeding dams,
The dying bleat of harmless lambs,
Call for revenge.   O, stupid race!
The heart that wants revenge is base."
   "I grant," an ancient Ram replies,
"We bear no terror in our eyes;
Yet think us not of soul so tame,
Which no repeated wrongs inflame;
Insensible of ev'ry ill,
Because we want thy tusks to kill.
Know, those who violence pursue
Give to themselves the vengeance due;
For in these massacres they find
The two chief plagues that waste mankind.
Our skin supplies the wrangling bar,
It wakes their slumbering sons to war;
And well revenge may rest contented,
Since drums and parchment were invented.

THE SHEPHERD'S DOG AND THE WOLF

A Wolf, with hunger fierce and bold,
Ravag'd the plains, and thinn'd the fold:
Deep in the wood secure he lay,
The thefts of night regal'd the day.
In vain the shepherd's wakeful care
Had spread the toils, and watch'd the snare;
In vain the dog pursu'd his pace,
The fleeter robber mock'd the chase.
  As Lightfoot rang'd the forest round,
By chance his foe's retreat he found.
"Let us awhile the war suspend,
And reason as from friend to friend."
  "A truce," replies the Wolf.   "'Tis done."
The dog the parley thus begun.
"How can that strong intrepid mind
Attack a weak defenceless kind?
Those jaws should prey on nobler food,
And drink the boar's and lion's blood.
Great souls with generous pity melt,
Which coward tyrants never felt.
How harmless is our fleecy care!
Be brave, and let thy mercy spare."
  "Friend," says the Wolf, "the matter weigh;
Nature design'd us beasts of prey;
As such, when hunger finds a treat
'Tis necessary Wolves should eat.
If mindful of the bleating weal,
Thy bosom burns with real zeal:
Hence, and thy tyrant lord beseech;
To him repeat the moving speech;
A wolf eats sheep but now and then,
Ten thousands are devour'd by men.
An open foe may prove a curse,
But a pretended friend is worse."

THE MASTIFF

Those who in quarrels interpose,
Must often wipe a bleeding nose.
A Mastiff of true English blood,
Lov'd fighting better than his food.
When dogs were snarling for a bone,
He long'd to make the war his own:
And often found when two contend,
To interpose obtain'd his end;
He glory'd in his limping pace;
The scars of honour seam'd his face;
In ev'ry limb a gash appears,
And frequent fights retrench'd his ears.
 As, on a time, he heard from far
Two dogs engag'd in noisy war,
Away he scours and lays about him,
Resolv'd no fray should be without him.
 Forth from his yard a tanner flies,
And to the bold intruder cries,
 "A cudgel shall correct your manners:
Whence sprung this cursed hate to tanners?
While on my dog you vent your spite,
Sirrah! 'tis me you dare not bite."
To see the battle thus perplex'd,
With equal rage a butcher vex'd,
Hoarse-screaming from the circled crowd,
To the curs'd Mastiff cries aloud:
 "Both Hockley-Hole and Marybone,
The combats of my dog have known.
He ne'er like bullies, coward-hearted,
Attacks in public to be parted.
Think not, rash fool, to share his fame;
Be his the honour or the shame."
 Thus said, they swore, and rav'd like **thunder,**
Then dragg'd their fasten'd dogs asunder;
While clubs and kicks from ev'ry side
Rebounded from the Mastiff's hide.

All reeking now with sweat and blood,
A while the parted warriors stood,
Then pour'd upon the meddling foe;
Who, worried, howl'd and sprawl'd below.
He rose and limping from the fray
By both sides mangled, sneak'd away.

THE OWL AND THE FARMER

An Owl of grave deport and mien,
Who (like the Turk) was seldom seen,
Within a barn had chose his station,
As fit for prey and contemplation.
Upon a beam aloft he sits,
And nods, and seems to think, by fits.
So have I seen a man of news,
Or Postboy, or Gazette peruse;
Smoke, nod, and talk with voice profound,
And fix the fate of Europe round.
Sheaves pil'd on sheaves hid all the floor.
At dawn of morn, to view his store
The Farmer came.   The hooting guest
His self-importance thus express'd:
   "Reason in man is mere pretence:
How weak, how shallow is his sense!
To treat with scorn the Bird of Night,
Declares his folly or his spite.
Then too, how partial is his praise!
The lark's, the linnet's chirping lays
To his ill judging ears are fine;
And nightingales are all divine.
But the more knowing feather'd race
See wisdom stamp'd upon my face.
Whene'er to visit light I deign,
What flocks of fowls compose my train!
Like slaves, they crowd my flight behind,
And own me of superior kind."

The Farmer laugh'd, and thus reply'd:
"Thou dull important lump of pride,
Dar'st thou, with that harsh grating tongue
Depreciate birds of warbling song?
Indulge thy spleen.   Know, men and fowl
Regard thee, as thou art, an Owl.
Besides, proud blockhead, be not vain
Of what thou call'st thy slaves and train.
Few follow wisdom or her rules;
Fools in derision follow fools."

THE CUR, THE HORSE, AND THE SHEPHERD'S DOG

A Village-cur, of snappish race,
The pertest puppy of the place,
Imagin'd that his treble throat
Was bless'd with music's sweetest note;
In the mid-road he basking lay,
The yelping nuisance of the way;
For not a creature pass'd along,
But had a sample of his song.
  Soon as the trotting steed he hears,
He starts, he cocks his dapper ears;
Away he scours, assaults his hoof:
Now near him snarls, now barks aloof;
With shrill impertinence attends;
Nor leaves him till the village ends.
  It chanc'd, upon his evil day,
A Pad [1] came pacing down the way;
The cur, with never-ceasing tongue,
Upon the passing trav'ller sprung.
The horse from scorn provok'd to ire,
Flung backward; rolling in the mire
The Puppy howl'd and bleeding lay:
The Pad in peace pursu'd his way.

[1] A Nag.

A Shepherd's Dog, who saw the deed,
Detesting the vexatious breed,
Bespoke him thus: "When coxcombs prate,
They kindle wrath, contempt, or hate;
If thy vile tongue had judgment ty'd,
Thou had'st not like a puppy dy'd."

THE OWL, THE SWAN, THE COCK, THE SPIDER, THE ASS, AND THE FARMER

An Owl of magisterial air,
Of solemn voice, of brow austere,
Assum'd the pride of human race,
And bore his wisdom in his face.
Not to depreciate learned eyes,
I've seen a pedant look as wise.
    Within a barn from noise retir'd,
He scorn'd the world, himself admir'd;
And, like an ancient sage, conceal'd
The follies public life reveal'd.
    Philosophers of old he read,
Their country's youth, to science bred,
Their manners form'd for every station,
And destin'd each his occupation.
When Xenophon, by numbers brav'd,
Retreated, and a people sav'd,
That laurel was not all his own;
The plant by Socrates was sown.
To Aristotle's greater name
The Macedonian ow'd his fame.
    Th' Athenian bird, with pride replete,
Their talents equall'd in conceit;
And, copying the Socratic rule,
Set up for master of a school.
Dogmatic jargon, learn'd by heart,
Trite sentences, hard terms of art,
To vulgar ears seem'd so profound,
They fancy'd learning in the sound.

The school had fame : the crowded place
With pupils swarm'd of every race.
With these the Swan's maternal care
Had sent her scarce-fledg'd cygnet heir :
The Hen, tho' fond and loth to part,
Here lodg'd the darling of her heart :
The Spider, of mechanic kind,
Aspir'd to science more refin'd :
The Ass learn'd metaphors and tropes,
But most on music fix'd his hopes.

The pupils now, advanc'd in age,
Were call'd to tread life's busy stage ;
And to the master 'twas submitted,
That each might to his part be fitted.

"The Swan," says he, "in arms shall shine :
The soldier's glorious toil be thine."

"The Cock shall mighty wealth attain :
Go seek it on the stormy main."

"The court shall be the Spider's sphere :
Pow'r, fortune, shall reward him there."

"In music's art the Ass's fame
Shall emulate Corelli's name."

Each took the part that he advis'd,
And all were equally despis'd.
A Farmer, at his folly mov'd,
The dull preceptor thus reprov'd :
"Blockhead," says he, "by what you've done,
One would have thought 'em each your son ;
For parents, to their offspring blind,
Consult nor parts, nor turn of mind ;
But ev'n in infancy decree
What this, what t'other son shall be.
Had you with judgment weigh'd the case,
Their genius thus had fix'd their place ;
The Swan had learnt the sailor's art :
The Cock had play'd the soldier's part ;
The Spider in the weaver's trade
With credit had a fortune made ;
But for the fool, in ev'ry class
The blockhead had appeared an Ass."

X. FABLES FROM LESSING

THE LION AND THE HARE

A Lion once honoured a Hare with his friendship. "Is it really a fact," demanded the Hare, "that the crowing of a miserable Cock is sufficient to compel you Lions to take to flight?"

"Such is undoubtedly the case," replied the Lion; "and it is a general remark, that we large animals are usually possessed by some trivial weakness. You must have heard for example that the grunt of a Pig causes astonishment and fright in the Elephant."

"Indeed!" interrupted the Hare. "Ha! now I can understand why we Hares are so terribly afraid of the Dogs."

THE ASS AND THE RACE-HORSE

An Ass undertook to run a race with the Horse. The result was as might have been expected, and the Ass got laughed at. "I now see what was the matter with me," said the Donkey; "I ran a thorn into my foot some months ago, and it still pains me."

JUPITER AND THE HORSE

"Father of man and beast," said the Horse, approaching the throne of Jupiter, "it is said that I am one of the noblest of the creations with which you have adorned the world, and my vanity bids me believe it. But do you not think my form still capable of improvement?"

"And what dost thou suppose would improve thee? Speak; I am open to instruction:" said the gracious Deity, smiling.

"Perhaps," continued the Horse, "I should have more speed if my legs were longer and more slender; a long swan-like neck would add to my beauty; a broader chest would increase my strength; and, once for all, since you have destined me to carry your favourite, man, it might be as well if the saddle, which the benevolent horseman supplies me with, were a part of my being."

"Good," pursued Jupiter; "have patience a moment!" and, with a solemn air, the god spake the word of creation. The dust became animated, organised matter was combined; and suddenly stood before the throne, the frightful Camel.

The Horse saw, shuddered, and trembled from excessive disgust.

"Here are longer and more slender legs," said Jove; "here is a long swan-like neck; a broader chest; a ready created saddle! Dost thou desire to be endowed with a similar form?"

The Horse still trembled.

"Go," continued the deity, "and this time the admonition shall suffice without the addition of punishment. To remind thee occasionally, however, of thy audacity, this new creation shall continue to exist!"— Then, casting a sustaining glance upon the Camel, Jove continued—"and the Horse shall never perceive thee without fear and trembling."

THE NIGHTINGALE AND THE PEACOCK

A sociable Nightingale found amongst the songsters of the grove plenty who envied her, but no friend. "Perhaps," thought she, "I may find one in another species," and flew confidingly to the Peacock.

"Beautiful Peacock! I admire thee."—"And I thee,

lovely Nightingale!"—"Then let us be friends," continued the Nightingale; "we shall not be envious of each other; thou art as pleasing to the eye as I to the ear." The Nightingale and the Peacock became friends.

THE HORSE AND THE OX

A brave Lad flew proudly along on a high mettled Courser: A wild Ox called out to the Horse: "Shame on thee! never would I be governed by a Boy!"—"I would," said the Horse; "for what honour should I acquire by throwing him off?"

THE PHŒNIX

Many ages had now passed away since the Phœnix had been seen in the world: at last he appeared. Immediately all the different kinds of animals, both birds and beasts, flock around him. Astonished at his beauty, they stared and admired, and broke out into great praise. But in a short time, the wisest and most prudent amongst them began to look upon him with an eye of compassion, and they sighed: "O unhappy Phœnix! Fate has been hard to him. He has neither mate nor friend. He will never know the pleasure of loving, or of being loved."

THE NIGHTINGALE AND THE HAWK

As a Nightingale was chanting his accustomed notes, a Hawk pounced upon him. "Since thou singest so charmingly," said he, "thou must be a delicious morsel!" Did the Hawk say this out of spite, out of scorn, or out of simplicity? I can't tell. But I heard a person say, yesterday: "That lady, who is so fine a poet, must undoubtedly be extremely handsome;" and certainly he said it through simplicity.

THE GOOSE

The feathers of a Goose put the newly-fallen snow to the blush. Proud of this dazzling gift of Nature, she considered herself intended for a Swan, rather than for that which she was. Accordingly, separating herself from her companions, she swam, solitary and majestically, round the pond. She now stretched her neck, the treacherous shortness of which she endeavoured to obviate with all her might. Now she tried to give it the graceful bend, which designates the beautiful Swan the bird of Apollo. But in vain, it was too stiff, and with all her pains, she remained a ridiculous Goose, without inspiring a single beholder with the least idea of her resemblance to a Swan.

How many geese are there, without wings, who, for similar assumption, become laughing-stocks to their neighbours!

THE SPARROWS

An old Church, in the chinks of which the Sparrows had built innumerable nests, was repaired. As it stood in its new lustre, the Sparrows returned to look for their old dwellings; but they found them all bricked up. "Of what earthly use," cried they, "can so large a building now be? Come, let us leave the useless heap of stones to its fate!"

THE SPARROW AND THE OSTRICH

"You may boast as much as you please of your strength and size," said the Sparrow to the Ostrich, "but you will never be so good a bird as I am; I don't fly far, 'tis true, and that only by starts; yet I do fly, and you cannot do any such thing."

THE OWL AND THE TREASURE-SEEKER

A certain Treasure-seeker who was a very unreasonable man, ventured among the ruins of an old castle, and perceived there an Owl which had caught a half-starved Mouse to devour it. "Is that fitting," said he, "for the philosophical favourite of Minerva?"—"Why not?" replied the Owl; "because I am fond of quiet meditation, can I therefore live upon air? though I am well aware that mankind frequently condemn the learned to such diet."

MEROPS

"I wish to ask you a question," said a young Eagle to a thoughtful and very studious Owl.

"It is said there is a bird called Merops, which, when it rises into the air, flies with its tail first, and the head looking down to the earth. Is it a fact?"

"By no means," said the Owl; "it is only a silly fiction of mankind. Man is himself a sort of Merops; for he would most willingly soar towards Heaven without losing sight of the world for a single instant."

THE ASS AND THE WOLF

An Ass had the misfortune to be met by a hungry Wolf. "Have mercy on me," said the trembling animal; "I am a poor sick beast; look what a great thorn I have run into my foot!"

"Really, you quite grieve me," replied the Wolf. "Conscientiously speaking, I feel myself compelled to put you out of your misery."

He had scarcely spoken, when he tore the supplicating Donkey to pieces.

THE KNIGHT IN CHESS

Two Boys playing at Chess, having lost a Knight, put a mark on a spare Pawn, and agreed it should pass for one. "A word with you," cried the old Knights to the new one : "whence come you, Mr. Upstart?" "Silence!" said the Boys; "does he not give us the same service as you do?"

HERCULES

When Hercules was admitted into Heaven, he made his obeisance to Juno before any other deity. All Olympus and Juno were struck with amazement. "What," cried every one, "do you give precedence to your enemy?"—"Yes, even to her," replied Hercules. "It was mainly her persecutions which gave me the opportunities of achieving those deeds by which I have rendered Heaven so much service."

Olympus approved of the answer of the new god, and Juno became reconciled to him.

THE WOLF ON HIS DEATH-BED

A Wolf lay at the last gasp, and glanced at the events of his past life. "True, I am a sinner," said he; "but let me still hope, none of the greatest. I have done harm; but also much good. Once, I remember, a bleating Lamb, which had wandered from the flock, came so near me, that I could easily have throttled it; and yet I did nothing to it. At the same time I listened to the jeers and jibes of a Sheep with the most surprising indifference, although I had no watchful Dogs to fear."

"I can explain all that," interrupted his friend the Fox, who was assisting in preparing him for death. "I have a distinct recollection of all the attendant circumstances. It was precisely the time that you so lamentably choked yourself with the bone, which the kind-hearted Crane afterwards drew out of your throat."

THE LION WITH THE ASS

As Æsop's Lion was going to the forest in company with the Ass, who was to assist him with his terrible voice, an impertinent Crow called to him from a tree : "A pretty companion ! Are you not ashamed of yourself to be walking with an Ass? "—"Whomsoever I can make use of," replied the Lion, "I may very well allow to walk by my side."

Thus think the great, when they honour a common man with their company.

THE ASS WITH THE LION

As the Ass was going to the forest with Æsop's Lion, who made use of him instead of a hunting-bugle, he was met by another Ass of his acquaintance, who called to him : "Good morning, brother ! "—"Impertinent scoundrel ! " was the reply.

"And wherefore? " said the former. "Because you are walking with a Lion, are you any better than I? anything more than an Ass? "

THE TWO DOGS AND THE LAMB

Hylax, of the race of Wolfhounds, guarded a gentle Lamb. Lycodes, who also in hair, muzzle and ears more resembled a Wolf than a Dog, espied him and rushed upon him. "Wolf," said he, "what are you doing with this Lamb? "

"You are a Wolf yourself," returned the latter (the Dogs both mistook each other). "Depart, or you shall find that I know how to take care of it."

Lycodes, however, would take the Lamb by force from Hylax. Hylax was equally determined to keep it, and between these excellent protectors the poor Lamb was torn in pieces.

THE FOX

A Fox, closely followed by the Hounds, saved himself
by springing on to a wall. In order to get down with
ease on the other side, he caught hold of a Thorn-bush,
and arrived safely at the bottom, with the exception of
being severely scratched by the Thorns. "Wretched
help," cried the Fox, "why could you not render assistance, without injuring those who relied upon you?"

THE SHEEP

As Jupiter was celebrating his marriage festival, and
all the animals had made offerings to him, Juno missed
the Sheep.

"Where is the Sheep?" enquired the goddess.
"Why delays the pious Sheep to bring us its humble
offering?"

The Dog stepped forward and said: "Do not be
angry, goddess! This morning have I seen the Sheep.
It seemed very sorrowful, and wept bitterly."

"What may have caused its grief?" asked the
goddess, already moved with compassion.

"'Wretched creature that I am!' it said; 'I have
neither milk nor wool; what shall I offer the great
Jupiter? Must I alone appear empty-handed before
him? Rather will I go to the Shepherd and beg him
to sacrifice me on Jove's altar!'"

At this moment the Shepherd's prayer accompanying
the scent from the sacrifice of the devoted Sheep, arose
through the clouds. Could tears have bedewed celestial
eyes, Juno would have wept for the first time.

THE THORN

"Just inform me," said the Willow to the Thorn,
"why you are so anxious to seize the clothes of man-

kind as they pass by you? Of what use can they be to you?"

"None," said the Thorn. "Neither do I wish to take them from him; I only want to tear them."

THE NIGHTINGALE AND THE LARK

What should we say to the poets who take flights beyond the understanding of their readers?

Nothing but what the Nightingale said one day to the Lark. "Do you soar so very high, my friend, in order that you may not be heard?"

SOLOMON'S GHOST

A venerable old Man, despite his years and the heat of the day, was ploughing his field with his own hand, and sowing the grain in the willing earth, in anticipation of the harvest it would produce.

Suddenly, beneath the deep shadow of a spreading oak, a divine apparition stood before him! The old Man was seized with affright.

"I am Solomon," said the Phantom encouragingly. "What dost thou here, old friend?"

"If thou art Solomon," said the owner of the field, "how canst thou ask? In my youth I learnt from the Ant to be industrious and to accumulate wealth. That which I then learnt I now practise."

"Thou hast learnt but the half of thy lesson," pursued the Spirit. "Go once more to the Ant, and she will teach thee to rest in the winter of thy existence, and enjoy what thou hast earned."

THE FAIRIES' GIFT

Two benevolent Fairies attended at the birth of a Prince, who afterwards became one of the greatest Monarchs his country had ever boasted.

"I bestow on my *protégé,*" said one, "the piercing eye of the Eagle, from whose view not the smallest Fly can escape in this extensive kingdom."

"The gift is noble," interrupted the second Fairy. "The Prince will become a discerning Monarch. But the Eagle is not blessed with his keen sight merely to discover the smallest Fly; he possesses also a supreme contempt for chasing them. And this gift do I bestow on the Prince."

"Thanks, dearest sister, for this wise restriction," resumed the first Fairy. "Nothing is more true than that many would have been much greater kings, if, with their extreme penetration, they had less often made use thereof on the most trifling occasions."

ÆSOP AND THE ASS

"The next time you write a fable about me," said the Donkey to Æsop, "make me say something wise and sensible."

"Something sensible from you!" exclaimed Æsop; "what would the world think? People would call you the Moralist, and me the Donkey!"

THE ARCHER

An Archer had an excellent Bow made of ebony, which would carry an arrow true to the mark from a great distance. Consequently he held it in great estimation. Once, however, as he considered it attentively, he soliloquised: "You are still a little too thick; and possess no decorations save your polish. What a pity!—But that may be remedied," he pursued. "I will go to the cleverest Artist, and let him carve it ornamentally."—Without losing a moment, he set out; the Artist carved a complete hunt on the Bow; and what could be more appropriate on a weapon of the chase?

The Man was rejoiced. "Ah! my dear Bow," said he, "you deserve these embellishments!" Wishing again to essay its powers, the spans the Bow and snaps it in two.

THE BEASTS STRIVING FOR PRECEDENCE

IN FOUR FABLES

I

A serious dispute arose among the Beasts, as to who should take precedence of his neighbour. "I propose," said the Horse, "that we call in Man to adjust the difference; he is not one of the disputants, and can therefore be more impartial."

"But has he sufficient understanding for it?" asked the Mole. "It appears to me that it must be very acute to detect all our deeply-hidden perfections."

"That was well thought of!" said the Marmot.

"Undoubtedly!" exclaimed also the Hedge-hog. "I can never believe that Man possesses sufficient penetration for the task."

"Silence!" commanded the Horse. "We know well enough, that he who can place least reliance on the merits of his cause, is always the readiest to doubt the wisdom of his judge."

II

Man, therefore, was constituted arbitrator. "Another word with thee," said the majestic Lion to him, "before thou pronouncest judgment! By what standard dost thou intend fixing our relative worth?"

"By what standard? Doubtless," replied the Man, "according as you are more or less useful to me."

"Excellent!" returned the offended Lion. "How much lower in the scale should I rank than the ass! Man! thou canst not judge for us. Quit the assembly!"

III

The Man retired. "Now," said the sneering Mole (and the Marmot and Hedge-hog again chimed in with their friend), "dost thou perceive, friend Dobbin? the Lion also thinks that Man is not fit to be our judge. The Lion thinks like us."

"But from weightier reasons than ye!" said the Lion, glancing contemptuously at the speaker.

IV

The Lion continued: "The struggle for precedency, now I consider all the circumstances, is but a sheer waste of time! Whether you regard me as the highest or the least, is perfectly immaterial. Enough, I know my power!" Thus speaking, he rose, and left the assembly.

He was followed by the sage Elephant, the fearless Tiger, the grave Bear, the cunning Fox, the noble Horse; in short, all who felt their own worth, or thought they felt it.

Those who went away last, and murmured most at the breaking up of the assembly, were—the Ape and the Donkey.

THE BENEFACTORS

"Have you in the creation any greater benefactor than me?" asked the Bee of a Man.

"Most undoubtedly," replied the Man.

"Name him!"

"The Sheep! For his wool is necessary to me, and your honey is only a luxury. And I will give you another reason, Mrs. Bee, why I consider the Sheep a greater benefactor than you. The Sheep gives me his wool without the least trouble or danger; but when I take your honey, you keep me in constant apprehension of your sting."

THE BLIND HEN

A Hen who had lost her sight, and was accustomed to scratching up the earth in search of food; although blind, still continued to scratch away most diligently. Of what use was it to the industrious fool? Another sharp-sighted Hen who spared her tender feet, never moved from her side, and enjoyed, without scratching, the fruit of the other's labour. For as often as the blind Hen scratched up a barley-corn, her watchful companion devoured it.

THE STATUE OF BRASS

A Statue of Brass, the masterpiece of an excellent Artist, happened to be melted down by a terrible fire, and in that condition, fell into the hands of another Statuary. His happy chisel produced another; the subject whereof was different from the former, but the workmanship was full as exquisite, and the expression equally noble. Envy saw it, and gnashed her teeth. At last she endeavoured to console herself by saying : "This Statue is passable; but the workman would not have made it, if he had not found the metal of the old one."

THE TWO DOGS

"How greatly our race has degenerated ! " said a travelled Poodle. "In a remote quarter of the globe which men call India, Dogs are still found of the right sort; Dogs, my friend, you will scarcely credit me, and yet I have seen it with my own eyes, which are not afraid of a Lion, and will even attack him in the boldest manner possible ! "

"But," said a sedate Pointer to the Poodle, "do they overcome the Lion? "

"Overcome him?" was the answer, "why, I can't exactly pretend to say. Nevertheless, only think, to attack a Lion!"

"Oh!" pursued the Pointer, "if they don't overcome him, your boasted Dogs in India are no better than we: though undoubtedly they are infinitely more stupid."

THE EAGLE

"Why do you rear your Eaglets in such elevated situations?" said a Man to the Eagle. The latter replied, "Would they venture so near the sun when arrived at the years of maturity, if I built my nest on the ground?"

XI. FABLES FROM KRILOF

THE RAIN-CLOUD

A great Cloud passed rapidly over a country which was parched by heat, but did not let fall a single drop to refresh it. Presently it rained a great shower into the sea, and then began boasting of its kindness in the hearing of a neighbouring Mountain. But the Mountain replied, "What good have you done by such generosity? And how can one help being pained at seeing it? If you had poured your showers over the land, you would have saved a whole district from famine. But as to the sea, my friend, it has plenty of water already, without your adding to it."

THE CUCKOO AND THE EAGLE

The Eagle promoted the Cuckoo to the rank of a Nightingale. The Cuckoo, proud of its new position, seated itself on an aspen and began to sing. After a time it looked round : all the birds were on the wing, some laughing, others abusing it. The Cuckoo grew angry and hastened to the Eagle, complaining against the birds.

"Have pity on me," he said; "by your command I have been appointed Nightingale to these woods. But the birds laugh at my song."

"My friend," said the Eagle, "I am a king, but I am not God. I can order a Cuckoo to be styled a Nightingale, but I cannot *make* a Nightingale out of a Cuckoo."

THE MONKEY AND THE SPECTACLES

Once a Monkey in his old age became weak-sighted. It had heard men say that this misfortune was of no great importance; only one must provide oneself with glasses. So he got half-a-dozen pairs of Spectacles, turned them now this way, and now that, put them on the top of his head, fastened them to his tail, smelled them, licked them; still the Spectacles had no effect on his sight.

"Good lack!" it cries, "what fools they be who listen to all the nonsense men utter. They have told me nothing but lies about the Spectacles." And then he threw them hard upon a stone, so that they were broken to bits.

So we speak ill of the things we do not understand.

THE ASS AND THE NIGHTINGALE

An Ass happened to see a Nightingale one day, and said to it : "Listen, my dear. They say you have a great mastery over song. I have long wished to prove

if your talent is so great as they say." On this the
Nightingale began to show her art: whistled in countless ways, sobbed, sustained notes, passed from one
song to another; at one time let her voice die away,
and echoed the distant murmur of the reed; at another
time poured through the wood a shower of tiny notes.
There was no one that did not listen to the song: the
breezes died away, the birds were hushed, the cattle
lay down on the grass; scarcely breathing, the Shepherd revelled in it, and only now and then as he listened
did he smile on the shepherdess.

At length the singer ended. Then the Ass, bending
its head towards the ground, observed—

"It's tolerable. To speak the truth, one can listen
to you without feeling weary. But it's a great pity
you don't know our Cock. You would sing much
better if you were to take a few lessons from him."

At this the Nightingale flew very far away.

THE COMB

A Mother one day bought a strong Comb to keep
her boy's hair in order. The Child never let the new
present go out of his hands; whether playing or learning his alphabet, he was always passing the Comb
through his golden hair. It was a wonderful Comb!
it never pulled out his hair, nor got caught in his curls.
One day it happened that the Comb was mislaid, and
the Boy went to play and romp about, till his hair got
all a-tangle. Scarcely did his Nurse touch it, than he
began to howl: "Where is my Comb?"

At last it was found; but when they tried to pass it
through his hair, it could not be moved either back-
wards or forwards, but it pulled his hair out by the roots,
till the Boy cried: "How wicked you have become, my
bad Comb!" To which the Comb replied—

"I am now just the same as I ever was. The fault
lies with your hair, which has got all a-tangle."

The Boy, at that, threw the Comb into the river,
where the Naiads now comb their beautiful hair with it.

XII. FABLES FROM TOLSTOI

THE WATER-DEMON AND THE PEARL

A Man one day was rowing on the sea, and dropped a costly Pearl into the water. He thereupon put in to the shore, and began to bale up the water, and pour it out on the land. This he did for three days without cease.

On the fourth day a Water-Demon came out of the sea and asked why he was drawing off the sea-water? The Man answered, "I am drawing the water because I have dropped a Pearl into it." The Water-Demon then asked him how soon he would stop?

"I will stop," he said, "when I have dried up the sea."

The Water-Demon thereupon dived down again into the sea, fished up the Pearl, and gave it to the Man.

THE MONKEY

One day a Man went into the woods, cut down a tree, and began to saw it up. Raising the end of the tree upon a stump, he sat astride it, and began to saw. After he had sawn a little, he drove a wedge into the slit, and went on sawing; then he took out the wedge and again drove it in, farther down.

All this while a Monkey was sitting on a tree and watching him. At last the Man lay down and went to sleep. Then the Monkey descended, and, sitting astride the tree, tried to do the same. But when she took out the wedge, the tree sprang back and caught her tail, whereupon she set up a piteous cry, and began to tug at her tail in vain.

At the noise, the Man woke up, and after beating the Monkey, made her captive with a rope.

THE WOLF AND THE BOW

A Hunter one day went out with Bow and Arrows. He managed to shoot and kill a Goat, which he threw on his shoulders and began to carry along. But spying a Boar, he threw down the Goat, and shot at the Boar and wounded him. The Boar then rushed at the Hunter, and after goring him to death, himself fell dead by the Man's side.

Scenting the blood, a Wolf came to the place where the Goat, the Boar, the Man, and his Bow all lay. The Wolf was glad, and said, "Now I shall have enough to eat for a long time. I will not eat everything at once, but little by little, that nothing may be lost. First I will eat the tougher things, and then I will dine on what is soft and sweet."

Then he began to gnaw the sinews of the Bow; but when he bit through the string, the Bow sprang back and struck him so violently, that the blow killed him.

Then the other Wolves, that had scented a feast from afar, came in their numbers, and ate up the Hunter, the Goat, the Boar, and their fellow Wolf.

THE CORN-CRAKE AND HIS MATE

A Corn-crake had made a nest in a meadow late in the year, and at mowing-time his Mate was still sitting on her eggs.

Early in the morning the Peasants came to the meadow, took off their coats, whetted their scythes, and started one after another to mow down the grass and lay it in rows. The Corn-crake flew up to see what they were doing, and when he saw a Peasant swing his scythe and cut a Snake in two, he rejoiced and flew back to his Mate, and said: "Have no fear of the Peasants! They have come to cut the Snakes to pieces."

But his Mate said, "The Peasants are cutting the grass, and with the grass they are cutting everything in their way—the Snakes, the Corncrake's nest, and the Corn-crake's head. My heart forebodes nothing good: but I cannot carry away the eggs, nor fly from the nest, lest I chill them."

When the mowers came to the Corn-crake's nest, one of the Peasants swung his scythe and cut off the head of the Corn-crake's Mate, and put the eggs in his bosom, and gave them to his children to play with.

THE WOLF AND THE HUNTERS

A Wolf devoured a Sheep. The Hunters caught the Wolf and began to beat him, whereupon he cried: "In vain do you beat me: it is not my fault that I am grey; God made me so." But the Hunters said: "We do not beat the Wolf for being grey, but for eating the Sheep."

A